D1423814

THE MURDERED SCHOOLGIRL

Maria Black, Head of Roseway College for Young Ladies, and solver of crimes, is faced with a problem after her own heart when young Frances Hasleigh arrives at the college. Within days the girl is found hanged in a neighbouring wood, in circumstances that seem to be devoid of clues and without motive. When Scotland Yard is called in, Maria applies her own unique system to find a way through a maze of intrigue — and uncovers the murderer . . .

JOHN RUSSELL FEARN

THE MURDERED SCHOOLGIRL

Complete and Unabridged

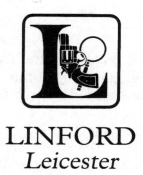

LINFORD
Leicester

First published in Great Britain

First Linford Edition
published 2008

British Library CIP Data

Fearn, John Russell, *1908 – 1960*
  The murdered schoolgirl.—Large print ed.—
Linford mystery library
  1. Women school principles—Fiction
  2. Murder—Investigation—Fiction 3. Detective
and mystery stories 4. Large type books
  I. Title
  823.9'12 [F]

  ISBN 978–1–84782–370–0

Published by
F. A. Thorpe (Publishing)
Anstey, Leicestershire

Set by Words & Graphics Ltd.
Anstey, Leicestershire
Printed and bound in Great Britain by
T. J. International Ltd., Padstow, Cornwall

This book is printed on acid-free paper

1

Maria Black, M.A., rose to her feet from behind her massive desk as her two visitors entered. She was an impressive, strong-featured woman, gowned in black silk, with her black hair drawn into a bun at the back of her well-shaped head. From the way she stood, from the aura of mystery she emitted, it was perfectly clear that she alone was the ruler of the college.

'I am afraid,' she said, smiling, 'that the porter gave me no names, merely referring to two people wishing to see me urgently . . . Do come in, won't you?'

She came from behind her desk, shook hands cordially, and nodded to two chairs. When the girl and her escort — a middle-aged man in high ranking military uniform — were seated, she returned to her seat and fingered the slender gold of her watch-chain as it glittered against her dress.

'I am afraid, Miss Black, that this visit

1

is somewhat sudden,' the military man smiled. 'I am Major Hasleigh, and this is my daughter, Frances.'

Maria's keen blue eyes regarded her. She seemed young — perhaps sixteen — a pale-faced blonde with regular features and very wide grey eyes that appeared utterly innocent. Knowing girls, however, Maria Black reserved her judgment.

'Briefly,' Hasleigh went on, 'I have had the misfortune to lose my wife and be ordered to join my unit abroad immediately. Formerly, while my wife lived, Frances here was able to have her education at a local day school. Now, however, the home is sold up and I have to depart — so I am in a pretty big predicament. I felt I must leave her in good hands, and having heard excellent reports on Roseway college — and yourself, madam — I thought I would like to hand her into your care.'

'I see,' Maria nodded thoughtfully.

She decided that he was of very uncertain age, good-looking in a way, with a face so red that he lived up to the traditional cartoons of majors the world over. His thick grey hair set him at about fifty. He had a grey moustache, too — and yet somehow his features were curiously young. Altogether he was not easy to assess.

'I'll just fit into whatever regulations there are, Miss Black,' Frances said anxiously. 'I know that it is an intrusion to burst in early in the summer term like this and expect to be enrolled but — Well, I just can't be left alone! It was my idea really that I be sent here. I'll not be any trouble, really!'

'The military authorities are so ruthless,' the major sighed. 'I have only about twelve hours in which to turn round.'

'Quite,' Maria nodded. 'I appreciate your position — and in these war-time days it behoves us to help each other as much as we can. I am willing for that reason to waive our usually strict rules. You would wish to domicile here right away, Frances?'

The girl nodded eagerly.

'Hmm . . . ' Maria took a syllabus from the desk drawer. 'You may wish to study these terms and conditions, major, while I make inquiries as to vacancies — '

He nodded and took the folded card from her. Turning to the house telephone Maria said briefly: 'Ask Miss Tanby to step along to my study, will you please?' Replacing the receiver, she glanced at the girl.

'Where have you been receiving your education up to now, Frances?'

'Elmington High School. You may not know it, though, ma'am; it is only a little place, Elmington. A Surrey village.'

'No, I don't know of it,' Maria admitted. 'I — '

'If you will excuse me, Miss Black,' Major Hasleigh interrupted, putting down the syllabus, 'these terms are quite acceptable. Money is no object. As much as you require in advance just as long as my little girl is happy and safe, as I know she will be with you . . . I am telling you this before your — er — Miss Tanby arrives.'

'Miss Tanby is my Housemistress,' Maria explained, and at that moment there came a knock on the door and the pale but deadly efficient Eunice Tanby came in.

'You wish to speak to me, Miss Black?' she asked, glancing at the visitors.

'I do, Miss Tanby — on a rather urgent matter of placing a new pupil. Meet Major Hasleigh and his daughter Frances . . . Miss Tanby, my Housemistress.'

Tanby smiled with colourless lips; then Maria got to her feet.

'I was wondering, Miss Tanby, if there is room in Study F in the New House for this young lady? I assigned two pupils to it only the other day — '

'Yes, Miss Black — Beryl Mather and Joan Dawson.'

'Splendid! That leaves room for one more . . . Three to a study is the general rule,' Maria explained, turning. 'Well, Major, that settles everything.'

'I'm so glad,' he said earnestly. 'As to the terms — '

'I am sure we can attend to that most satisfactorily,' Maria interposed. 'Miss Tanby, I will leave Miss Hasleigh in your care. Have her bags taken to Study F, show her the room yourself, and then I feel certain that in your own inimitable way you will make her feel at home

. . . Thank you for coming so promptly.'

Tanby shrugged, accustomed to abrupt dismissals. She waited while the girl took leave of her father — yet endearing though it was, Maria noted they did not kiss each other . . . Then Tanby took the girl's arm and led her from the room.

Maria sat down again, her cold eyes on the major's face.

'I am prepared,' he said, 'to pay a year's fee in advance. It may be at least a year before I am back in England — '

'That's very generous of you,' Maria said, 'but it also raises a point which I must clarify, Major. Your daughter might be taken seriously ill — she might be injured or even killed in an air raid; or unwittingly get involved in criminal circumstances. If that should happen, to whom am I to turn?'

'Good Lord!' The major gave a start. 'Air raids apart I am sure there is no need to fear. She is a healthy girl and very quiet. As for criminal circumstances — Really, Miss Black!'

'Such things have happened,' Maria stated, unmoved. 'It is one of the regulations set down by our Board of Governors. Take a small instance. If your daughter were down with double pneumonia and I had no relative to contact, where would I be?'

'I see,' Hasleigh muttered. 'Well, I am not allowed to hand on my own address abroad with my unit for security reasons — but I'll tell you what you can do!' His eyes gleamed in sudden inspiration. 'In case of emergency call on my sister-in-law — Mrs. Clevedon, The Willows, Sundale, Essex. As the wife of a big financier she will have plenty of influence in case of anything — er — criminal,' he finished, drily.

'Much obliged, Major.' Maria made a note of the address. 'I have to do it because in war-time — forgive me — you might never return — '

He laughed. 'I'm fully aware of that. As to other matters on the financial side, just communicate with this bank and they will attend to it.'

Maria took the cheque he had written out — an account drawn on the Elmington Branch Bank, Surrey. She nodded, then said:

'I shall need your daughter's ration book and identity card if you please. So many regulations these days, unhappily.'

'Yes, of course.' He pulled out his wallet and handed them both over. Both ration book and identity card had a new label on the front, reading — *Frances Hasleigh, c/o Roseway College, Sussex.*

'So you anticipated results, Major?' Maria smiled.

'I did, yes. I had Frances transfer her address the moment she thought of coming here. It was a risk — but it came off I'm glad to say.'

Maria put the cards in her desk drawer; then as she and the major reached the door of her study she said casually:

'Since you are liable to be away a long time, Major, perhaps you would like to carry in your memory a picture of where your daughter will work, play, and sleep?'

'Well, I — ' He hesitated. 'I don't want to take up a lot of your time on account of my sentiment, Miss Black.'

'Not at all; daughters are very precious . . . Just come with me.'

Maria swept out into the passageway and thereupon began a majestic parade. There was something magical about the way under-teachers, stray pupils, and occasional members of the domestic staff fell away from about her as she advanced.

In turn she took the major at a rather breathless speed to the classrooms — where a dead silence descended while she explained the finer points — then up to the long, cool Sixth Form dormitory, shaded against the blaze of the summer sun; and up again to the solarium and gymnasium, with its endless equipment for improving the physique and maintaining the health. It was in this big room, with its trapezes and parallel-bars, that the major gave a sharp glance at three instruments standing against the wall.

'Are those ultra-violet machines?' he asked quickly.

Maria nodded. 'A most useful adjunct of modern science, Major, and used by quite a lot of my pupils, especially those with inherently pale skins who feel they might improve themselves by a little — hmm! — tan.'

'My daughter is never to use one!' Major Hasleigh declared harshly.

Maria raised her eyebrows. 'My dear Major, it is purely a matter of personal choice. None of my pupils is forced to use ultra-violet. If your daughter does not wish to make use of the treatment, that is her own affair entirely.'

'I am worried that she may be forced into it. There is that kind of thing to reckon with among girls.'

'I presume,' Maria said, rather coldly, 'that there is a definite reason for this rather — er — arbitrary request?'

'A medical one. Something she doesn't know about.'

Maria shrugged. 'As you wish, Major. I will give definite instructions of your wishes to the Housemistress and the physical instructor . . . Now, shall we proceed?'

'Yes, of course.'

But for the major all interest seemed to have gone. Besides, Maria took him from place to place with such speed that he had hardly time to absorb the virtues of the swimming bath, the dining room, the chapel, and other amenities. He was quite breathless by the time he was conducted back to the steps of the main building and given Maria's firm handclasp as his farewell.

From the top of the School House steps she watched him go across the quadrangle — then she returned to her study and sat down.

Pondering, she studied the cheque again. Finally she made up her mind and rang up the bank itself in Elmington, Surrey, and for some reason she felt quite rebuffed when she learned that the account of Major Hasleigh was completely in order.

'Extremely peculiar,' she muttered. 'Maybe I need the opinion of a second person — '

Once again she summoned Miss Tanby over the house telephone, and like the slave of the lamp the Housemistress reappeared with silent promptness.

'I have had to leave the Sixth Form in the middle of its history lesson, Miss Black,' she announced anxiously.

Maria smiled. 'My dear Miss Tanby, with history changing every day I am sure it will have to be rewritten anyway . . . Sit down, please. I feel the need of one of our little confabs.'

'Very well, Miss Black,' Tanby answered, folding her angular figure on to a chair.

'You know, for instance, that I have the rather disturbing weakness of being in love with criminology — '

'Yes, Miss Black, I know all about your private hobby — your study of crime, your deductive capacities, your passion for the unusual . . . I even remember,' she added in a hushed voice, 'how you solved the mystery of your brother's death in America last summer — calling yourself 'Black Maria' and enlisting the help of a — er — Bowery thug for the purpose.'

'That,' Maria sighed reminiscently, 'was a truly glorious vacation, and I really did enjoy myself in the company of Mr. 'Pulp' Martin. However, that is behind us, Miss Tanby, and thanks to your silence no girl in this school — or the public either — knows that I solved that mystery. It would hardly do for the girls to know: they might start calling me 'Black Maria' to my face!'

Miss Tanby shifted uneasily.

'Tell me, Miss Tanby, what do you think of a man whose high colour smears when he gets warm?'

Miss Tanby frowned. She had never studied the colour of men very closely: they had never given her the chance. 'I don't quite understand, Miss Black — '

'I am referring to our departed friend, Major Hasleigh. There is something distinctly peculiar about that upright military gentleman! Something that arouses my suspicions . . .'

'I thought he seemed a very respectable gentleman,' Tanby said timidly.

'Respectable, I grant you — but most unorthodox! I was struck from the moment I first saw him by his very high colour. It was not the pink and purple bloom of cardiac trouble, nor the brick-red or nut-brown of exposure to the elements. No, it was an odd shade of matt red, rather like the colouring matter some young ladies put on their legs in these days of stocking shortage . . .' Maria coughed a little and halted. 'It was utterly unnatural! So, rather at the expense

13

of my own legs and heart, I gave him a miniature marathon round the school's appointments to see what happened when he really became warm,' Maria smiled wickedly. 'As he left I was rewarded with the amazing sight of seeing white trickles in the redness about his forehead! His colour was *applied*, and in places perspiration removed it. Normally I should think he is fairly pale.'

Tanby simply sat and said nothing. Maria gave her an irritated look. 'Well?' she asked.

'I'm sorry, Miss Black, but I was just wondering if there is really anything significant about it. Presumably the major thinks sunburn powder makes him attractive.'

'Sunburn powder?' Maria repeated.

'Quite different from the lotion used for legs,' Tanby explained. 'The leg lotion doesn't have to smear because of rain; but sunburn powder is used very often by people with pale skins to — er — enhance their attractiveness . . . ' Tanby stopped as though she were astonished at her own revelations; then she added mildly, 'I've

14

seen the powder and the lotion both advertised.'

'And no doubt have used them,' Maria commented drily. 'However, we are not here to discuss feminine frivolities or the virtues of cosmetics. What I want to know is why a military man should be so effeminate as to use such a powder. I suspect, too, that his hair was powdered, though I could not exactly blow on it to find out. So, Miss Tanby, a man with powdered face and hair and an intense dislike for ultra-violet equipment suddenly arrives and places his daughter with us, leaving a year's fee in advance. It is, to say the least of it — peculiar.'

'Surely, then, you should have refused to take his daughter?' Tanby asked, rather bluntly.

'I could hardly do that because her father powders his face and hair, could I? He paid the fees by cheque, which I find is quite genuine . . . ' Maria gave a little sigh, 'I suppose that I am so accustomed to looking for peculiarities in people that I am making a mountain out of a molehill . . . All the same, I would like to know why he doesn't wish his daughter to undergo ultra-violet ray treatment at any time. It is such a stimulating process, too. There have been times when the girls have been in class when I have myself — Hmm, we have no need to go into that . . . You will see to it, Miss Tanby, that the girl does not have the treatment if you can prevent it, and if any of the girls try and make her she is to report it to me.'

'Yes, Miss Black,' Tanby nodded.

'Thank you for listening to my little — er — investigative talk. I find you a great help at such times. Amongst other things, keep your eye on this girl Frances. If she proves as unique as her father she will be well worth watching.'

Tanby waited, then seeing the imperious nod of the hair bun she went out silently . . . Alone again, Maria's thoughts were not on the biology class she was due to take at three o'clock. They were on the address of Hasleigh's sister-in-law, which she had scribbled down.

'Prominent financier,' she mused. 'I wonder if prominent enough to be in *Who's Who?*'

Evidently not, for all her searching failed to reveal any trace of the name. It seemed reasonable enough that a house with such an impressive address should have a telephone, anyway, so she dialled inquiry and asked for the number. Politely she was advised that 'The Willows, Sundale, Essex,' was not listed.

'Extraordinary!' Maria muttered, 'or is it?'

She turned next to her index of British schools, but she failed to trace the girl's previous seat of learning — Elmington High School. Small the place might be, but every college and school in the country was included here, as she well knew.

'Maria, you are learning things,' she muttered. 'Out of nowhere, literally, you've got a new pupil. Maybe Major Hasleigh handed to me what the films call a — ah — 'bum steer', so he could get out without evading my questions. However, there are other ways yet.'

Accordingly she sent a telegram to the sister-in-law over the phone, reading

— Are you relative of Major Hasleigh? Reply to Black, Roseway College, near Langhorn, Sussex. Then, satisfied that she had done all she could for the moment she hurried off to take the biology class.

The girls, however, found that their empress was right off her form. She even muffed that technical bit about the sub-clavicle artery, which was her favourite bit of bonework. They little knew that her eyes and mind were trained on the school gates, through the big classroom window, otherwise they might have understood.

When the telegraph boy did eventually appear Maria had moved on to the Fourth Form. She brought the lesson to a hurried close, then hastened to her study just as the porter was bringing the telegram in. She took it from him, dismissed him briefly. Then when she had the buff form in her hand she frowned over it.

It had a blue ink rubber-stamp right across it — UNDELIVERABLE. ADDRESS UNKNOWN.

'Extraordinary, even incredible,' she reflected. 'A girl from nowhere, indeed, whose associations seem to have melted like her father's sunburn. Definitely I must keep an eye on her — definitely!'

2

All unaware of the effect she had produced on her crime-sensitive Headmistress, Frances Hasleigh domiciled herself in Study F the moment she had freshened up and placed her belongings in the dormitory locker assigned to her by Miss Tanby. There were no studies for her until tomorrow, so until classes were ended for the afternoon she spent a little while tidying up the none too orderly study, a job she had just completed when Beryl Mather and Joan Dawson entered, their textbooks slung in leather straps over their shoulders.

'Well!' exclaimed the dark girl, throwing down the books. 'A newcomer, eh? How are you? I'm Joan Dawson.'

Frances shook hands. 'I'm Frances Hasleigh. Glad to know you both — '

Beryl Mather, 13 stone of a girl, shook hands, too. 'Call me Tiny,' she grinned. 'Everybody else does. If you ever need my proper name it's Beryl Mather — '

Frances studied her big, round, grinning face — then she looked back at Joan Dawson. She was very different — slim, graceful, rather thin-featured, with expressive dark eyes and a general alertness of manner.

'I haven't been here so long myself,' Joan sighed. 'I'm not very struck on it, either. The nearest boys' college is fifteen miles away and the cinemas all have ancient films. Buried alive, I call it'

'Boys don't interest me,' Frances said quietly. 'If I have any male company at all I like intelligent men — full of brains.'

Joan raised her eyebrows. 'Hmm . . . Anyway, it's time we had some tea. We can either have what we've collected for ourselves — no easy job in these rationing days — or else we can take what the dining-hall provides. It isn't compulsory, like dinner. What's your fancy?'

'Chicken and champagne,' Frances shrugged. 'Otherwise I'll share whatever you've got. I've had no time yet to do any shopping of my own.'

'Tiny does ours,' Joan smiled. 'Food is

about the only thing she lives for.'

'And a thin time I'm having!' Beryl objected, putting the kettle on. 'Still, maybe I'll keep body and soul together somehow — '

Joan laughed, but Frances Hasleigh did not even smile. Instead she turned and looked thoughtfully out of the window. Joan Dawson frowned. This new girl seemed to have precious little to say, and she was decidedly unemotional considering her surroundings were strange to her. There was rather an odd expression on her face, too, as though she were under some kind of strain. Pretty enough, however, with her clear grey eyes, fair hair, and straight features. Yet, somehow, there was something very mature about her. She had neither the poise nor the figure of a girl of sixteen —

'Where did you go to school before?' Beryl asked.

'Elmington High School,' Frances answered absently. 'You probably never heard of it.'

'No, I never have,' Joan said. 'Not that it matters — '

Frances looked from one girl to the

other. 'We three are more or less compelled to live together, so maybe I'd better make one or two things clear now. You won't find me very good company. I talk very little and avoid contacts as much as possible. I do not like frothy young men, but I do like brainy ones. If you don't pester me with silly questions, I shan't pester you, and if you find I have odd habits and do odd things that will be my own affair, for which I'll take full responsibility. That understood?'

Joan frowned. 'Yes, of course, but we aren't the ones who can cause you much trouble. Don't do anything to upset Miss Black or Tanny. They're mustard — especially Black Maria.'

Frances said nothing. She had retired into that strange shell of reserve again. She resumed gazing through the window until a prod in the back reminded her that tea was ready.

'You're a queer one,' Beryl remarked, taking her chair. 'I never heard a new girl get things off her chest so quickly. Here, try the salmon-paste — or have a teacake?'

'Teacake,' Frances said absently. 'And a drink of tea.'

Joan and Beryl exchanged glances, then presently it seemed to become too much for the sharper girl.

'Look here, Frances, if there is any sort of trouble you're in we'll be only too glad to help out — if we can. We don't mind you wrapping yourself up in yourself, but don't do it too much, will you? It gets on one's nerves a bit, and I'm a pretty nervy customer at the best of times.'

'I just want to think — and hard; and I can't do it if you two insist on pestering me. Just leave me alone!'

'What's to think about?' Joan asked, mystified. 'In this place everything is done for you. We don't think; we just obey — or Heaven help us!'

Frances ate silently for a while, then: 'If I wanted to ask a pretty brainy man about the exact position of the star Sirius, whom would I approach?'

Joan set her teacup down and Beryl nearly choked over her sandwich.

'Why do you want to know that?' Beryl asked blankly. 'Who cares, anyway?'

'I do!' Frances retorted irritably. 'I'm simply asking a straightforward question. I happen to be interested in astronomy, you see — '

'The only stars I like are on the films,' Beryl said pensively. 'Tyrone Power, and Errol Flynn, and — '

'Will one of you please answer my question?' Frances insisted sharply.

'You're not a teacher, you know!' Joan said indignantly. 'Answering your question, I should think Mr. Lever would be your best bet. Young — about twenty-four, waiting to be called up, and positively bulging with brains. You say you like that sort, so there it is.'

'How do I find him?' Frances asked quickly.

'You don't! He's only visible in the classroom when taking science. The rest of the time he is over on the staff side of the building. Very strict regulations, you know. Too many attractive young ladies about for any looseness.'

'Yes, I should think he ought to be able to answer my question very easily,' Frances nodded. 'Thanks for telling me

— albeit belatedly. Now to something else. How often is one allowed to leave the school? In the evening, I mean.'

'You can go to Lexham, the nearest town, once a week if you get a permit from Miss Black,' Joan answered. 'Otherwise our activities are limited to Langhorn — the village. When you go to Lexham you have to be in here by ten-thirty. With Langhorn the limit is eight-thirty. Langhorn has a cinema, anyway, and that's something.'

Frances gave a rather tired smile. 'You were right, Joan, when you said things were slow around here. I like a bit of bright life now and again, so if at any time you wake up in the dorm and find a bolster doing service in bed for me, don't be surprised.'

'Do as you wish, of course,' Joan shrugged. 'But if you are ever caught breaking bounds it may mean expulsion. You know that don't you?'

'I know. But I have my own reasons for being a roamer.'

'Not all the girls will be as loyal to you as we will,' Beryl pointed out. 'We have our sneaks and tittle-tattlers.'

'I'll risk it,' Frances said calmly.

Joan shrugged again and went on with her tea. It was no use trying to argue with this odd girl. So quiet and innocent, yet obviously knowing her way about, it was hard to read her. Certainly she did not behave with the usual self-conscious shyness of a new girl: she was entirely self-possessed.

'We're going up into the solarium after tea,' Beryl said, looking longingly at the remaining cake. 'Coming? Give you a chance to meet the others.'

'Depends what you do there,' Frances replied.

'Anything you want,' Joan shrugged. 'Either lie in the evening sun and think out your future, or else have a bit of exercise with the medicine ball, dumb-bells, parallel-bars, or — Well, you can please yourself.'

Frances thought it out, then nodded — so some fifteen minutes later found them up in the solarium where several girls had already congregated. Some were writing letters; some were practising their own variations on physical culture; still others were sitting about and talking. But practically all of them paused in sudden interest at the sight of the new girl in the Sixth.

It certainly put ideas into the mind of Vera Randal, the head girl of the Sixth Form, to which position she had climbed mainly by literal force of arms. Tall and massively built, she came ambling forward as she saw Joan pointing out the various virtues of the big place.

'Who's the little stranger?' she asked Joan.

Joan turned sharply and looked up at the big, domineering face with its thrush-like speckling of freckles.

'I'm Frances Hasleigh,' the girl herself said, quietly.

'Well, well — quite a high-sounding name! Know any tricks?'

'A few,' Frances answered, her voice still calm.

'Then don't try them on me!' Vera Randal advised. 'I'm the head girl of the Sixth Form and in case you get any queer ideas beforehand I'm telling you that I have a way of dealing with shrimps like you if they try and upset my authority . . . But you wouldn't try and do that, would you?'

Frances did not answer and deliberately turned her back. The girls glanced at each other as Vera Randal's face reddened.

'I'm talking to you! You! New girl!'

Frances turned languidly. 'Oh, I'm sorry. I thought you'd finished long ago. You are head girl and you don't allow shrimps like me to block your path. All right. Now what do we do?'

Breathing deeply, Vera gazed at the cynical grey eyes; then suddenly she looked round on the others.

'Impudent for a new kid, isn't she?' she sneered. 'But she'll learn! All right, it's time for our usual half-hour's ultra-violet. Come on, everybody!'

There was a general scurrying to the dressing rooms. Joan caught Frances's arm tightly.

'Come on, Frances — this way. It will tone you up a bit. You have a pretty pale skin, come to think of it — '

'Just a minute!' Frances shook herself free. 'What exactly are we going to do?'

'Take sunray treatment. There are the machines over there by the wall. Ultraviolet. It's grand stuff if you know how to use it — '

'Not if I know it!' Frances said abruptly, her mouth setting firmly — then she looked round as the big hand of Vera Randal fell on her shoulder.

'Won't do, newcomer!' she announced. 'We all do it, and My Lady Highbrow isn't going to be the exception! Come on and get into a swimsuit — '

'I said I wasn't going to!' Frances retorted. 'Just leave me alone!'

'I don't stand disobedience, especially from a new kid!' Vera snapped. 'And you're going to do as I say!'

With that she whirled Frances forward resolutely, but the girl did not go very far. Suddenly she halted herself, turned round, and caught the big girl by the wrist. Before she knew what was happening Vera had whirled round, over Frances's head, and landed with a terrific thump on the floor matting.

'Sorry,' Frances said, straightening up, 'but I meant what I said. I am not going to take ultra-violet treatment — '

She headed towards the door, then, as she reached it, she paused and looked back.

'That's one of my tricks,' she explained drily, smiling at the astonished, dishevelled Vera. 'Ju-jitsu. Why don't you try it yourself some time?'

'Of all the confounded . . . ' Vera breathed, then she blinked as the door closed sharply and Frances departed.

★ ★ ★

Mr. Robert Lever, aged twenty-four, proud of his moustache and his prowess in the various branches of science, was deep in Einstein's *Relativity* when there came a gentle knocking on his study door. He looked up, put on the plain-lensed glasses he wore to convey a more mature aspect, straightened his ruffled black hair, then bade the visitor enter.

He tried to imagine who it might be at this hour of eleven-thirty. Surely none of the domestics, and even less likely to be a teacher —

To his astonishment a pale-faced, blonde-headed girl came in, a light blanket coat enveloping her slender figure up to her chin, just as though she was prepared for some kind of pretty cold vigil.

'Mr. Lever?' she asked, closing the door.

'Why, yes. I — er — ' He stopped and looked at her anxiously. 'I am afraid I haven't had the pleasure of meeting you before. And I think I ought to tell you that this is a dangerous violation of the college rules.'

'Yes — I know. I'm Frances Hasleigh, a new pupil here. I want to ask you a question. I'm told that you are pretty good at astronomy.'

'Well, I know a little about it, certainly. But — but you can't come here like this! If it were found out I'd lose my position — '

Frances smiled with her colourless lips. 'Since you are liable to be called up soon, would that matter anyway? Wouldn't you rather help a much puzzled girl even if it means the risk of discharge?'

He looked at her fixedly as though trying to imagine what she meant — then, struck with a thought, he went over and locked the door.

'This is really terrible,' he said, returning to face her. 'If you want to ask me a question do so in a whisper, and then go! Now, what is it?'

Frances seated herself with a certain air of possession. And looking at her there were few thoughts of science left in the mind of Robert Lever. He knew only two things — that he was in decided danger and that she was extremely pretty.

'Mr. Lever,' she said, 'I want to know the position of Sirius.'

'Good Heavens!' he exclaimed blankly.

Frances raised her eyebrows. 'Isn't it a natural question for a student of astronomy to ask?'

'Oh, yes, I suppose it is — but at eleven-thirty at night when you should be in your dormitory . . . I can show you a stellar map giving its exact position at this time of the year. Or I can draw you a design if you wish.' Lever turned to his desk and began to rummage. 'Hmm — how annoying. I must have left my fountain-pen in the form room again . . . '

'Don't you think it better, Mr. Lever, if you showed me the star in the sky itself?' Frances murmured. 'It's a glorious night, and with everything blacked out it helps the study of the stars enormously.'

'Does it?' he asked weakly, glancing at the curtained window.

'I don't think a window view would be much use,' Frances said. 'The buildings will hide the view a lot. We'll have to go into the quadrangle. After all, it won't take a minute to solve my little problem.'

'But, hang it all, Miss — er — Hasleigh, why do you want to know such a thing anyway?'

'Just interest,' Frances shrugged. 'And because I am a pupil in a seat of learning I expect you to help me. If you don't . . . Well, of course, I could hint to Miss Black that I had been here and — '

'I'll show you with pleasure!' Lever interrupted hastily, and realized now why she was so wrapped up. She had obviously planned beforehand to reach her objective. So he got into his own coat, opened the door softly, and peered down the dimly lit corridor.

'Nobody saw you come here?' he whispered.

'Not so far as I know. I had to find my way with a torch, but I had a pretty good idea where your study was — '

'This way,' he said, and, taking her arm, he led her silently down the corridor and so finally out into the quadrangle. It was dark, starlit, surrounded by the blacked-out mass of the college buildings.

'Now, which is it?' Frances asked, looking skywards.

'There!' Lever pointed upwards and the girl angled her head closer to him, apparently to get in line with his hand. Finally, as she searched in vain, he caught her shoulder and moved her towards him gently.

'There! See? Right between those two stars — '

Then he broke off in horror at a sudden cough from the gloom. A torch gleamed into life and behind it was a dim figure. Lever was on the point of making a dash for it, but the girl caught his arm tightly.

'I hope, Mr. Lever, that you have a satisfactory explanation for this conduct?'

The voice was acid, and the figure behind the torch proved to be Miss Tanby, an overcoat thrown hastily about her shoulders. She flashed the beam into both faces steadily.

'I — er — I don't know,' Lever gasped helplessly.

'I see. Then perhaps you will have time to clear your mind a little by the time we reach Miss Black's study. Come with me, please — both of you. Fortunately Miss Black has not yet retired — '

The dazed science master and Frances Hasleigh were escorted across the quadrangle to the School House. It had all happened so swiftly that Lever just did not know what he was doing; but Frances, for her part, did not seem to be in the least worried. The most concerned over the business was clearly Miss Tanby. There was even triumphant glee in the way she knocked on the door of Maria's study.

'Come in!' she bade imperiously, and the three entered to find her reclining in the armchair holding a volume entitled *A.B.C. of Tracking*. She laid it aside at the vision confronting her.

'Why, Miss Tanby, whatever is wrong?'

'I don't want to think the worst, Miss Black, but unfortunately I have to,' the Housemistress replied. 'Not twenty minutes ago Vera Randal came to my study and informed me that she had seen Hasleigh here leaving the dormitory, putting a bolster dummy in her bed. I felt it my duty to look into it immediately. I had hardly reached the quadrangle before I found Hasleigh here with Mr. Lever. And — and they were . . . well, embracing!'

'I deny that!' Lever retorted. 'I was merely showing the young lady the exact position of Sirius.'

'So Vera Randal was awake, eh?' Frances murmured, reflecting. 'I wasn't quite sure — '

Maria rose, her face stern. 'This

infraction of the rules is bad enough in your case, Hasleigh — a newcomer to the school. But it is far worse in yours, Mr. Lever! You are fully conversant with the regulations. What is your explanation?'

'I have already given it, Miss Black,' he answered quietly. 'This young lady came to my study about eleven-thirty with a request to be shown the exact position of the star Sirius. I suggested I could do it with a star-chart, or draw a design for her — but she insisted on us going into the quadrangle to look at the sky. So I showed it to her. Then Miss Tanby came up.'

'And what is this about an — hmm! — embrace?' Maria asked coldly.

'Just mistaken appearances, that's all. I was trying to direct Miss Hasleigh's eye to the right point in the sky.'

'Huh!' sniffed Tanby, then fell silent as Maria gave her a glance before turning to Frances.

'Well, Hasleigh, is this correct?'

'Not altogether,' she answered slowly. 'I *did* ask Mr. Lever about the star Sirius, certainly — but when we got out into the

38

quadrangle he started making love to me. I was trying to hold him back from kissing me when Miss Tanby came up — fortunately!'

Lever stared at her blankly. '*I* made love to you! But, good Lord, I never heard such a lie in my life! I — '

'You knew perfectly well that you had no right to leave your dormitory, didn't you?' Maria demanded, and Frances nodded slowly.

'Yes, Miss Black, I knew it. But the Sirius problem was worrying me. And in new surroundings I didn't feel I could settle, either. I wanted fresh air. So I decided to kill two birds with one stone. I could not see that I was doing anything really wrong. It was Mr. Lever here who spoilt it by his love-making.'

Maria reflected, fingering her watch-chain. Then: 'Since you are fully aware of the rules, Mr. Lever,' she said, 'I have no alternative but to ask you to leave this establishment. Your duty when this girl came to you was to telephone across to Miss Tanby and report that Hasleigh was out of bounds. You did not do that — and that condemns you. You will kindly make arrangements to leave within twenty-four hours and I will communicate with the Board of Governors concerning salary in lieu of notice. I will not for one moment tolerate this fraternity between pupils and teachers of opposite sex. That is all.'

Lever clenched his fists and looked at Frances bitterly.

'I could take this better if you were not such a cheap, rotten little liar!' he breathed. 'Many a man would slit your throat for this.'

'I will thank you to leave, Mr. Lever,' Maria said coldly.

He gave her one look, then turned and went, slamming the door.

'I'm sorry, Miss Black,' Frances said quietly. 'I suppose I did transgress, but I never thought it would turn out as it did.'

'I am prepared,' Maria said, 'to make allowances for your un-accustomedness to this college. Had you been here some little time expulsion would have followed automatically. As it is, I shall levy the punishment of a week's confinement to the school area in the hope that you will learn more clearly that whilst here you have got to obey the rules. If you ever transgress again you know the penalty. Now return to your dormitory at once!'

'Yes, m'm,' Frances said, her voice low. Then as she turned to go Maria gave her pause.

'A moment, Hasleigh. Just why does the star Sirius so concern you?'

'Oh, I — I just wondered which it is,' she shrugged. 'There is nothing more in it than that, m'm.'

'Hmm . . . ' Maria tightened her lips. 'Very well, you may go.'

As the door closed Tanby moved forward urgently. 'Miss Black, it's not my place to question your judgment, of course, but I must say that I expected you would expel that girl. This deliberate infraction of the rules is probably only the beginning! A girl who will do that so shamelessly will probably do it again and again!'

Maria smiled faintly. 'Surprisingly enough, Miss Tanby, I agree with you — but if I were to expel her how would I do it? Her rather — er — peculiar father is probably out of the country by now, her mythical relations are non-existent. As far as I can see she has nowhere to live but here. If I were to expel her when she has nowhere to go I would lay myself open to censure from the Board of Governors. I am bound by the same law as landlord and tenant: I cannot expel a pupil who has no home to return to . . . With Mr. Lever it is different. I expect he will join up. If I had not discharged him the Board would have reprimanded me.'

Tanby rubbed her pointed chin worriedly. 'I wish I could make out what kind of a girl this Frances is,' she muttered. 'She certainly does not behave like any ordinary pupil. So tremendously assured . . . Why don't you ask her about her dubious connections?'

'Chiefly because I have no legal right to do so yet — and also because she intrigues me . . . ' Maria sat down again at her desk. 'To be truthful, Miss Tanby, I find it most interesting to have somebody peculiar right in my own college, instead of having to go and find them, as I did when I went to America last year.'

Tanby gave her a sharp look. 'Miss Black, I do believe that you have kept this girl on here just to — to satisfy your whim for solving mysteries!'

Maria gave a grave smile and picked up her *A.B.C. of Tracking* again.

'The hour is getting late, Miss Tanby, and I have a chapter of this to re-read yet. I think perhaps we had better discuss again after a night's sleep.'

After Tanby left Maria sat on reading a few minutes, then she lowered her book. Unlocking her desk drawer she brought out a black leather bound book. In a moment she had it open, skipped through the pages referring to the murder of her brother in America, then stopped at the page she had headed *The Hasleigh Puzzle*. So far she had not made a very extensive entry —

A new girl has been enrolled today — Frances Hasleigh. Pretty blonde, a trifle cynical, and unusual in manner. Her father is even more unusual. Is sunburned, and yet it washes off! Hates ultra-violet machinery if it is to be used on his daughter. Has given me the names of relations which do not exist!

Picking up her pen Maria made further notes —

Frances Hasleigh has deliberately broken the rules and visited the science master, Mr. Robert Lever, at 11.30 p.m. She says the reason for her mission was to find out the exact position of the star Sirius. Does this mean anything? Have been compelled to discharge Lever and confine Frances to the school buildings for one week. This young lady definitely intrigues me.
Time of entry: 12.7 a.m.

'And somehow,' Maria mused, 'I think it has only just begun. I am psychologist enough to know that she is not an ordinary schoolgirl. Not by any means! Manner, figure, deportment — they are all against it ... Most extraordinary! Most!'

3

For three days of the week's confinement to college Frances Hasleigh made no effort to break the sentence. She had become entirely reserved and spoke only when spoken to, except for occasional outbursts of icy invective against Vera Randal, who never lost an opportunity to remind Frances of her infraction — being careful, however, not to go too far. She remembered the heavy fall on her back in the solarium.

Then, on the night of the third day, Joan Dawson awoke abruptly about one in the morning to find the girl fully dressed and gliding towards the biggest window at the far end of the dormitory.

'Frances!' she called softly. 'Where are you going?'

'A walk,' came the laconic answer. 'Stick up for me if anybody finds I've gone. I've left a bolster — '

Then, silently, the window opened and

45

a dim figure was visible for a moment sliding on to the stone balcony outside. Obviously Frances was using the big drainpipe method of exit this time.

Joan peered through the window. Her bed was right against the centre window and without any effort she could see across the quadrangle to the big bulk of the School House. There was a moon getting up, and by its murky silver light she presently saw Frances's figure move swiftly across the open space below into the shadows — then she lost sight of her.

Joan gave a start as the light at Vera Randal's end of the dormitory suddenly gushed into being. She was sitting up in bed with her big freckled face shining with triumph.

'Put that light out!' Joan cried. 'The curtains aren't drawn! Blackout — '

Since Vera took no notice Joan hopped out of bed and covered the windows quickly. By this time the whole dormitory seemed to be awake.

'I heard what she said!' Vera cried. 'Off again, is she? Well this time it will finish her! I'll get her kicked out of the school for this! Throw me about the solarium, will she!'

'Shut up!' hissed Molly Webster, one of her study mates. 'You'll be having Tanny here in a minute!'

'Let her come!' Vera snapped. 'If she doesn't, I'm going to her.'

Vera got decisively out of bed, put on slippers and a dressing gown. She headed towards the door, but before she reached it Joan and Beryl Mather had caught her arms tightly.

'Wait a minute, Vera!' Joan insisted. 'If you keep on running to Tanny with stories you're liable to get yourself labelled as a sneak, and you know what that will mean. You just won't be head girl any longer!'

Vera hesitated, looking across at Molly.

'We can settle this between ourselves,' Molly said. 'Anyway, Frances didn't get expelled last time, so she probably won't this. I think she's one of Black's favourites — '

'That isn't true!' Joan said hotly. 'And since it seems to get on all your nerves, why don't you have it out with her

47

personally when she comes back? That's only right!'

'Listen to little Joan standing up for wayward little Frances,' Vera sneered. 'It makes me sick! You, and Tiny there, and Frances are as thick as thieves. Why don't you share your joys and sorrows with us? And another thing, Joan, when are you going to share that parcel you got this morning?'

'I can't share it,' Joan retorted. 'It was a pair of stockings and I'm sticking to it!'

'One day,' Vera mused, her eyes narrowing, 'I'm going to take you apart, Joan! But first I'll deal with Frances! Just wait until she gets back!'

She put the light out again, drew the curtains away from the windows once more, then back to bed to wait. The example set the other girls did likewise.

It was nearly an hour later before Frances reappeared at the big window and opened it silently. Just as carefully she closed it and began to glide across to her bed; then there was stealthy movement in the dark and she found herself surrounded with torch-beams playing on her face.

'Well, Miss Gadabout, what this time?' Vera demanded. 'Been out with your precious science master again? He's still in the village, you know, even if he has quit the school. I saw him this afternoon when I went shopping.'

'Is it any business of yours where I've been?' Frances asked, in that quiet, insolent voice she had.

'As head girl of this class it definitely is! I'd have reported it to Miss Tanby right away but for — my sense of honour . . . And don't smile like that, either! You can't keep on breaking rules when it is my job to see that they're kept!'

'I'm afraid you take an awful lot on your shoulders,' Frances said coolly, taking off her overcoat and returning it to her locker. 'And don't keep flashing that beam in my face, please. Or are you playing at gangsters?'

'That's it!' Vera whispered. 'Give me one chance and I'll break your neck one day, Frances — believe me!'

Frances sat on the side of her bed and began to undress leisurely. The torches had been extinguished now, but she could see the girls hovering over her in the moonlight.

'You're all very tiresome,' she sighed. 'If I feel like going out for a walk in the moonlight, I'll go! Anyway, Vera, a girl with a cloddish mind like yours can't be expected to feel as I do. My father is a traveller and a soldier, remember. I get the wanderlust from him.'

'You're not going to call me a clod and get away with it!' Vera snapped.

'Oh, why don't you leave her alone?' growled Cynthia Vane, her other study mate. 'I don't like her either, but why do we have to lose our sleep just because of that? If she wants to creep about, let her!'

'Anyway,' Molly Webster said, 'one would think you'd never broken a rule in your life, Vera! I've been here long enough to know that you've broken every rule in the book in order to be top girl. Let's get back to bed — '

Vera hesitated, then with memories of her fall in the solarium at the back of her mind she relaxed and nodded slowly.

'All right, we'll go back to sleep. Otherwise there will be some questions asked if we're tired in class tomorrow. But I'm not finished with you yet, Frances Hasleigh! I know what you want — to be in my place. And that issue's got to be decided! Before I'm finished with you you'll be on your knees begging for mercy!'

Frances did not answer. Undressed by now, she climbed into bed, drew the covers over her and remained silent. Grim-faced, Vera plodded back to bed. The group broke up and retired again.

After her one infraction Frances did not break the rules again during the rest of her week's punishment — but whether it was because she was uncertain of what Vera Randal might do was not entirely clear. She said so little, even to her two study mates, and by now they had become her bosom friends. They both gave every impression of liking her really, despite her rather queer temperament.

The only thrill the girls got as the week ended and Frances found herself free again — on probation anyway — was the arrival of a new science master, by the name of Clive Whittaker. All hopes of a young man rather less dull than Robert Lever were realised when into the classroom to take biology there walked one afternoon a man of perhaps twenty-eight, tall and stooping, clean-shaven, with black wavy hair and a rather pale face. Somehow he looked delicate, or else it was an impression conveyed by his bent shoulders.

But he knew his job, as the girls soon found out — and to their delight he treated them, in every Form, with an easy courtesy calculated to get the best out of their studies. There was none of the dull recital of facts that had made Robert Lever so outstandingly uninteresting.

For some reason, Frances came to life in real earnest when he took the class. Her usual languid contempt entirely disappeared and instead she had brightly sparkling grey eyes and a merry smile. It was most extraordinary, and more than one girl noticed it, too. Then, when she was only listening to Whittaker instead of answering his scientific posers, Frances sat looking at him with a kind of awed reverence that made more than one girl nudge another and then stifle a giggle.

It was finally Joan Dawson who brought the matter to a head when the class was over on the Monday afternoon. She, Frances, and Tiny Mather were strolling out of the School House into the warmth of the sunlit quadrangle.

'I suppose,' Joan said, 'that it's your weakness for brainy young men that makes you go cow-eyed when you see Whittaker?'

'I think he's just marvellous,' Frances said simply. Joan and Beryl glanced at each other.

'But he's got round shoulders!' Beryl protested.

'Ah, but his *mind*!' Frances said dreamily.

'Well — er — would you like to tell him so?' Joan asked drily. 'Here he is now — approaching. Looks as though he's going out.'

'Hey, Frances, just a minute!'

She turned at the sharp command and saw that Vera Randal, Molly Webster, and Cynthia Vane were hurrying towards them. In a moment or two they had caught up.

'Well?' Frances asked calmly. 'What is it, head girl?'

'Don't try and be funny with me! I want to know if you have the nerve to decide our differences right away? There is only room for one head girl, and the issue's in doubt. If I am the head girl you have got to obey me. If you can defeat me you can take my place and I obey you.'

Frances raised her eyebrows. 'Sounds quite primitive — like apes fighting for the kingship. Well, what am I to do? Knock the confounded stuffing out of you?'

'You're welcome to try,' Vera sneered. 'I've a suggestion to make. We've got an hour before tea. Come out to Bollin's Wood and bring your two pals here as your seconds — and I'll bring Molly and Cynthia as mine. We'll thrash it out. If you can get me on my back and keep my arms pinned to the ground while ten is counted I'll admit you're the new head girl — '

As Frances reflected, Clive Whittaker came past. He nodded and smiled.

'Lovely day, sir,' Frances smiled.

'Delightful,' he agreed, and it seemed to the other girls that he gave her an odd look. 'Just on my way to do some shopping in our thriving village . . . And you girls take care you don't start damaging each other,' he added. 'I heard what you said, Randal — and it sounded most aggressive. After all, this *is* a school for young ladies . . . '

Then he was on his way again towards the school gates, leaving Frances looking after him.

'When you've quite finished mooning, what about it?' Vera demanded.

'It's the accepted idea,' Joan said quickly, as Frances gave her a look of inquiry. 'I really think you ought to do it!'

'All right,' Frances shrugged. 'Let's be off!'

With that she linked her arms through those of Joan and Beryl and led the way to the gates, followed at a distance by the hefty Vera and her two stooges. A ten-minute walk down the lane brought them to the stile leading into Bollin's Wood — a deep mass of shady under-growth at this time of year, the ground a solid carpet of ferns, long rank grass, and twisting brambles.

The girls went on until they were well within the wood's depths, then in a little clearing, just within sight of the River Bollin, Vera called a halt, motioned her two friends on one side.

'Now,' she breathed venomously, 'it's my turn! I'm not going to fight you, Frances, because I can't do ju-jitsu like you can. That wouldn't be fair play — but I'm going to make you smart for the way you've treated me! Right!' she broke off suddenly. *'On her!'*

Utterly unprepared for an onrush by three at once, Frances went crashing over to the ground with the girls on top of her. Joan and Beryl rushed to her assistance immediately, but they could do very little, particularly against Vera. In perhaps thirty seconds Frances was stretched out flat, her shoes taken off, her ankles corded together and her hands tied behind her. For good measure a gag was added and tied tightly in her mouth. Three to two was more than they could handle, especially against a heavyweight like Vera.

They, too, lost their shoes and found themselves bound and gagged in double quick time.

'There!' Vera breathed, standing up and taking the three pairs of shoes Molly Webster had collected. 'This is going to be Lesson One! You can get from here to the lane without shoes, and I hope you enjoy it! You'll find your shoes by the stile, and if none of you are too good on your feet for the next week we'll quite understand. The gags are so you can't yell for help, like the rotten little cowards all of you are . . . All right, girls, come on!'

Molly and Cynthia nodded and followed their leader out of the clearing. As Vera had promised, she put the shoes by the stile, then she and her two consorts went across to the sunny grass bank on the other side of the lane. They sat down with a certain air of resolve, prepared to watch the fun.

Ten minutes passed and the wood remained quiet. The three looked at each other in vague surprise, shifted their positions, then relaxed and waited again.

'Even if they take all night we're not

going in after them,' Vera stated flatly. 'They might spring a trap and do the same to us. I wouldn't put anything past Frances — '

'Taking a long while, anyway,' Cynthia Vane said. 'I'm not going to get much fun out of this if they don't hurry up! 'Sides, I want my tea.'

'Tea can wait for a treat like this,' Molly Webster said, leaning back on the grass.

So another twenty minutes passed without anything happening.

'I suppose,' Cynthia said doubtfully, 'we shouldn't — ?'

'No!' Vera retorted. 'And shut up!'

But even Vera began to become uneasy when a full hour and a half had gone by and the girls had not appeared. At the most Vera had reckoned her painful idea of a joke would not take more than thirty minutes . . .

'Oh, confound them!' she said at last, getting to her feet impatiently. 'They must have gone the other way without their shoes, or something, just to spite us. We'd better look. Come on.'

She led the way across the lane, over

the stile, then re-entered the wood warily. The shoes were still there by the stile, as they had been throughout the full period. In the wood itself there was dead silence, save for the rustling of the leaves in the wind. The chill of evening was on it now, too.

'Gently,' Vera cautioned, as the others caught up with her. 'Be ready for anything — '

But nothing untoward occurred. Until finally they came through the last bushes surrounding the little clearing — They stopped dead, paralysed at the sight that had burst upon them. Sheer horror absolutely held them rigid. They wanted to run, to scream, to cry out — but they couldn't do any of these things. They could only go staring and feel their mouths get dry and their faces hot.

Lying flat on the ground, obviously unconscious, were Joan Dawson and Beryl Mather, still bound and gagged as before. This in itself was unexpected and unpleasant enough — but the worst sight of all was of Frances Hasleigh hanging from the lowest branch of a nearby tree, her hands still corded behind her and her feet a good six inches from the ground. She even swayed gently in the wind, a terrible puppet at the end of a rope.

'Oh!' Vera gulped, perspiration standing out in big drops on her colourless face. 'Oh, God, she's — *She's been hanged*!' she screamed abruptly. 'Quick — get out of here — !'

Her own blind panic was as nothing compared to Molly's and Cynthia's. They swung round and raced for their lives back to the lane, tripping and falling as they went, blundering out at last over the stile . . . Here, after a moment or two of stormy breathing, they began to collect their wits.

'What — what on earth do we do now?' Molly stammered. 'Something terrible's happened — and we'll be blamed for it!'

'We didn't do it, you idiot!' Cynthia shrieked, visibly shaking with fright.

'We've got to tell Miss Black,' Vera said. 'We'll have to! Come on — '

So they turned and ran all the way back to the school, came through the gates like track runners, to be followed by the amazed stares of the girls lounging about the quadrangle. Breathless and dusty, the three finally reached Maria's study and blundered in after each other without as much as a knock.

'Girls! Girls!' Maria cried imperiously, jumping to her feet. 'Such unseemly behaviour! Remember where you are!'

'It's — it's Frances!' Vera babbled, 'She's been hanged!'

'She's been *what*?'

'She's hanging there in Bollin's Wood,' Cynthia Vane went on hysterically. 'We've just seen her! Tied up to a tree by her neck. Her wrists, and ankles, bound. A gag in her mouth — And Joan Dawson and Beryl Mather are there, too, senseless. Oh, this is awful . . . I think I'm going to faint.'

'Steady, girls,' Maria breathed, her face sternly set. 'Steady, I say! This is a desperately serious matter . . . Here, I'll come back with you right away.'

She turned, slipped on her hat and coat, then accompanied the girls outside. The stares were more prolonged than ever at the sight of the usually majestic

Maria speeding along with her hat slightly awry and three chattering girls with her.

In seven minutes flat they were at the site of the tragedy, and Maria paused for a moment as the terrible scene confronted her. Then, getting a hold of herself, she went over to the hanging girl and stared up at her. There was not the least doubt of the fact that she was dead. Her eyes were starting horribly and her face had the dull purple tint of strangulation. Across her mouth, wedged between the teeth, was the rough gag . . . Maria gave a little shiver, then felt the girl's tied hands. They were warm.

'Webster,' she said briefly, turning to the startled Molly, 'go to the village police station immediately and fetch Inspector Morgan back with you. Tell him what has happened and ask him to fetch a doctor with him. Hurry!'

'Yes, Miss Black!' And the girl went at top speed.

Then Maria transferred her attention to Joan and Beryl. Joan did not seem far from recovering consciousness but Beryl was out cold. Maria's hand detected the lump on the back of the fat girl's head, which had obviously been the cause of her collapse. As far as Joan was concerned there was no such evidence: perhaps shock had done it in her case.

In a few moments both girls were unfastened, Joan proving the easiest to untie. Maria went to work to revive them while Vera Randal was sent to the nearest house in the lane for water. In ten minutes both girls were looking about them, dazed and breathless.

'What on earth happened — ?' Joan whispered moving stiffly. 'I was — Oh, I remember! Something hit me in the jaw! Oh, it's you, Miss Black!' Startled realisation of something wrong came suddenly into her pale face. Her eyes moved and rested finally on the swinging body. *'Ohh!'* Her voice was a screech. 'It's — it's Frances! Look — *look* — !'

'Steady, steady,' Maria murmured, patting her arm. 'Just keep a hold on yourself, my dear — and don't look towards that tree more than you have to — '

'But — but she's hanging!' Beryl

Mather whispered, staring at the body as though trying to understand it. 'How is she — ?' Then suddenly it dawned on her what horrible implication was behind it and her big body started to shake with something between tears and explosions of fear.

Altogether, Maria had her hands full for the next few minutes trying to force both girls to calm themselves. Gradually they did so: they could do little else in Maria's masterful presence,

'You were hit on the head, Beryl, weren't you?' Maria asked.

She nodded painfully. 'And it still aches horribly, m'm. I was trying to free myself when something hit me on the head and I passed out.'

'Free yourself?' Maria repeated sharply.

'All three of us were left tied up,' Joan said looking up at Vera Randal. 'Then we had our shoes taken off and were left to walk or jump back to the stile by the lane — '

'Indeed!' Maria turned a grim face to Vera. 'From the look I saw Joan just give you, young lady, I imagine you had something to do with the matter?'

'Yes,' the big girl acknowledged sheepishly. And without any further hesitation she told the whole story, finishing lamely, 'It was only meant as a joke — and it finished like this!'

Maria tightened her lips then she glanced up at sudden sounds in the undergrowth and three figures appeared — Inspector Morgan, whom she knew quite well, Dr. Roberts, who did most of the local police medical work, and the still scared Molly Webster.

'This is a pretty horrible business, Miss Black,' Morgan said, his eyes on the body. 'This girl has been telling me all about it — '

'I left the body as it is until you have examined it,' Maria answered, then she stood at the side of the inspector and watched as Dr. Roberts studied the body intently from various angles. At length he gave a nod.

'We can take it down now, Inspector,' he said. It was no easy job. Morgan had to climb up the tree and along the branch to grapple with a thrice-knotted cord, while the doctor supported the body from below to take off the strain. But it was done finally and the late Frances Hasleigh was laid down gently in the undergrowth and the cord and gag were removed . . . Then came the task of unfastening her hands. Here again there were tight triple knots to wrestle with.

'Somebody certainly didn't mean her getting free,' Morgan breathed finally, when at last the job was done. 'All right, Doctor, it's your province now.'

Roberts nodded and went to work. It was nearly ten minutes later before he had finished his diagnosis.

'Obviously death from strangulation,' he said grimly, getting to his feet. 'She has been dead for a little over an hour. There is also a faint bruise on the back of her neck under each ear. They were inflicted before death. Near as I can judge they might have been caused by the pressure of somebody's hand . . . That's about all I can tell you — Oh, except for one thing.' Roberts picked up his bag and glanced across at Maria.

'This was about the oldest pupil you

ever had in your college madam. From her teeth and general development I judge her at least twenty-three. Does that interest you?'

'Definitely it does,' Maria nodded, 'but it does not entirely surprise me. I had already suspected it.'

'Up to you now, Inspector.' Roberts turned to go. 'I'll see you in the Coroner's court. Good evening, Miss Black — '

For a moment the inspector stood frowning thoughtfully.

'The body will either have to be taken back to your school, Miss Black, or else to the mortuary until her parents can be fetched . . . Which do you suggest?'

'The mortuary hardly fits the case, Inspector,' Maria replied, reflecting. 'After all, the college is — or was — her home for the time being, and it is there she should be taken now. But I must ask you to bear in mind that I have hundreds of girls under my care, so please wait until darkness has fallen, then have her brought in an ambulance. I'll meet you at the school gates at ten o'clock and we'll have her locked in a private bedroom in the visitors' wing. I am sure that that will be best.'

He nodded. 'Very well. I'll see to that and notify the Coroner. For the moment I just want the immediate details. Who found the body in the first place?'

'We did,' Vera Randal volunteered, nodding to her pals. 'We were playing a joke on Frances and her two friends here. We left them bound and gagged, then took their shoes and put them by the stile in the lane. We wanted them to hop their way out of the wood . . . When after an hour and a half they didn't appear we thought there must be something wrong — We found Beryl and Joan unconscious and Frances hanging on that tree branch.'

Morgan nodded slowly, jotting down notes in the fading light. 'You provided the ropes for this — er — joke?' he asked coldly.

'Only for the hand-tying,' Vera said quickly. 'We never saw that long silky cord which Frances had round her neck. And we didn't tie her hands that tightly, either. Somebody else must have re-tied her wrists when we'd gone.'

'I see . . . What was the deceased's full name, Miss Black?'

'Frances Hasleigh, Inspector — but there is a definite amount of peculiarity attached to her parentage. In fact I think we might have a private chat about her connections up at the college. How about tonight after you have brought the body home?'

'Maybe it would be as well,' he agreed. 'In the meantime I'll have a look round here with what daylight there is left. I'll see you at ten o'clock then, Miss Black, outside the gates.'

She nodded and jerked her head imperiously to the girls.

'This way, girls — if you two are fit to walk?' she added with a glance at Joan and Beryl.

They both nodded, apparently forgetting for the moment they had no shoes on. Joan had hardly taken one step forward before she gave a yelp of anguish and sat down quickly, holding her foot.

'Thorns!' she gasped painfully. 'Nearly cut my foot to ribbons! Vera, you rotten beast, you — ! Sorry, Miss Black,' she broke off, as Maria gave her a grim look.

'Vera, fetch those shoes immediately,' Maria snapped. 'And if you ever dare to think of such an escapade again I'll demote you to a lower form and take away all your privileges. Hurry, girl! It's getting dark!'

Vera went and returned quickly. Thankfully Joan slipped her shoes on, and Beryl did likewise — but even so Joan walked gingerly and with obvious pain after her adventure with the thorns. Maria watched her gravely as she came hobbling up. Beryl Mather however, did not seem in the least troubled, ambling along with her usual side-to-side motion.

'What do I do with these, Miss Black?' Vera asked, holding out Frances's shoes.

'I'll take them,' Maria responded, then she led the way over the stile and into the lane. Here she looked round on the serious faces. 'Girls, I have something to say to you. This terrible affair is going to mean an exhaustive police inquiry, of course, involving all of you. Whatever may transpire you must tell the truth every time. Never mind what revelations it may mean — such as your rather vindictive joke conception, Vera. Don't try and evade anything. Lastly none of you are to breathe a word of this to any of the other girls. What information they may glean from the newspapers does not require colouring by you. Is that understood?'

'Yes, m'm,' they answered in chorus.

'Good! And not a word must be said about the ambulance tonight. I shall severely punish any of you who dare disobey!'

Maria led the way back to the school as the darkness was closing down, left the girls to scatter to their own quarters and went along to her study. She found Miss Tanby waiting there.

'Oh, so here you are, Miss Black! I've been waiting to ask your opinion of this chemistry thesis by Pragnell of the Fifth. I think she — '

'Murder — sure as fate!' Maria breathed, laying Frances's shoes down gently on the desk and getting out of her hat and coat.

Tanby gave a start. 'Mur — murder?'

'Miss Tanby, prepare yourself for a

shock!' Maria turned and faced her across the desk. 'Frances Hasleigh has been murdered!'

Tanby felt behind her for a chair, sank into it, clearly shocked.

Briefly Maria outlined the facts, then she sat down at her desk. 'In other words, Miss Tanby, I am face to face with murder right on my own home ground, as it were, and one of my own pupils as the victim! The tragedy and horror of the thing apart I cannot help but welcome the chance it gives me . . . Though I must say I never quite expected that strange girl to finish up so violently, or so suddenly.'

'But what are we going to do?' the Housemistress bleated. 'Think of the scandal! This school will be the main topic of conversation from one end of the country to the other once the news is published . . .'

'That is to be expected,' Maria shrugged. 'One cannot have a pupil murdered without the Press extracting glory from the fact. Fortunately the urgency of the war will keep us off the front pages, anyway. My immediate duty is to advise the Board of Governors as to what has happened, then communicate with the parents of the five other girls involved and make the facts as clear as I can . . . The trouble is that Vera Randal and her two friends may have laid themselves open to arrest unless they can fully satisfy the police that they had nothing to do with it.'

'Yes,' Tanby admitted, bewildered, 'I suppose that's true. But I'm sure they wouldn't do such a thing!'

'Unfortunately, Miss Tanby, the police will not just take your word for it. Anyway, you have the facts, and now I shall give you your orders. All talk of this matter among the girls is to be ruthlessly stamped out, and the visitors' wing is to be out of bounds to everybody except you or me. As I have told you, the body will be placed in Room 10 in the visitors' wing until it is decided what is to be done . . . Is that quite clear?'

'Yes, Miss Black. And you?'

'I shall write to the various parents immediately and then try and get in touch with Major Hasleigh through his bankers. For the moment, that is all. Most of my duties I shall have to turn over to you, Miss Tanby, for from what I can see I am going to be very busy — very.'

The Housemistress nodded and left the study dazedly. Maria sat in thought for a while — then out came her inevitable black book. She wrote swiftly:

The mystery surrounding Frances Hasleigh has now developed into a tragedy. She was found hanging today in Bollin's Wood following a joke (so called) by three girls of the Sixth. Two points are interesting: 1. The rope about the wrists and the neck was knotted in a rather strange fashion — three times. And 2. She was a woman of 23 and not 16 years of age. Shall have to look into this matter privately, for I cannot think at this stage who would want to kill the girl. All I can recall, indeed, is the threat of Robert Lever that 'many a man might slit her throat for telling lies as she did.' Must look further. The time is 9.0 p.m.

Next, she turned her attention to typing out letters to the various parents concerned, including a letter to the head of the Board of Governors. Altogether, with the amount of thought she put into them, it took her an hour. Then she collected them all, put on her hat and coat, and went with them to the school mailbox, thereafter taking up her position inside the gateway to wait her appointment with Inspector Morgan.

4

The Inspector arrived dead on time and, shielded from prying eyes by the blackout, the body on the stretcher under a sheet was conveyed by two attendants to Room 10 in the visitors' wing — Room 10 being one of the highest in the building. The windows having to be left open, Maria was taking no chances of any inquisitive pupils getting up to their tricks.

Then, the door locked and the ambulance men dismissed, she went back to her study with Inspector Morgan.

'I've informed the Coroner, Miss Black,' he said, taking a chair and looking at her across the desk. 'I suppose the inquest will be in a day or so. Meanwhile, I'm afraid I've a few more questions.'

'I expected it,' Maria shrugged.

'You realise, Miss Black, that those three girls who found the body are in a most unenviable position?'

'Yes, but if it can be arranged that I take the full responsibility for their good behaviour I'd be glad of it. After all, Inspector, I have a school on my hands.'

'I appreciate your difficulties. But we'll come to that in a moment. Have you got in touch yet with the parents or guardians of the girls concerned?'

'I have written to them. I didn't telephone, because I am not a believer in ill-considered statements, especially where murder is concerned. Anyway, we shall be hearing from them promptly enough.'

'And the parents of the deceased?'

'There, Inspector, we have a difficulty. The girl apparently had no mother living, and her father is a major who was ordered abroad by the military authorities on the very day Frances came here — ten days ago.'

'But — her home? She must have lived somewhere!'

'I gathered the major broke up his home on the death of his wife — the home being in Elmington, Surrey. Knowing he would have to go abroad at short notice he enrolled his daughter here so that she could be safe while he was absent. He left the name and address of his sister-in-law in case of any trouble while he was away. I regret to say that the sister-in-law does not exist.'

Morgan frowned. 'In plain language, Miss Black, you were duped and now have a murdered girl with no traceable parents on your hands?'

'The only connection I have is with the major's bank,' Maria said. 'They surely ought to have his address . . . '

Maria drew out the memo she had made of the address and handed it over. Morgan studied it, then:

'I must have the girl's identity card and ration book, too, if you don't mind. They should be foolproof in tracking her former address.'

Maria nodded and handed them across to him.

'I suppose the major's cheque for school fees cleared all right?' Morgan queried.

'Definitely, and his bank assured me his account is in order.'

'I see . . . ' Morgan leaned forward

toward the desk. 'Just what did he look like — this Major Hasleigh?'

'Rather like the popular conception of a major. Tall and erect, very red face, and grey hair and toothbrush moustache. He had a quiet voice, however. Wearing military uniform, of course.'

'Nothing to make him conspicuously identifiable, then?'

Maria thought of the sunburn that had proved impermanent, but shook her head. That had been her own little bit of research.

'Those two girls who were found lying bound and unconscious — what can you tell me about them? I shan't have them brought here for questioning at this hour so I'll rely on your information. Are they — trustworthy?'

'As far as I know,' Maria shrugged. 'Joan Dawson, the dark one, came here as a pupil shortly before Frances Hasleigh. Her father is an industrialist and extremely wealthy, while her mother is the owner of a big chain of dress salons. People in quite a high niche of society.'

'And the stout girl?'

'Beryl Mather? She is the daughter of a brewer in a big way of business. Not really brilliant, perhaps, but perfectly honest — as also is Joan, as far as I know. Joan is a girl of remarkably quick wits, so my teachers tell me. In fact, Inspector,' Maria went on, 'you can check up on the parents and private history of each of the girls concerned — including the three who found the body — Vera Randal, Molly Webster, and Cynthia Vane. I know their parents personally. Despite their crude idea of a joke, they would never have had anything to do with the deliberate murder of a fellow-schoolgirl.'

'I am afraid the law and Superintendent Vaxley will want more proof than just that,' Morgan said quietly.

Maria frowned. 'Superintendent Vaxley?'

'I have referred this matter to Scotland Yard. I can see from the start that my training has been too limited to grapple with a case like this . . . I spent this evening going over the wood with a couple of my men. Believe me, armed with torches and covering nearly every inch of ground, we did not find a single clue as to the attacker. There seems to have been no murderer, and even less motive — Well, it's up to the higher-ups as far as I am concerned. All these facts you have given me I am handing over to the Superintendent when he arrives. It's pretty obvious that the inquest will mean a verdict of murder — probably against person or persons unknown — so the sooner the job is started the better. I expect Vaxley will arrive some time during the night and start work tomorrow. His first call will be on you, Miss Black.'

'I'll be delighted to meet him, Inspector,' Maria smiled, though inwardly she was not at all keen. She saw in the approaching shadow of Superintendent Vaxley a possible check to her own ways of looking into things.

'As to the dead girl herself,' Morgan went on, 'what kind of a girl was she? Did she give any reason to make you suspect she might have a tragedy ahead of her?'

'No,' Maria answered calmly, without embellishment. The news that Morgan was not going to handle the case anyway had led her to sudden reserve.

Morgan got to his feet. 'I think I have all the details I want for the Superintendent to start on, Miss Black, thank you — Oh, there is a pair of shoes which belonged to the deceased. I must have them to put with these . . . '

He laid an envelope on the table and brought out the silken rope with which the girl had been hanged, together with the smaller cords that had held her wrists and ankles. Maria looked at the silk rope keenly for a moment.

'Would it matter if I — look at it?' she asked.

'By all means — but handle it carefully. Hold only the ends.'

'Thank you . . . Oh, here are the shoes.'

Maria laid them in front of him, and he examined them closely. For her own part she got to her feet, took the silk rope over to the big reading-lamp and studied it intently beneath it. Morgan was still pondering the shoes. Quickly she drew out a pair of small nail scissors and snipped about four inches off the rope end, thrusting it into her tight-fitting cuff. Then she returned slowly to the desk.

'Interesting rope,' she said, 'but unfortunately it can't talk.'

'No reason why it can't with the right instruments,' Morgan smiled. 'Just the same as these shoes . . . '

Maria looked at them, and at the maker's name on the lining. It made her frown for a moment — *Facile-pied, Paris.*

'French,' Morgan nodded, seeing her look. 'Maybe the Super will squeeze some juice out of the fact . . . Well, madam, I must be off!'

She helped him put the shoes and ropes in his big envelope, then saw him off the premises. Returning to her study she looked at her watch.

'Ten-thirty-two. Hmmm . . . Still time for a little investigation work before this superintendent person gets here tomorrow.'

She put away the pilfered rope into her desk drawer, then donned her overcoat and beret, armed herself with torch and umbrella, and so left the college silently before the moonrise.

Within fifteen minutes, without encountering anybody, she was in Bollin's Wood, treading as softly to avoid the crackle of undergrowth. Presently she reached the pitchy dark clearing of the afternoon's tragedy.

'For a crime to be committed and leave not a single clue is manifestly impossible,' she muttered. 'Baxter in his *Crime Without Clue* is adamant on that point . . . Now, what have we?'

Switching on her torch, she began to prowl, poking at the leaves and grass with her umbrella ferrule. She soon found the spot where Joan and Beryl had been lying: the grass had not yet straightened from the weight of their bodies, especially Beryl's — and a little further away there was another flattening where Frances had presumably been lying when the ill-natured joke had started.

The trouble, from Maria's point of view, was that the three had had no shoes on, so they could not have revealed footprints even if they had got to their feet and moved. Stockinged feet in dry leaves and soft grass — with no sharp heel imprint — would obviously be impossible to trace. Of course, there was another factor. If any of them had got to their feet, bound, they would have moved in leap-frog jumps, and therefore their impact with the ground might have left a trace . . . But there was nothing. Not a sign. It seemed that they had never moved from where they had fallen.

But if somebody had hanged the girl they must have come into the clearing! Unless they, too, had been without shoes, which was hardly a practicable theory.

Maria pondered this with her torch switched off and the darkness all about her — then she moved to the spot directly under the tree branch on which Frances had been hanged. Here again there was no sign of anything, no hint of anybody having stood under the branch and perhaps having lifted the girl up to her doom.

'Peculiar,' Maria muttered.

She moved to the tree itself, then with the help of her umbrella crook she hauled herself into the tree and struggled up to the first limb. Switching on her torch she gazed steadily along the branch. It was not very long, and of the thin, highly flexible type. In the approximate centre of it the bark had been scored off to reveal the bright green beneath, obviously where the rope had been tied round and the swinging of the girl's body had produced a rubbing movement on the rope. Nothing significant there: it was only to be expected.

But there, at the far end of the branch, there was something else! A second scoring of the bark, and of a much thinner width.

In a moment Maria was scrambling back down the tree, hurried along the ground to the end of the branch and then pulled it down to her with her umbrella handle. It bent easily enough and she had it in her hands in a matter of seconds. In her torch-beam she studied the scoring carefully, then again using her umbrella handle she allowed the branch to go up and down like a pump-handle.

'Excellent,' she murmured. 'The act of pulling on this makes a difference of six inches of height to the corpse! Hmm! Definitely worth considering . . . '

She went back once more to the tree.

But though she went over it thoroughly she found no trace of anything that might have a relation to the crime.

So, finally, she began to retrace her way, presently coming to the mass of footprints in the soft ground near the stile where the marks left by the girls, herself, and the police were all interwoven. Not that they interested her: the one thing rooted in her mind at the moment was the second scoring on the tree branch . . .

It was nearing midnight when she returned to her study, but she made no preparations for retirement.

'Why *three* knots,' she mused, twisting her watch-chain in her fingers.

She recalled the moment when she had untied the wrists of Beryl and Joan as they had lain on the ground. Those knots had been single ones, and by no means tight: just the kind of knots any schoolgirl would tie. Probably, if there had been no attack on them, all three girls could have released themselves from them pretty rapidly . . .

With Frances it had obviously been a case of her wrists being re-tied for security reasons. Her wrists had been crossed behind her and most securely bound, with that final triple-knot to make doubly sure. The rope that had hanged her had also had the same style of knot.

'Which proves,' Maria reflected, 'that the person who attacked Frances wanted to be sure she couldn't get free — that the said person also provided his or her own rope for the hanging. And that proves — what?'

Maria got up and went to her bookcase, took out the *General Encyclopaedia* and began a study of Section 'K' wherein three pages were devoted to every kind of knot, with illustrations. There was the reef knot, the bow knot, the Boy Scout knot, the treble knot —

She caught her breath sharply and studied the descriptive matter under the illustration. Here before her was an exact duplicate of the very knot she was worrying about . . . over, under, over — pull! The reading was quite informative:

'The triple or treble knot is used in some forms by the marine services

— and, in wire, by the electrical professions. By electricians it is used also as the basis for plaiting triple electric flex wire when there is positive, negative and earth.

'By the triple knot being used it is impossible for the cord or whatever it may be, to come unfastened from its support, because should the topmost knot loosen the second one tightens up, which in turn secures the third. The triple knot is also used sometimes in emblem form by girls' and boys' forestry organisations . . . '

Maria laid the book aside and pondered for a while.

'Marine services? Electrical professions? Who fits into those categories? Nobody that I know of, unless — Good Heavens! Unless Mr. Lever might be included in the electrical professions. He is quite a capable young scientist. And there *did* seem to be some sort of connection between him and Frances apart from his threat about throat-slitting. On the other hand there is an electrical connection with the peculiar Major Hasleigh himself — his dislike of ultra-violet machines. Dear me, this is most interesting . . . '

She put the *Encyclopaedia* away and then brought out her diary of the case, bringing her conclusions up to date:

Frances Hasleigh was murdered this afternoon somewhere between 4.30 and 6.30. Hanged, the murderer providing his own rope. Superintendent Vaxley of Scotland Yard is to take the case over . . . For myself I have very few conclusions on the matter as yet. The lack of motive is my main stumbling block, and I cannot imagine as yet how the murderer did the job without leaving footprints.

Have particular interest in a second scoring in the tree branch on which Frances was hanged. Is it possible that this held the rope by which the branch was pulled down? Or, even, did Frances hang herself. If so, how did she tie her own hands so securely?

Clues — such as they are: Shoes

made in Paris, triple knots on hanging rope and hand tie. Must look into this much more thoroughly. Cannot think who would want to hang the girl.

The time is 12.30 a.m.

She put the book away, then pondered the other angles she had in mind. One was the name of the makers of the girl's shoes — *Facile-pied*, or Easy Foot, to which she decided to devote her attention later; and the other was the piece of rope she had snipped off the main exhibit Morgan had lent her.

Taking it from her desk drawer, she studied it. It was unlike any rope she had seen before — fairly thin, but enormously strong and made up of hundreds of silk fibres woven into a taut mesh. Certainly it was not the sort of cord to find in general use, even in peacetime.

Putting it carefully in an envelope she picked it up and left her study, en route for the laboratory on the other side of the quadrangle. Here there were instruments that could tell her far more than the naked eye.

As she crossed the gloomy quad she fancied she caught sight of a dim figure disappearing round an angle of the School House buildings. She stopped uncertainly, and watched intently. But the figure did not appear again.

'Steady, Maria,' she told herself. 'Probably just the night watchman . . . '

She was quite convinced it had not been, however. She continued on her way to the laboratory. Once inside she drew the blackout blinds and switched on the lights. It did not take her very long to have her piece of silk rope under the high-power microscope. The fine but tough fibres leapt into instant relief.

They showed up like stout cords, and with them was something else — fine hairy tendrils of various colours, green, blue, yellow, the merest whiskers even under the microscope and therefore totally invisible to the naked eye.

Maria pored over them, trying to decide what they might mean. Knowing the scientific fact that silk attracts silk, if electrically charged, it seemed logical to her to assume that they had been rubbed off by the rope wherever it had been prior to the hanging.

'Even from Frances's own dress perhaps if it happened to have been dragged across her before she was hanged,' Maria mused, her eyes narrowed. 'Possible — and it means an unpleasant job for you, Maria! Take a look at what the girl is wearing. Pink, I think, but you had better be sure.'

She put the piece of cord back in its envelope, thrust it in her pocket, then left the laboratory. A few minutes later she entered the dimly-lit deserted visitors' wing and took out her bunch of keys, inserted the appropriate one in the door of Number 10. Quietly she moved inside and went across to the window to draw over the curtains.

Then she switched on the light, and got the surprise of her life!

The mattress on which the body of Frances Hasleigh had been lying was empty! There was no sign of the girl anywhere . . .

Recovering from her mental shock, Maria checked up on the room number again. This was the original room all right, and only she had the key.

The door showed no signs of having been tampered with — but in any case the unknown body-snatcher had had no need to bother with it since the window had been — and still was — wide open. That it was five floors from the ground had evidently not proved a deterrent.

Maria went silently back to her study for a torch and magnifying glass, then she began a thorough examination of window and sill. Here, for once, clues were all over the place. A rope had obviously been used for there were plain evidences of rope shreds in the woodwork at the bottom of the window-frame, as well as a clean smear across the paint where the rope had been paid out as Frances Hasleigh's body had presumably been lowered into the quadrangle.

'But what on earth for?' Maria frowned, straightening up. 'And where is it now?'

She locked the window tightly, left the room and secured the door — and so made her way out to the quadrangle. As she had expected, there were no clues here on the hard concrete. She looked about her in the blackout, but there was no sign of anybody or anything.

'But, Maria, you saw somebody for a moment,' she mused. 'A vague, indeterminate figure to be sure — but it was *somebody* — and going towards the School House apparently. Most peculiar . . . '

Two courses seemed open to her — either to arouse the school with a general alarm, which would set at naught all her hopes of secrecy over this mysterious tragedy; or else to wait until the morning and conduct a search in the daylight on her own account. The only thing against this latter course was that in the meantime the body-snatcher might take the corpse far away — even perhaps to another town. Maria then decided such a removal was hardly possible. Nobody could move the body of a dead girl any great distance without attracting attention, especially with the alertness of the countryside due to war emergency. Home Guards, or even alert fireguards, might ask questions.

Altogether, it seemed reasonably sure to her that the body could not be far away, and that the morning was the time to get moving . . . So she returned to her study, stifling a yawn as she closed the door. She had become intolerably sleepy by now, was surprised to find it was nearly half-past two.

She toyed with the idea of watching the window of Room 10 across the quadrangle from her study here, in the event of the body being returned, but Nature had a stronger demand to make and instead of doing anything of the sort she fell asleep in her chair.

When she awoke again it was nearly four o'clock and she was stiff and cold. She gave a little shiver and stretched herself.

She felt somewhat refreshed. Beyond a slight weariness of limb she felt ready for action again. So she made herself a pot of tea on the little electric ring and then settled down to think as she drank slowly.

She spent a few minutes writing down her impressions, added 4.15 a.m. at the end of them, then considered. Her original idea of checking the silk fibres in the hanging rope against the dress Frances had been wearing had been scotched utterly by the girl's disappearance.

'It has got to be checked!' she decided. 'Not that it can lead anywhere definite as far as I can see. Any of those girls might have had the rope against them — No, not any of them, come to think of it. It could easily have trailed across Joan and Beryl as they lay on the ground, or across Frances herself — but Vera, Molly, and Cynthia were never anywhere near it, so they say. Hmm — I must look into it as soon as propitious.'

She looked at the trade name of the shoes, which she had jotted down on her memo-pad. Taking the *Trades Directory* from the bookcase she went through it carefully. Practically all shoemakers in the British Isles were listed, but there were none for France.

'Only to be expected, with those vile Nazi people in control of the country,' Maria sighed, putting the book away — but for all that the thought of France gave her the feeling that for the moment she was on the edge of something vital. But nothing seemed to click in her mind.

She thought next of the silk shreds in the hanging rope. She had no idea if the girls in question — Beryl and Joan — would wear the same dresses today, considering the dirt they had collected in the clearing. And by day the lockers in the dormitory would be secured and the appropriate keys with the girls. In fact, the dresses might disappear into the laundry basket before Maria even had a chance to see them. Unless —

Maria smiled as she got to her feet. By night, as she well knew, the lockers would be undone with the keys on the locks —

'It won't do anybody any harm for once to miss some sleep, and we may as well be prepared for incendiaries . . .'

She left the study and made her way silently to the corridor leading to the Sixth Form dormitory. There she decisively pressed her finger on the fire-alarm button. The noise was terrific in the sudden quiet; and in a few moments the girls — and Eunice Tanby from her own room in a more distant section of the building — came literally tumbling into view, rather wild-eyed, half-dressed, but with no signs of panic. In other parts of the building there were also the sounds of running feet and shouting voices.

'Practice fire drill!' Maria stated calmly. 'I regret the inconvenience, girls, but a fire will not consider our sleeping hours when it comes. To your stations! Miss Tanby, take charge of this sector. I will see how the other forms are faring and tell them what is afoot.'

'Yes, Miss Black.' The Housemistress clapped her hands sharply. 'Get moving, girls. Four of you to the east wall fire hose; four of you to the two stirrup pumps on the lower landing — '

Maria hurried along the corridor, ostensibly to the stairs leading to the lower corridors. But on the way she detoured by the door of the Sixth Form dormitory, glanced back at the busy, grumbling girls who were not in the least concerned with her movements.

Reaching the dormitory and headed straight for the lockers labelled 'Joan

Dawson' and 'Beryl Mather.' Just as she had expected the keys were in the locks. She opened both doors and peered within. Immediately she saw the dresses inside she recalled the ones she had seen the two girls wearing. Beryl's had been a champagne-coloured one with a blue collar and Joan's, somewhat creased and mud-stained, was vari-coloured silk! In fact, an exact match of the shreds that had been on the hanging rope.

Maria suddenly alerted at the chattering voices becoming louder down the corridor. She closed both doors, and hurried outside.

She pretended a great interest and authority in the fire-drill — but was glad when it was over, so she could think over what she had found. She made a note of it in her book:

Silk strands on hanging rope coincide with the material of Joan Dawson's frock. Is this worth considering?

'Definitely so!' she decided. 'But how does it fit into the pattern?'

Rather than flog her brain any further on the problem, she busied herself for the rest of the time until rising bell in working out a timetable for Miss Tanby, whereby the worthy spinster would be able to take over the temporary duties of Headmistress. Maria's mind was on other things that she would have to do — things far more important than imparting learning to young ladies who were more interested in the hockey field anyway.

5

The moment breakfast was over and she had taken prayers in the chapel, Maria summoned Joan Dawson and Beryl Mather to her study. They arrived promptly and stood waiting in some anxiety in front of her big desk.

Maria noted that they were indeed wearing different dresses to the previous day, then she sat back and interlocked her fingers in front of her.

'Joan,' she said quietly, 'this little talk is not between pupil and Headmistress, but between — shall I say — friends?' She gave a rather dry smile. 'The same applies to you, Beryl. Now, I want you both to be very frank with me so that I may know how to act when Superintendent Vaxley of Scotland Yard arrives. You will undoubtedly be questioned, and if I know in advance what is coming I may be able to help you.'

'We'll tell you anything we can, Miss

Black,' Joan said earnestly, and Beryl Mather nodded her unruly head.

'Tell me, then, didn't either of you see or hear somebody prior to being rendered unconscious in the clearing?'

They both shook their heads firmly.

'Tell me exactly what you did when you were left bound by Vera Randal and her friends. You first, Beryl.'

'Well, all three of us were lying on the ground,' Beryl said slowly. 'Joan was on one side of me, and Frances on the other. I tried to get to my feet and just couldn't — I — er — am a bit stout, you see.

'Frances seemed to have the idea of us standing back to back so that we could untie each other's wrists. She got up finally, and so did Joan here. She and Joan were back to back, unfastening each other's wrists. I had my back to them, of course, but Frances had no sooner shouted that her hands were free and the gag out of her mouth before something struck me a terrific welt on the head and I was knocked out cold. The next thing I remembered was you bending over me, Miss Black.'

Maria's cold eyes turned to Joan. 'This something that hit Beryl must surely have been seen by you, Joan. What was it?'

'I don't know, Miss Black,' she answered quietly. 'I had my back to both Beryl and Frances. My wrists being untied, I was busy with my ankles when Beryl must have been knocked out. The only one who could have seen what hit Beryl was Frances — I think she must have done, for I heard her give a little gasp. I didn't think anything of it and never bothered to look round. I'd freed my ankles and had half got to my feet when I was hit a real smack under the jaw. Everything went black. Whoever it was must have come up from behind me and knocked me out before I could see who it was.'

'Hmm . . . ' Maria said. 'But you believe that Frances *did* know who it was?'

'I think so, but . . . ' Joan shrugged. 'She is dead, so what can we do?'

'In which case,' Maria mused, 'the unknown rebound Frances and you. He made a thorough job of Frances, but was not very concerned over you, presumably because you were unconscious anyway. Beryl had not been untied before she was stunned . . . You say you fancied Frances gave a little gasp. In that case she got the gag out of her mouth?'

'She was entirely free, Miss Black — except for her ankles.'

'Those were left tied just as Vera Randal had done it,' Maria answered. 'They were not tied by the same person as the one who tied the wrists and the — the hanging rope.'

Maria got to her feet and began to pace slowly up and down.

'Tell me, Joan, did you touch that hanging rope at any time?' she asked abruptly.

'Good Heavens, no!' the girl cried, aghast. 'How could I?'

'Well, it touched you, my dear. In fact, I think it trailed over you at one point. You see, I happen to know that strands of that many-coloured silk frock you were wearing yesterday are imbedded in the rope.'

Joan's eyes widened and her face seemed to go paler. She seemed to make an effort to collect her thoughts. 'I — I've no idea how that could have happened. Since I was unconscious, how *could* I know?'

'Naturally, you couldn't,' Maria shrugged. 'I merely mention it so you will be ready for the question if Superintendent Vaxley should spring it on you . . . '

The two girls exchanged glances. Maria came back to her desk again.

'I think,' she said quietly, 'that there's something you should know . . . The body of Frances Hasleigh has disappeared!'

'From — from Room 10?' Beryl Mather gasped.

'Exactly. It was presumably lowered from the window of that room and taken — I know not where. There are many places where it might have been taken in a place as extensive as this one. Places where I cannot go without — er — raising inquiry. Are either of you girls willing to undertake a search for it, notifying me the moment you find it? I am right outside my authority in asking you to do it, but if it is not found there may be unpleasant repercussions.'

'We'll look for it!' Joan answered promptly. 'Do we stay off lessons to do it?'

'You have this morning in which to search,' Maria said gravely. 'Report to me if you find it. If you don't, then come to me here just before dinner bell and tell me where you've looked.'

This was enough for them and they turned to leave the study. Beryl Mather went with her usual rolling motion, but Joan limped badly. Evidently her feet were giving her a good deal of trouble. Maria watched them from the window as they went out into the quadrangle on the first stage of their search.

She reflected she had taken a long chance — then just as she was going to turn away. She gave a start. A figure had just come through the gateway. She could distinguish a check suit, green pork-pie hat, a red tie . . . She gave a little gulp as the visitor hailed the two girls and spent a few moments talking to them. From the amount of arm-waving that went on it was pretty clear he was asking directions — and getting them.

'No — it isn't possible!' Maria breathed. 'Mr. Martin is in New York — '

But she kept her eyes fixed on the figure just the same. He swaggered up to the steps of the School House and entered. Maria got back to her desk hurriedly just as there came a knock on the door.

'Come in,' she bade, rather breathlessly.

An impudently grinning red face angled round the door. Then the vivid hat came off and upstanding carroty hair was revealed, sweeping back from a broad, intelligent forehead.

'Black Maria!' he exclaimed, striding in and shutting the door with a bang. 'Say, I'd know your puss anyplace! Hi-ya!'

Maria shook the big paw he held out, her eyes travelling over the expanse of face, the appalling suit, the various colours of shirt, tie, hat —

'Mr. 'Pulp' Martin!' she whispered. 'I thought I'd left you in the Bowery where I solved the mystery of my brother's death . . . Sit down, won't you?'

'Them was the days, eh?' he grinned, half sitting on the desk. 'You and me running around Maxie's Dance Hall, me swiping Ransome across the kisser, you falling in the docks. Swell stuff while it lasted. But I guess you're wondering how I found you? There ain't much to it, really. I came over to this country of yours a few months back, just when war started. Things got kinda hot down my way and I figured I'd better blow until the heat was off. I came over here as a volunteer for the American Air Force — you know how I love a scrap. But I got rejected on account of there's something screwy about my feet. Me, a reject! So I've been doin' a bit of potterin' down London way in the Civil Defence — not as a regular, though . . . Then, swipe me flat, if I didn't read in last night's paper about a murder happening up this way — a kid from the school of Miss Maria Black found with her neck stretched. I figured there could only be one Maria Black so I hopped a train and came right over to see if I could do anything. I got the address of this college from the station. We sort of worked okay together before, remember? Anyway, I asked those two pieces outside where I could get the low-down on you, and here I am. You know me when it comes to service — '

'Quite!' Maria gave a little cough. 'Frankly, I don't know whether you are a gift from Heaven to me or just a rather — ah — embarrassing intruder. You see, things are so much different here to what they were in the States. Nobody knew me there, outside my relations, but everybody does so here, and for various reasons I must not be seen associating with you too closely.'

'I get it,' he nodded promptly. 'Don't worry, Maria, I'm quick on the uptake. You're a big dish of stew over here and I'm not. Okay by me. I'll find a squat somewhere in the village. You can always give me the old one-two when you want me . . . Know any place where I can hit the hay and grab a bite to eat while I'm around here?'

'You might try the Fox Hotel in the village, Mr. Martin. I think there will be room there. They are on the telephone, too, in case I need you urgently.'

Pulp gave her a keen look of his intense blue eyes.

'Look, Maria, what's the set-up in this murder, anyway? It didn't say much in the paper. Anything I oughta know?'

'Simply a matter of hanging, Mr. Martin. A new pupil is left with me, a pupil who seems to have no home connections, and she is found hanged on a tree branch with a bruise mark behind each ear. No clues in the wood where the tragedy happened. There are a lot of other details, of course, but those are the salient points. The rest will come out at the Coroner's inquest.'

'Mmmm — quite a poser for England's greatest woman criminologist, huh? Remember you telling me you was that? And I figure it's true, too. The old neck stretch and pan handle grip, eh?'

'The *what* grip?' Maria frowned.

'The pan handle grip. Ain't the proper name for it but that's what me and the boys call it. It's a grip that can put anybody to sleep for minutes or hours, depending on the pressure. Finger and thumb behind the ears in just the right spot stop the circulation to the brain and the guy — or dame — just passes out cold.'

'Ah! Upon my word, Mr. Martin, you have a most uncanny gift of dropping in with suggestions at the right time. Tell me, could anybody use this — hum! — pan handle grip?'

'Sure — provided they'd learned it beforehand. Just what you might call knack.' Pulp's eyes brightened. 'Say, think I've got something to help you?'

'It's possible, Mr. Martin!' Maria answered. 'I see that I may need you after all — there is little pleasure in working on a case alone. One's views become clogged . . . Suppose I give you a retainer fee?'

He grinned and shrugged. 'I've got my own ways of gettin' flush, I guess, but a bit on the nose wouldn't hurt. I'm yours for the old price — five dollars a day, or night.'

Maria got up with a grave smile, went to her safe, took some treasury notes from a steel cash-box and handed them over.

'There you are, Mr. Martin. Now do me the favour of getting along to the Fox before anybody sees you here. If you can't get fixed at the hotel let me know over the phone where you finally settle.'

'It's a date,' he nodded, sliding from the desk. 'Don't you fret, Maria — we'll get this monkey business in the bag same as we did before . . . Be seeing you.'

He picked up his hat and turned to the door, just as Miss Tanby knocked and came in. She stared blankly at the loud suit and grinning red face.

'Pulp Martin's the name, sister,' Pulp explained blandly. 'You and me'll be ringing doorbells before you know it — '

'Great Scot!' Tanby gasped, and stared after his massive figure; then, rather bewildered, she came forward into the study where Maria stood eyeing her in some amusement.

'That, Miss Tanby, is Mr. Martin,' she said gravely. 'A — er — rather overpowering personality, but about the most honest trickster I ever met. Chivalrous to women; violent to men. In a word, my assistant.'

'*That* man!' the Housemistress gasped. 'Is he the one who helped you in America?'

'Exactly — and do not judge too readily by appearances. He is in England through various circumstances . . . Anyway,' Maria rose, 'I presume you wish to see me, Miss Tanby?'

'It's Superintendent Vaxley, Miss Black. He's just arrived. He got into the New House by mistake just as I was — '

'The details are quite irrelevant, Miss Tanby. Please show him in.'

Tanby nodded and went back to the doorway. She motioned into the corridor and as Superintendent Vaxley came in she went out and closed the door. Maria moved forward to clasp the extended hand.

'Miss Black, this is a pleasure indeed!'

Vaxley was a tall man — very tall — with a face as thin as a pedigree greyhound, a straight, inquisitive nose, and pointed chin. His eyes were tiny and sparkling, like little sapphires; his mouth generous. His greying hair was nearly non-existent over the temples.

'Delighted to know you, Superintendent,' Maria said majestically. 'Be seated, won't you?'

He whipped up the tails of his roomy raglan coat and sat down. 'Speaking unprofessionally for a moment, Miss Black, I have often wanted to make your acquaintance — though I never thought it would be in such tragic circumstances ... I have heard of your — er — unofficial work, you know.'

Maria gave a little start as she sat down opposite him.

'I don't quite understand, Superintendent.'

'Perhaps you will when you know that Inspector Davis of New York is a cousin of mine. Believe me, I have heard quite a deal about you from him, especially about your unorthodox way of handling that gangster, Hugo Ransome. You clapped him in jail a year ago when all the police in New York had their hands tied. That, to my mind, is an achievement for an unofficial investigator to be proud of.'

Maria gave one of her rare warm smiles.

'Purely in the course of another investigation,' she shrugged. 'However, you have taken rather a worry from my mind. I am, of course, deeply interested in the mystery which has descended right into my own school, and I was rather afraid that a man of law as prominent as yourself would look askance on my little researches. Now I feel — '

Vaxley interrupted her with a laugh.

'My dear Miss Black, whatever you do will receive no check from me: I might even learn a thing or two. I got myself assigned specially in this case for the interest of meeting you. A headmistress with a detective *alter ego* is something new — to me, anyway. And your past work shows you are no dabbling amateur.'

Maria gave a little cough of embarrassment. 'Purely a hobby Superintendent, and I trust you will respect my confidence in never revealing it as anything else but that. I have a Board of School Governors to please, remember . . . Now, shall we get down to the matter on hand?'

Vaxley nodded and took out his notebook. Briefly, he recited a detailed list of the facts that had been gleaned by Inspector Morgan. When he had finished he looked up with those keen little eyes.

'Quite correct,' Maria agreed; then she looked rather troubled. 'But I have found one or two things out for myself. Am I to mention them or try and work out my own line of research?'

'You are certainly not to withhold any vital evidence,' Vaxley replied. 'But whatever matters you find which only you think are vital evidence — that is, sidelights on the obvious — are your own gain or loss. In any case, you'll not find Scotland Yard exactly lacking when it comes to analysis.'

Maria's eyes twinkled. 'To clear my conscience, Superintendent, I'll tell you everything I know and we can each put our own construction on it. So here you are — Frances Hasleigh was hanged with a thrice knotted silk rope: her wrists but not her ankles were also thrice knotted: her ears had bruise marks at the back of them: her shoes were made in France; she was afraid of ultra-violet treatment: the rope that hanged her has silk shreds in it which tally with the material of a frock worn by one of the two girls who were unconscious while she was hanged. Last of all, the tree branch on which she was hanged has scored marks at the *end* of it

117

as well as in the centre where her body was suspended. Score marks being slightly smaller. That is as far as I have got — up to now.'

Vaxley nodded slowly and looked at his report again. 'I have it here from the doctor about the bruise marks behind the ears. Not done with an instrument and possibly done with a finger and thumb — before death . . . There is no undue significance in that, Miss Black. Obviously the killer rendered the girl unconscious before killing her.'

'Said killer has left no footprints in the clearing,' Maria commented; at which Vaxley smiled.

'He could not have flown, Miss Black — and if there are no footprints there will be other traces. As to the triple knots they may have a special meaning all their own. I'll decide that later on when I've thoroughly examined the rope. The shoes? Well, to trace the makers would have been easy if France had not fallen. Even if we could trace them I cannot see they can tell us much, unless it be a flashback on the girl's history. As to the ultra-violet treatment — that is interesting . . . ' Vaxley rubbed his pointed chin. 'Interesting, yes — but remote . . . And you say the silk rope has the shreds of a silk frock worn by one of the three girls, has it? How did you get the chance to examine the rope so closely?'

Maria smiled. 'You have your methods, Superintendent: I have mine. I am simply stating a fact, for you to follow or discard as you wish. My guess is that the rope trailed over one of the girls — Joan Dawson, to be exact — as she lay senseless on the ground.'

'A very likely explanation,' Vaxley agreed. 'As to the other marks on the tree branch I'll form a better view when I've seen it . . . You see, Miss Black, you have the advantage of being able to form a theory, however complex, and follow it out to its conclusion. We of the law are more hidebound; we have to show a result. We deal in the concrete and you in the abstract. Thanks, though, for all this information. For the moment I have a different line to follow — '

Maria feared he was going to suggest

that he view the body — but to her relief he took another angle.

'Obviously, the one thing lacking at the moment is the motive. That girl must have had a merciless enemy, and it is my job — and yours, if you wish — to find out who it was . . . First I'd like to see these three girls who played the trick on the dead girl and her friends.'

Maria nodded and picked up the house-phone. When she had given her orders she asked a question.

'You have a detailed list of the various parents, I take it?'

'Yes. A check-up is already being made on them, though we are obviously dealing with quite respectable families.'

'Possibly a whole host of parents will descend on me before long,' Maria sighed. 'I had to write to them all, and I expect rapid answers. All except the parents of Frances Hasleigh, of course. There, Superintendent, we face a profound problem.'

He nodded grimly. 'Yes: I'm coming to that later — '

He paused as there was a knock on the

door. At Maria's command to enter Vera Randal, Molly Webster, and Cynthia Vane came in sheepishly. It was quite a change to see Vera Randal looking scared for once.

'I shan't keep you long, young ladies,' Vaxley said, his little eyes darting from face to face. 'I am afraid you have some questions to answer about that little joke you played on your schoolmates. A very reprehensible sort of joke it was, too!' he added sternly.

'Yes, sir,' they said in chorus, with obvious repentance.

'Tell me, when you had bound and gagged Frances and her two friends, what did you do then?'

'Took their shoes away from them and put them by the stile in a heap,' Vera answered quickly. 'Then we sat on the bank on the opposite side of the road to watch them hop into view. But they didn't! After about an hour and a half we decided that we'd better look. That was when we found out what — what had happened.'

'And during that time you didn't hear

anybody or see anything?'

'Nothing at all,' Vera replied, and her two friends nodded their heads vehemently. 'The wood might just as well have been empty.'

'And those shoes were never touched at all?'

'No sir — not at all. Miss Black found them when we dashed back with her to the wood.'

Maria nodded her head silently as Vaxley glanced at her. Then he reflected for a while.

'You three girls did not like Frances Hasleigh, did you?' he asked finally. 'Or her two friends?'

The three looked rather startled for a moment, then Vera took the bull by the horns as usual.

'We didn't like Frances, no — or Joan, either. Beryl we just didn't like because she tagged along with those two. Frances didn't behave like an ordinary schoolgirl — she was too beastly cocky and self-assertive. As head girl of the class it was my job — and it still is — to keep the other girls in order. I had to do something to make her see who was boss and so I — or rather we — tried our 'breaking in' ceremony.'

'Hmmm' Vaxley said. 'And Joan? Had you something against her, too?'

'Nothing much. She had a parcel from home the other day and wouldn't tell us what it was at the time. That sort of blacklisted her among the girls. We share our joys and sorrows as a rule and anybody who doesn't is in for a bad time. She finally admitted it was a pair of stockings — '

Vaxley frowned pensively and Maria made a brief note of her own on her scratch pad. Then at length Vaxley spoke again.

'I consider that all of you have behaved most vindictively,' he snapped, and it was surprising how his generous mouth tightened into a hard line. 'You realised when you thought out this deplorable scheme that those girls could have had their feet severely lacerated before they reached their shoes, didn't you?'

'They might have got free,' Vera retorted

'And they might not! You have a queer sort of mind, young lady! It wants taking in hand. However, that is not my business. I merely point out that a girl so cruel might not be averse to inflicting torture — for that is what your scheme amounted to.'

Vera's red face went redder and her eyes blazed a challenge.

'Are you trying to suggest that *I* hanged Frances?' she shouted. 'You can't do that! I didn't, I tell you! I was seated on that bank in the lane the whole time.'

'Can you prove it?' Vaxley asked quietly.

'Of course. Molly and Cynthia were with me — '

'Their evidence is valueless because they are as involved as you in this case. What outsider can you produce to prove that you were sat on the bank?'

The three looked at each other helplessly.

'I see,' Vaxley said, pondering. 'All right, since you can't answer the question I shall have to look into it further. All three of you girls are in a decidedly awkward predicament, and your best way to help yourselves is to tell all you know . . . You said, Miss — er — Randal, that Frances Hasleigh was not like an ordinary schoolgirl. What exactly do you mean by that? Did she break the rules, or something?'

'She twice broke bounds at night to go for a canoodle with our ex-science master,' Vera sneered, hardly caring what she said after the verbal thrashing she had received.

'Don't exaggerate, girl!' Maria snapped. 'There was only one instance where she — '

'Twice!' Vera hooted. 'Another time you didn't know of!'

'Don't dare raise your voice to me, Randal,' Maria said icily. 'And explain yourself. What other occasion are you referring to?'

'It was during the time you gave her house detention. She went out one night and I was going to report it, but the girls talked me out of it. We decided to teach her in our own way, hence the initiation ceremony in the wood.'

'At what time did she leave, and when

did she come back?' Vaxley asked.

'She left the dormitory by the big window about one o'clock, and came back an hour later. She wouldn't say where she had been, but it was pretty obvious to all of us.'

'Why obvious?' Vaxley asked.

'She is referring to her escapade on her first day here,' Maria answered. 'Frances sought out the science master, Mr. Lever, on a pretext — some astronomical question or other — and my House-mistress, Miss Tanby, surprised the pair of them together in the quadrangle in the small hours. It was Randal here who passed the information on. I had to dismiss Lever immediately and I gave Frances house detention for a week. Having only just arrived and having no apparent home either I just couldn't expel her. Randal means, I think, that she and the other girl thought Frances had gone for a second rendezvous with the science master.'

'What else should she go out for?' Vera demanded.

'There are sometimes more reasons

than the obvious one,' Vaxley said. 'As for you girls, you can go. I'll probably have another chat with you later.'

Maria gave a curt nod of dismissal and the three trooped out looking rather troubled. When the door had shut Vaxley gave a faint smile.

'It is possible, Miss Black, that you will have three model pupils there for a little while to come. You can usually get the full story out of a bullying type like this girl Randal if you scare them to death — '

'You don't think that any of them did it, then?' Maria asked in relief. 'I am thinking of the scandal to the school — '

'Not them! The Vera Randal sort never do. This was planned by an ice-cool mind, not by a vindictive bully. A severe punishment later on might help her and her two cat's paws to appreciate the virtues of decent behaviour . . . But this science master interests me. You say you discharged him. Do you know where he went?'

'I cannot be sure of that, but I think he took a room in the village. Anyhow he had that in mind when he left . . . Frankly

I am rather surprised at the new turn in events. I never even suspected that Frances broke bounds twice.'

'I'll have him picked up,' Vaxley said. 'What does he look like?'

In detail Maria described him and the superintendent made a note, and then asked quietly:

'Do you think there was any connection between him and this unfortunate girl? She was, as we know, quite a fully-grown woman and may even have been secretly married to this scientist.'

Maria shrugged. 'I just don't know. All I *do* know is that she got Mr. Lever into the quadrangle on the pretext of wanting to know the position of Sirius. She may have really wanted to know, or it may have been an excuse. As yet I haven't formed an opinion.'

Vaxley smiled slightly. 'No wonder Inspector Morgan got into deep water! But to every pattern there are the pieces . . . Anyway, I think I'd better examine the body and then question the two girls who were knocked out. I believe you had the body put in your visitors' wing?'

Maria tried not to look anxious. 'Yes — yes, of course. But first, Superintendent, tell me something. Did you check up on Major Hasleigh's bank?'

'We did. There was an account in that bank in his name, but your cheque for fees when passed left only a few pounds surplus. Hasleigh gave the bank his address in Elmington, which we find does not even exist. In other words, he left the money in the bank to be immediately taken out — the very next day in fact. Purely backing for getting his alleged daughter into this school . . . We have a warrant out for his arrest for misrepresentation and the War Office has been asked to check their files in order to trace him. Another thing, the ration book and identity card of the dead girl are forgeries. We've a suspect for who did them, but we can't get any proof. There's a good deal of it goes on if you know the right places to go . . . Briefly, Miss Black, the whole thing was a put-up job with murder at the end of it.'

'I think,' Maria said slowly, 'that 'Major' Hasleigh will never be found. And

I have my doubts if he was a father at all, much less Frances's.'

Vaxley was about to ask her to elaborate, then something in her expression deterred him.

'I know — you have your own theory,' he smiled. 'So be it. You have the advantage of pursuing your own angles: we have the advantage of all the machinery of the law to enforce our wishes. That makes us about equal. Now, about the body?'

'Yes — the body — '

Maria hesitated, glancing through the window, she gave an unnoticed sigh of relief. Joan Dawson and Beryl Mather were just hurrying up the steps of the School House. Since it was well before dinner-bell they had obviously found something. In a few moments they were knocking on the study door.

'Come in,' Maria bade gravely.

'Miss Black, we — ' Joan began eagerly, but Maria cut her short.

'I think, Joan, it must be pretty obvious to you that I have a visitor. Whatever you have to say can wait until later — Oh, the parcel!' she broke off, with an air of understanding. 'You found out where it was delivered?'

Beryl looked rather blank, but Joan nodded quickly.

'Yes, Miss Black — here's the address — '
She scribbled a few words on a sheet of paper from the desk. Maria took it from her, tried not to look startled at the four words — *'In the chapel crypt'* — then folded the note and put it away in her desk drawer.

'All right, girls, thank you,' she nodded. 'We will see to it later . . . Now, Superintendent, I am at your service.'

As the girls went out Vaxley asked sharply: 'Shouldn't those girls be at lessons, Miss Black, instead of tearing about the damp regions of the school?'

Maria gave him a glance as she accompanied him out into the corridor.

'Damp regions, Superintendent?'

'Both girls' stockings had damp smears on them; there were dewdrops glistening in their hair. I saw it distinctly in the sun through the window — ' Vaxley broke off and smiled. 'I have the oddest feeling that you are not playing the game entirely square with me, Miss Black! Did that note really refer to a parcel? And those two girls were Frances's unfortunate friends at the time of her murder, weren't they? You called one of them Joan.'

'Yes, they are the two girls,' Maria nodded ruefully. 'I see that I must not try and hide things from you, Super. Frankly, the body of Frances Hasleigh disappeared last night from Room 10 where I had had it placed. I went to see if it was all right, and it had gone! I put those two girls on the job of trying to find it before you arrived, and they have evidently succeeded. That note said — *In the chapel crypt.*' As to the why and wherefore concerning the removal of the body I know no more than you.'

Vaxley's lips tightened a little. 'So somebody is interested in the dead body, eh? Somebody evidently on these very premises. And you set two pupils to look for the corpse — girls of sixteen at that. Most unorthodox, Miss Black.'

'I had my own reason for doing that,' she replied stubbornly.

'I shan't press you,' Vaxley smiled. 'Anyway, you could not have kept the body's removal a secret, because I knew it should have been in the visitors' wing . . . Anyway, suppose we try and find this wandering corpse together?'

They had come out into the sunny quadrangle by now. Maria led the way across to the chapel. They went through it, beyond the nave, and into the ancient crypt beyond. There was nothing here, but the heavy flagstone leading to the old abbey mausoleum — a relic of most ancient times — had been raised and was on one side.

Vaxley looked down at it, then Maria unclipped her fountain pen torch and gave it him. He led the way down a flight of stone steps into a mildewed area that reeked of wetness and the grave. The dampness Joan and Beryl had brought back with them was immediately explained away.

For a while the two stood looking round on the various burial plates and sarcophagi, then Maria nodded to the flat stone on top of the nearest sarcophagus.

The dead body of Frances Hasleigh lay there, the sheet that had formerly covered her now missing, her hands folded on to her breast. And here was a peculiar thing that Maria and Vaxley both noted at the same moment —

The girl's left forearm, to the elbow, was severely burned. From wrist to elbow it was black with blisters and the surface skin had peeled away. Even her dress, immediately underneath her forearm, was scorched and crinkled.

'Extraordinary!' Maria commented. 'This looks like deliberate mutilation of the dead, Super.'

Vaxley did not reply. He began to prowl round the body and studied it from all angles. Maria did the same. At length they looked at each other.

'Her feet are not scratched anyway,' Vaxley said. 'That seems to prove she did no walking in the clearing. Yet the legs of her stockings are torn — and the back of the heels. Seems she must have been dragged — '

'My view, too,' Maria acknowledged.

'But her arm!' Vaxley breathed, staring

at it. 'Was it like this before?'

'No, there was not a mark on her arms when she was found dead. This has happened since. It's rather a horrible discovery. Burning — Hmm! I wonder if ultra-violet — '

Vaxley gave a start. 'You did mention that, didn't you? But who the devil would want to steal a dead girl's body and then burn her forearm nearly to the bone? Again, there is a point, Miss Black. This may have been done by actual burning and not by ultra-violet radiation . . . Can ultra-violet make any impression on a corpse?'

'It can,' Maria said calmly. 'Ultra-violet tans the skin of either living being or dead one. The radioactive action is purely confined to the skin and the presence or absence of active blood circulation makes no difference. This burning could have been done by ultra-violet radiation on an extreme and prolonged scale.'

Vaxley looked back at the arm closely. It was set rigidly stiff by now, just as it had been placed when she had been laid on the mattress in Room 10.

'Quite a pretty girl,' he said reflectively, studying her face with its alabaster whiteness and closed eyes. 'Pity she had to die so horribly . . . Mmm, yes,' he mused, raising the blonde hair at the back of her ears and studying the tell-tale bruise marks now almost disappeared. 'I see now what Morgan meant . . . Well, Miss Black, she will have to be taken back to the visitors' room when the blackout is on. That is your best move. I will have a couple of men down here shortly and they will do the job for you. They can keep an eye on this place during the rest of today, too. In the meantime what has this place to tell us?'

He began to search the floor and the tablet on which the girl was lying, but the torch was not particularly bright and there was nothing unusual to be seen. Certainly no footprints with the damp there was clinging to the floor. Finally he gave it up and looked at Maria again.

'Reverting back to this ultra-violet business, Miss Black. You have ultra-violet lamps in the college, I presume?'

'Three — up in the solarium.'

'I'd like to see them. Who has charge of them?'

'The physical instructor and our new science master have equal responsibility, Super. One for the physical value thereof, and the other for the scientific possibilities.'

'Well, we'll go and have a look at these lamps, and have a word with the two men concerned as well.'

Maria nodded and led the way back up the steps to the crypt. Vaxley returned her torch, then took hold of the heavy flagstone and with an effort levered it into place.

'Damned heavy,' he panted, dusting his hands when it was back in position. 'I don't see how either of those two girls — or even both of them together — could ever have got it up. Of course, they could have noticed it because of the ring in it — Unless it was on one side like that when they found it. We must have a word with them as soon as possible.'

Maria led the way out of the crypt, through the chapel, and so finally back into the school. Before long they had reached the solarium and Vaxley went across to the ultra-violet machines against the wall.

'Easy enough to move,' he commented finally, 'but their power relies on the mains. How could one of them be used in the mausoleum where no power is laid on?'

'You think one of them was used, then?'

'Seems obvious to me. How otherwise was the burning produced? Of course, they might be battery driven — '

Vaxley went down on his knees and frowned as he studied the bolts holding the lamps to the floor.

'We're on the wrong horse here, Miss Black,' he growled. 'These lamps have not been moved for a very long time. Not a scratch on these nuts here and the enamel not even disturbed. No, these certainly were not used . . . Yet,' he went on, getting up again, 'it seems logical to infer that for some reason somebody wanted to use ultra-violet on the dead body of that girl and could only do it in a place likely to be undisturbed — way under the chapel crypt, for instance.'

'I think that, too,' Maria nodded. 'But since these machines were not used and there is no power in the mausoleum to generate them anyway, we are brought back to the theory of some battery-driven lamp.'

'Right,' Vaxley nodded. 'Which would be a pretty heavy job. Still anybody who could shift that flagstone could easily move heavy batteries . . . I think the best thing we can do is have a word with the two men connected with these lamps. Maybe we could do it in your study?'

Maria nodded and preceded him on the journey back. It was not long before Clive Whittaker arrived in response to her summons over the house telephone. He seemed rather surprised as he glanced at Vaxley lounging in the armchair, but definitely he was not nervous. He stood waiting, a faint smile on his keen, clean-shaven face, his stoop shoulders bent as usual.

'I am Superintendent Vaxley of Scotland Yard,' Vaxley said briefly. 'I don't have to tell you, Mr. Whittaker, that a pupil of this college — Frances Hasleigh — was found hanged yesterday?'

'No, sir, you don't. I think that practically all the school knows about it by now — if not by word of mouth then from the newspapers. I first heard of it yesterday evening when I was working late in the laboratory. A girl brought me a science essay I had ordered her to do for disobedience in class and she let the information slip. She had heard it from somebody else — '

'Which girl was it?' Maria asked sharply.

'I believe it was Marsden, of the Fifth.'

'Mr. Whittaker,' Vaxley said, 'you are the science master here, and as such share the responsibility for the upkeep of the ultra-violet lamps in the solarium?'

'Correct,' Whittaker agreed. 'The physical instructor and I look after the lamps between us.'

'Just how extensive is your knowledge of ultra-violet, Mr. Whittaker?'

'As Miss Black and the Board of Governors know when I applied for the position here, I have certificates for my scientific prowess. I studied science in the Vienna Technical Institute — as it was then — the French College of Physics, and in the British Imperial Laboratories. I suppose I know pretty well all there is to know about ultra-violet.'

As Vaxley reflected, Maria made a brief note of her own on the scratch pad, then Vaxley spoke again:

'We have reason to believe that the death of Frances Hasleigh was, for some unexplained reason, connected with ultra-violet instruments. Last night the body of the dead girl was removed from the visitors' wing and taken down into the chapel mausoleum where the left arm was subjected to some kind of severe burning process. Can you throw any light on that?'

Whittaker shook his dark head. 'I'm afraid I can't, sir. It sounds like a most extraordinary business to me.'

'Very!' Vaxley agreed. 'Did you know Frances Hasleigh at all?'

'Only as a pupil — and not very well even then. After all, I have not been here long enough to get very well acquainted with anybody.'

'Quite so . . . Perhaps you can tell me if the girl evinced any particularly outstanding interest in science?'

'I cannot say that she showed any preference for any particular subject — unless it be astronomy. When it came to knowledge she had a good all-round scientific education. I never asked her a scientific question but what she could answer it.'

Vaxley nodded slowly, then: 'Can you tell me where you were last night between ten o'clock and rising-bell this morning?'

'I was in my study reading until eleven last night, after I had finished my laboratory work — then I went to bed. Of course, I can't prove it, because nobody called on me during that time.'

'I don't think we need worry over that, Mr. Whittaker,' Vaxley smiled. 'And don't feel alarmed. This is purely routine. That will be all for the moment, and thank you for being so frank.'

Whittaker turned towards the door, then he paused and looked back, frowning.

'I realise,' he said, 'that this ultra-violet

business causes a great deal of suspicion to attach to me, but I had nothing to do with that girl's death. I swear it to you!'

Vaxley smiled, but said nothing. With that Whittaker went out quietly.

'Well, Miss Black?' Vaxley asked presently. 'Did you glean anything?'

Maria merely shrugged. She had already decided it was her own business just how much she gathered. 'You wish to see the physical instructor?' she asked.

'Yes — and then those two girls.'

Again Maria got busy with her orders over the house telephone. The physical instructor was soon disposed of, however. He was not a resident teacher, anyway, coming to the college from the village every day to give his P.T. lessons. Nor for that matter was he a man of great genius. Brawn, and brawn only, was his strong point, and his blunt, matter-of-fact answers to the questions posed for him satisfied Maria at least that he was not even worth recording in the case. Certainly his knowledge of ultra-violet seemed to be limited to switching a button on and off after a given period.

Then came Joan Dawson and Beryl Mather. Freshened up after their mausoleum experiences they stood regarding Vaxley with anxious frowns.

'Are both you girls convinced that you did not see or hear anybody else in the clearing before you were attacked?' he asked them — and they nodded promptly and vigorously.

'The only one who could have seen anything was Frances,' Joan said, and then without being asked she went into a fully detailed account of the circumstances, just as she had related them to Maria earlier in the morning.

At the close of her story Vaxley rubbed his jaw. 'This morning you both found the missing body of Frances Hasleigh in the old abbey mausoleum, didn't you?' he asked

'Be quite frank, Joan,' Maria smiled. 'The Superintendent knows all about my asking you to search.'

'Oh, well then — Yes, we found it. It was only by chance, though. We had no footprints, or clues, to go on. It just seemed to me that if anybody wanted to hide a dead body they would probably choose a place where nobody would ever go. Beryl said that that might mean the old mausoleum. So we went there — and found Frances.'

'Did you find the flagstone to the mausoleum open or closed when you got there?'

'It was half open. That was what attracted our attention. It looked as though somebody had tried to put it back into place but had not had the time. Between us we pushed it far enough on to one side to enable us to get below.'

'I see,' Vaxley nodded. 'And did you notice anything odd about the body of Frances when you found her?'

'I did, yes,' Joan nodded. 'Beryl got scared when she saw the corpse, and ran for it. I felt a bit squeamish myself, but I couldn't help noticing that Frances's left arm was horribly burned.'

'Most observant,' Vaxley said approvingly; 'and I am going to ask you both to keep it strictly to yourselves . . . That will be all, girls, thank you.'

They nodded and Joan led the way to the door, limping. Vaxley frowned at her.

'What is the matter with your feet, young lady? I noticed you were limping when I saw you earlier on'

'Thorns in the clearing yesterday, sir,' Joan replied. 'I cut my foot pretty badly.'

'You'd better go along to the matron and have it seen to,' Maria said briefly,

'Yes, Miss Black,' Joan nodded, then she and Beryl went out and closed the door.

Vaxley glanced at his watch and rose to his feet. 'Well, Miss Black, I have been here quite long enough and it is close on dinner-time. Thank you for the courtesy you have shown me. I have learned all I need to learn here: the rest is a matter of routine. I'll examine the clearing after lunch, and if I reach any particular conclusions I'll let you know. And I'll send down those two men I promised . . . If you get into difficulties just contact me at the local police headquarters and I'll be over right away.'

Maria nodded and got up from her chair, shook the lean hand he held out to her. His little eyes searched her face for a moment.

'I do believe you've learned something from all this,' he said smiling.

'The observant person,' Maria murmured, 'learns something out of everything . . . So glad to have met you, Superintendent — Oh, by the way, in what position do I stand in regard to those various girls? Their parents will be bound to ask me. Are any of them likely to be put under police detention?'

Vaxley shook his head. 'Not on the present evidence. If it should threaten later I'll give you good warning. As long as they are here in the school and with your eye on them I will consider it sufficient.'

Maria saw him as far as the quadrangle, then she returned to her study and pulled her black book from the desk drawer.

'Before I forget,' she muttered. 'So many things crammed into one morning — '

She took up her pen and began to write swiftly:

Clive Whittaker (our new science master) got his degrees in Vienna, Paris, and Britain. Note the first two places. Connecting link: Frances's shoes made in France, and Whittaker also in France at some time. Did they know each other on the Continent?

Joan Dawson received a parcel of (alleged) stockings recently. Check up. Joan Dawson still limps.

Frances Hasleigh broke bounds twice. Find where she went the second time.

Following disappearance of Frances's body from Room 10, I have had her found again by Joan Dawson and Beryl Mather. Found in old abbey mausoleum with forearm (left) burned nearly to bone. Why? Ultra-violet?

Mausoleum flagstone could only be raised by a strong man — i.e. not by schoolgirls. Clive Whittaker seems at the moment to have no connection with all this, yet somehow —

Mr. Martin (Pulp) has arrived in England most unexpectedly, and I may have use for him.

The time is: 12.52 p.m.

Maria put her book away, then left the study with majestic strides to the staff dining-hall.

6

During dinner Maria spoke little: she was too busy planning her forthcoming activities. Immediately it was over she consigned her duties to Tanby and then went to her study and rang up Pulp Martin. Evidently he had succeeded in lodging himself at the Fox Hotel for he answered promptly enough.

In response to Maria's order to come over to the school right away, he complied within fifteen minutes and entered her study with the same bland cheerfulness as in the morning.

'Well, what's cookin'?' he asked, waiting as Maria armed herself with a powerful torch, a lens, and several empty envelopes.

'I am not cooking. Mr. Martin — only starting in real earnest to solve this mystery. So far it has all been fact gathering, so now begins my own method of check and counter-check. That is where you come in . . . At the moment I want to study the mausoleum where the body of Frances Hasleigh was taken by somebody unknown.'

'Taken?' Pulp repeated, frowning — so in detail Maria told him what had transpired.

'So that is why I want another look at the mausoleum before Vaxley's men get there,' she finished. 'I wish, too, I could decide who it was I saw in the quadrangle last night when the body disappeared. I saw somebody heading for the School House and I have blamed myself for not following up my advantage. However, maybe we can fit that piece in later . . . In your terse but expressive phraseology, Mr. Martin — let's go!'

Pulp accompanied her across the quadrangle. She did not try and conceal the fact that Pulp was with her. If even the celebrated Vaxley was prepared to allow her full scope, it was certainly nobody else's concern what she did. She felt she was as entitled as the law to look into the business with whomever she chose.

So they reached the crypt. There was

no sign of Vaxley's men having arrived.

'I need your help, Mr. Martin,' Maria said, nodding to the massive flagstone. 'Too much weight for me to haul about . . . Do you mind?'

He seized the iron ring in his big hands and heaved. Nevertheless, it made him breathe pretty hard to move that stone on one side, and when he had finished he mopped his brow with a green handkerchief.

'Tidy weight,' he panted.

'Which is rather interesting,' Maria murmured. 'This stone was either pulled on one side by a very strong man or else it was levered out of position.' She paused to study the edge of the stone with her torch beam. 'No — there are no signs here of anything resembling a crowbar having been used. That, in turn, seems to eliminate any of the girls as having been responsible and leaves — up to now — either our science master, Mr. Whittaker, or the physical instructor. Hmm . . . I do not regard the latter as even worth considering; yet on the other hand the science master, who I do think had something to do with this, is rather weak-looking with stooped shoulders. So, what have we?'

Pulp thought for a moment, then: 'Say, isn't there some kind of link-up? I mean, the body was lowered from a window five floors up, wasn't it?'

'Everything points to that, yes.'

'Okay, then, let's see the weight of the body, then I'll tell you what's buzzing round in my noodle.'

He took the torch away and led the way below, helping Maria down after him. Then when she had joined him he gave her the torch back and quite unconcernedly slipped his hands under the body and raised it gently in his arms, finally laid it down again.

'About twelve stone dead-weight and say nine alive,' he mused. 'That's a tidy weight, too. I figure that it would be just as tough to lower a body of this weight from a five-story window as it would be to raise that stone. So in both cases it was done by the same guy. To cut it short, Maria, you're looking for a guy who ain't no weakling.'

'Splendid!' Maria approved. 'That helps me a good deal.'

Pulp looked at the body again. 'I reckon there's something odd here,' he commented. 'If a rope was used to lower her, with her dead-weight hanging on it too, it should have creased this dress — but it looks okay to me all over. And unless the rope was brand new it would have left a dirty mark. This dress being pink it would have shown up. But it don't.'

Maria looked with him interestedly, then suddenly she straightened with a gleam in her eyes.

'I have it, Mr. Martin — the sheet! It was laid over her when she was in the visitors' wing and when she disappeared *it* disappeared too. It must have been tied in a broad band either round her waist or under her arms and then the rope was fastened to it. In that fashion there would be no creasing. I just wonder if it is about here somewhere?'

This started them both on a search and it was not very long before Pulp gave a whoop of delight and thrust his arm into a deep crevice in one of the farther corners. He pulled forth a dirty, crumpled sheet and spread it out.

In the torchlight they examined it. From the crosswise creases upon it, it was clear that it had been used as a noose round the girl's body, and at one part there were dirty smears where the rope had been fastened. But there was also something else — a curious spotting of coffee-brown marks as though a brush dipped in light brown paint had been flicked across it.

'What do you reckon it is?' Pulp asked curiously.

'Off-hand, Mr. Martin, I can't tell you — but maybe I will later. The Superintendent evidently missed looking in that crevice — and I'm glad he did. Here, hold it for a moment I wish to look a little further yet.'

Maria began to prowl round the raised sarcophagus on which the girl lay. But here there was not a trace of a clue as to who the body-snatching interloper had been. Finally Maria gave it up. She glanced up to find Pulp looking behind the girl's ears.

'The old pan-handle all right,' he said briefly.

'I think, Mr. Martin, we can make one or two deductions,' Maria said thoughtfully. 'First, you observe this girl's forearm. Obviously there was something on that arm that had to be obliterated — its burned condition proves it. But why such a thorough way of doing it? And why so much trouble to remove the body from the college? Plainly it was a job that could not be done in the school for fear of interruption. From that we can assume other things . . . A knife could have slashed this dead arm just as easily and would have been no trouble for the attacker to carry — but instead he — or she — chose this most elaborate, not to say unwieldy method. Link that up with the girl's professed dislike for ultra-violet radiation, and her so-called father's profound antipathy for it, and what have we?'

'Well, Maria, I got me brains in the right place so I'll tell you how I dope it out. Suppose there was somethin' on this arm that only showed up in this

155

ultra-violet stuff? Whoever wanted whatever it was — if you get me — got that
first and then burned the skin right away,
maybe by leavin' the ultra lamp trained
on it.'

'Right!' Maria cried. 'My view exactly.
Upon my soul, Mr. Martin your observa-
tional powers have greatly improved since
we worked together in America! That
must be it. But what could it be that
could only show up in an ultra-violet
light? We have nearly everything but that
— the girl's reluctance to use it, her
father's dislike of it, and now this. But
none of the violet ray machines in the
school have been moved, so another one
must have been employed.'

To Maria's surprise Pulp turned aside
and began a second search. Since he gave
no hint of what he was looking for she
stood aside and waited patiently — then
after perhaps ten minutes of careful
searching he directed her attention to a
corner of the mausoleum ceiling. She
studied it intently in the torchlight and
saw the glint of two strips of copper.
When she looked more closely she saw

there were two electric wires bared for about two inches along their length and held apart by a wedge of wood.

'There it is,' Pulp grinned. 'The electric mains pass under here to get to the college. I figured they might do because I remembered seeing a couple of power pylons as I came to the school.'

'Then there is power laid on here after all!' Maria exclaimed.

'Of sorts. Whoever did this filed away a piece of the lead conduit covering and bared the wire. That shows fair electric knowledge with live wires. I guess all he had to do was clip a coupla leads on these wires and he'd be all set to work his ultra-violet machine.'

'Which in turn shows he must have made it his business to study the mains layout of this college,' Maria mused. 'Really, Mr. Martin, I am much indebted to you and very angry with myself. Now I come to think of it there is a chart in the entrance hall showing the full electrical circuit of the college — for the use of the fire service in the case of a raid, you understand. Had I looked there — as our unknown body-snatcher obviously did — I could have seen for myself that there are wires down here ... Anyway, it narrows the field. We know how he got his power, and we presume he must have used a lamp of his own.'

'Yeah, that's how I figure it,' Pulp agreed.

Maria nodded to the sheet and he picked it up.

'Our next job is to analyse those brown stains,' she said briefly. 'Come — '

She led the way up into the crypt again, then just as Pulp had heaved the flagstone back into place there came the sound of heavy footfalls and two men came into view — plainclothes men, but with the unmistakable stamp of the law upon them

'Not before it is time, my men,' Maria said briefly, as Pulp rolled up the sheet under his coat. 'I have had to be on guard myself until you came — and a great deal of time I have lost, too!'

'Sorry, ma'am,' one of them said, touching his hat. 'We came the moment we were instructed.'

'Very well,' she nodded. 'Come, Mr.

Martin — ' And she walked on majestically towards the nave as the two men glanced at each other and then prepared to take up their positions.

Pulp grinned as he followed Maria out into the sunshine. 'You sure think of the cutest words to put the skids under the dicks sometimes. Wish I had your touch . . . Anyway, what's next?'

'The laboratory for analysis. It should be deserted at this hour.'

But when they entered they found Clive Whittaker present, busy with a series of bottles and test tubes. He gave a slight start as Maria arrived, glanced beyond her to Pulp then put down the test tube he had been studying into its rack.

'Busy, Mr. Whittaker?' Maria asked gravely, advancing.

'Just an experiment, Miss Black,' he shrugged. 'I have half an hour to spare before taking the Fourth in chemistry, so I thought I would fill in the moments.'

Maria's eyes went swiftly over the bottles he had had no time to conceal. Mercury fulminate, nitro-glycerine, starch, ammonia, nitrate of silver, and several smaller bottles of stuff which had only symbols to identify them and which she knew were not college property

'You have some rather dangerous ingredients here, Mr. Whittaker,' she commented. 'I sincerely trust you do not contemplate blowing us all up!'

He smiled oddly. 'There is little fear of that. Rest assured that I know what I'm doing. It's just that I am writing a book on explosives and like to analyse them in my spare time. Practical research, as it were.'

'Oh, I see — '

'I'll not take up the room if you are requiring the place,' he said, picking up his own various bottles and the test tube. 'I'll carry on later, after school hours.'

Since Maria said nothing he assumed correctly that he had taken the best course. He put his bottles away in a half-empty drawer, returned the now empty test tube to the wall-rack, then went out quietly.

'Peculiar,' Maria reflected, frowning at

the tube. 'And perhaps worth looking into — '

'Not with them ingredients!' Pulp said uneasily. 'I'm kind of allergic to the nitro-glycerine, Maria. If you're going to examine it let me take a powder — '

'I am not referring to the chemicals themselves,' Maria smiled, 'but to our young friend's actions. I think they might bear investigation . . . However, we have other things to deal with it the moment. Lock the door, and then let me have that sheet.'

Pulp nodded and complied, then he stood by and watched as she carefully scratched some of the brown, powdery substance from the sheet onto a micro-scope slide. She looked at it through the lenses for a while, shook her head, then tipped the powder into a minute quantity of water and added a few chemicals from the jars in the shelf. The final result she put into a beaker and then began slow and tedious analysis.

When finally she had finished she looked up with a gleam in her blue eyes.

'Metol quinol,' she announced. 'And in

case you don't know what that is, it is a perfect quick-acting developer for photographic plates. The formula as a rule is metol quinol, hyposulphate of soda, and clear running water — '

Maria paused and gave a decisive nod. 'Mr. Martin, we are compelled to accept the obvious. Part of the hypothesis is mine, and part of it is yours. Assume so far that a man of not inconsiderable strength took the body of Frances Hasleigh to the mausoleum, and there by means of ultra-violet process first brought into being something that was on her forearm, and then photographed it. There we have a dual motive for the mausoleum! One for darkness and the other for safety from prying eyes. We can also assume that photographic plates were used which were specially sensitive to ultra-violet — No, no, that is not right! They would not need metol quinol developer, but a totally different process in which bromide would figure largely. Hmm — '

Maria frowned for a moment, then worked her way out of the impasse.

'No — the photography would be normal and the light would no doubt be an ordinary torch. Using time exposure that would be simple enough since the subject was dead — immovable. Then, when the photograph was taken the development thereof took place. Let us say, though, that our body-snatching photographer *shook* the photographic plate, when developed, much as one does a wet brush. Spots of developer solution spattered unnoticed into the crevice wherein he had thrust the sheet . . . Then, satisfied he had a perfect negative, he turned on his ultra-violet machine again and burned the girl's arm until every trace of whatever was there was obliterated. Then — '

Maria shrugged. 'Well, maybe something scared him off, for he packed up in a hurry, forgot the sheet, did not stay to put the flagstone back, and just — vanished. There, I think, we have a workable theory. We don't know the culprit and we don't know what scared him away — but we are going to do our best to find out!'

'Yeah,' Pulp agreed. 'I guess it might be

the set-up at that. But who do you think done it?'

She smiled pensively. 'It is more than possible that — '

She paused as there came a sharp knocking on the laboratory door. Going over to it she unlocked it to find Miss Tanby outside, rather wide-eyed.

'Oh, here you are, Miss Black! I've had the staff trying to find you everywhere . . . The parents are here.'

'All of them?' Maria exclaimed, startled.

'Well, they seem to have arrived in a body. I showed them into your study.'

Maria sighed. 'All right, Miss Tanby, please tell them I will come at once — ' She turned back to Pulp regretfully.

'There it is, Mr. Martin — incessant calls on my time when I am — er — getting warmed up. However, I think we have made a good start.'

'You betcha!' he grinned. 'What's the layout now?'

'Take the sheet with you back to the Fox Hotel and keep it out of sight. I am glad Vaxley missed it — it gives me a decided advantage . . . He had the chance to find it, so that is his loss. I am wondering, however, if he saw those bare electric wires, but said nothing. No matter: you and I have our own views about them.'

'Okay, I'll be off,' Pulp nodded. 'And if you want me just give me a bell.'

Maria watched him go, then she left the laboratory and hurried to her room to make herself presentable for the task ahead of her.

★ ★ ★

Arriving in her study Maria found it rather overcrowded with four women and five men. At a glance she recognised Mr. and Mrs. Dawson, Mr. and Mrs. Randal, Mr. and Mrs. Vane, Mr. and Mrs. Webster, and Beryl Mather's father.

'Good afternoon, ladies and gentlemen. Quite a deputation indeed!'

'Just coincidence,' Joseph Randal said, in his heavy voice. 'There is only about one train a day in these times and parts and it seems we all made an effort to catch it.'

'Quite so,' Maria reached her usual chair and sat down. 'Your being all here makes matters easier for me. From my letters you understand the circumstances, but I thought a personal explanation might help.'

'It's a scandal!' declared Mrs. Vane agitatedly. 'We send our children here for education and the next thing we know there is a murder — and one of the pupils at that!'

'That,' Maria said gravely, 'is purely in the nature of things. A murderer does not pick his spot. Since your daughter, Mr. and Mrs. Vane, and yours, too, Mr. and Mrs. Randal and Mr. and Mrs. Webster, were directly concerned with the original prank which was the prelude to the tragedy, I thought you had better have the facts first-hand. If not from me, then you can contact Superintendent Vaxley of Scotland Yard at the local police headquarters. He has the matter in hand . . . First, though, let me hasten to assure you that though the law takes a grave view of the affair, of course, there is no question of any of your daughters being arrested. They were merely the perpetrators of a very inconsiderate joke, which ended tragically.'

Joseph Randal shrugged. 'Vera probably had a reason for what she did.'

'She was lucky, Mr. Randal, to escape expulsion,' Maria said icily. 'As the matter stands she is at liberty to continue her studies here if you wish it. If not — Well, it is for you to decide.'

'I think,' said Beryl Mather's rotund father sourly, 'a girl who will think up a deliberately vicious idea to inflict pain on her school comrades deserves not only expulsion but jail! Young upstart!' he snapped. 'What is more I would have demanded it if things hadn't gone this way.'

'You can't help young people playing jokes!' Mrs. Randal retorted. 'Vera is not the kind of girl to — '

Maria raised her hand. 'Please do not regard this matter as an issue over an ill-natured prank. Murder has been done, and an inquest will follow! All I require to know from you all is if you wish your various daughters to remain here? In any event, even if they leave, they will be summoned for the inquest.'

'Well,' declared Joan Dawson's father, his blue eyes troubled, 'if my girl is liable to get mixed up in nasty things like this, and murder to boot, it's about time we sent her to another school. Good Lord, she was knocked unconscious, bound and gagged — ! She might have been murdered, too! No, I think it is time to take her away. What do you think, Clara?'

The industrialist glanced at his thin-faced wife. So far she had sat in silence, her sharp blue eyes darting from one face to the other. Now, prompted by her husband, she spoke slowly and unemotionally.

'I am none too sure that I agree, Herbert. The tragedy is over and done with. I cannot see the point in Joan leaving now. Maybe it would be better to see what she herself thinks — '

Dawson shrugged, but did not answer. So Maria took up the house phone and gave the order for Joan to be sent in to her.

Immediately she arrived she went

straight over to her father and hugged him eagerly.

'Oh, dad, it's so wonderful to see you! And so unexpected, too — '

Dawson smiled and patted her shoulders affectionately, then she turned to her mother, gave her a most perfunctory kiss, and certainly no embrace.

'You are looking quite well, Joan, considering,' her mother said briefly. 'Now Miss Black has something to say to you.'

'Joan,' Maria said, 'do you, or do you not, wish to stay on here after what has happened?'

The girl's dark eyes became surprised. 'Stay? But, of course, I do, Miss Black!'

'Even after being attacked by those bullying young women!' her father exclaimed.

'That's an insult!' Joseph Randal shouted.

'I must insist that there be no personalities in this!' Maria interrupted. 'Joan — you wish to stay on?'

'Certainly I do, m'm. That joke Vera played was all in the way of school life, so it doesn't worry me a bit.'

'But you're still limping!' her father cried. 'Isn't it from that attack?'

'Well — in a way. I trod on some thorns without shoes and it left a nasty after-effect . . . I'll get over it. But I really want to stop, dad — if only to find out who killed poor Frances. She was Beryl's and my best friend.'

Her father looked at her puzzledly, but her mother gave a slow nod and tightened her lips. Maria watched the three faces intently as though a thought had struck her.

'I think, Joan, you are being very sensible,' her mother said finally. 'You stay!'

'Yes, mother,' Joan said meekly.

'Then I'll have to agree, too,' her father shrugged. 'Your mother and I are always in accord — '

'That being so, Joan, you may go,' Maria said; then as the door closed behind the girl she looked back at the group.

'Well, if she can stay on I cannot see what we others have to complain about,' Mrs. Webster shrugged. 'I think my husband and I will let Molly decide her own fate.'

'Good enough,' Webster himself nodded. 'If she doesn't want to stop she can write home and say so. I'm a busy man and can't afford to waste any more time. This coming down here has been a confounded nuisance!'

His remarks started them all off, but from the general confusion of remarks and cross talk it finally emerged that the various girls were to remain in Maria's care. And on this note she got rid of the adults as tactfully as possible and then returned to her desk to make a note or two. In her record book she made a note of her metol quinol discovery, and the unexpected chemical experiments of Clive Whittaker — then she added one sentence on a line to itself:

Blue eyes — blue eyes — brown eyes? Is this physically possible? Check.

'Better to put it that way,' she mused. 'Now things show a tendency to warm up a little there is no knowing who might decide to investigate the investigator. And if I left any clues as to my thoughts it would be a cardinal tragedy indeed!'

As she put her book away the telephone bell shrilled.

'Yes? Miss Black speaking — '

'Oh, hello, Miss Black! Vaxley speaking. I thought you would be interested to know that Robert Lever has been arrested and that he is being held on suspicion of the murder of Frances Hasleigh.'

'Robert Lever! My ex-science master?'

'The same. I don't mind telling you how it happened. When I visited the Bollin's Wood clearing this afternoon I found a fountain pen lying in the undergrowth, quite close to the tree where Frances Hasleigh was hanged. The pen was completely damning, for it had Lever's name engraved on it. My theory is that in stooping to fasten up the girl the pen dropped out of his pocket: the clip is loose anyway — '

'Very interesting,' Maria said pensively. 'And you say you have already found and arrested him?'

'No difficulty about it. Since being

discharged from Roseway he had been living in a combined room in the village prior to finding a fresh position or else being called up — '

'He admits that it is his pen?'

'Of course. He can hardly deny it with his own name on it. He has some rather unconvincing tale about leaving it in the Sixth Form room on his desk and forgetting in his hurry to claim it. That carries no weight with me. He admits, too, that he was in the neighbourhood of Bollin's Wood yesterday afternoon. He can't very well deny it either, for it seems that he took a boat out on the Bollin River about five o'clock. The local boatman has corroborated the fact.

'He admits he knew Frances Hasleigh, though only slightly, chiefly through that quadrangle escapade. The thing seems quite clear to me. He took the boat down the river, got off it and into the wood, and finding three girls all bound up, he knocked out two and avenged himself on the remaining one who had caused him to lose such a comfortable position in the college.'

'How did he know the girls would be there?' Maria asked.

'My guess is that he was rowing on the river and heard their voices — Vera Randal's especially. He then beached the boat, and entered the wood circuitously. There it is — revenge motive.'

'And do you believe it was he who moved the body to the mausoleum and burned the forearm?'

'I'm not sure of that yet,' Vaxley answered. 'I've only just begun to investigate, remember.'

'I presume,' Maria said, 'that Lever had the murder rope with him? The silk cord?'

'I have a theory for that, too. He says — and the boatman has verified it — that he had a bundle of textbooks with him. Lever denies that they were fastened up and the boatman cannot remember — but I believe that they were fastened together with that silk cord and that Lever hurried back for it when he saw his chance — and used it — '

'It is a hypothesis, of course,' Maria admitted, 'but I should go on investigating if I were you.'

'We'll do that all right,' Vaxley laughed. 'Meanwhile the evidence is strong enough to warrant his arrest. He'll appear in the coroner's court tomorrow afternoon. You will find yourself and those girls summoned, too, by tomorrow morning's mail. It will be held at Lexham.'

'I will be prepared for it, then — Oh, by the way, I suppose there is no sign of Major Hasleigh as yet?'

'Not a trace, but we haven't finished yet . . . Anyway, Miss Black, goodbye for the time being.'

She put the receiver back, and tightened her lips. Tomorrow there was going to be a hard day's work ahead of her. Lexham, the nearest large-sized town, was fifteen miles away, and naturally the girls in question would be in her care. And the day after that more time would be absorbed in the funeral of Frances, with part of the fees for her truncated schooling to pay for it. This meant, to Maria, that while she was hot on the scent she had one or two things to do almost immediately.

She picked up the telephone and once

more contacted Pulp Martin.

'Mr. Martin, we have important — even dangerous — work for tonight,' she said, as his breezy voice greeted her. 'Please be here about ten tonight when it is dark. Just tell the lodge-keeper who you are and I'll see that you are admitted.'

'It's a date, Maria,' his voice boomed. 'If it's a fight we are heading for I'm just achin' to mash some guy's kisser.'

'Hmm — quite!' Maria coughed. 'See you later, Mr. Martin.'

Satisfied, Maria put the receiver back and made her way from the study en route for tea.

7

Pulp Martin presented himself exactly on time and found Maria in her study attired in dark costume, black gloves, a beret and with a little bag in her hand, which he guessed contained her investigator's equipment.

'What's the set-up?' he asked eagerly.

'Mr. Martin, in order to further our investigation we — or rather you — will have to indulge in the — ah — pan handle grip.'

'Yeah? Who's goin' to get the works?'

'I am afraid that Clive Whittaker, our science master, is going to be the unfortunate recipient. I want him to sleep gracefully for about fifteen minutes while I go through his study and its effects. I believe that he has a lot to do with this murder.'

Pulp frowned. 'He don't look a strong guy to me, and that's what we're lookin' for, ain't it?'

'Appearances are deceptive. So come with me — and be very quiet.'

Pulp grinned and glanced down at his plimsoll shoes. Maria led the way out of the study. The girls had retired to their various dormitories by now, so the place was deserted. Without encountering a soul they passed silently down many corridors, then presently, as they gained the main corridor leading to the staff studies, she raised a finger to her lips.

'There — at the far end,' she whispered. 'That is Mr. Whittaker's study door.'

'Yeah, I see it. Suppose the door's locked? The other people in these studies might get nosy.'

'Try Whittaker's gently and see if it is unlocked. Knock, and see what reply you get. If it is unlocked signal me. If not, come back here.'

'Oke!' he nodded, and went on ahead of her.

She watched him intently from round the angle of the corridor. He knocked sharply on the panels three times, then as there was no response he tried the door gently. He looked round and shrugged his

178

big shoulders so Maria hurried forward and brought a bunch of keys from her pocket.

'I have duplicates for every door in the building,' she explained, turning the appropriate key in the lock. 'You go first. If he is there just — er — kosh him one! I must not be seen at any price.'

'You're on,' Pulp answered, and angled his massive body into the darkened room. Nothing happened, so Maria followed him, closed and relocked the door, then switched on the light.

'Mr. Whittaker has either retired early or else is perhaps engaged in further strange laboratory experiments. Anyway, I think we have time for a look round. If he should reappear suddenly you can still — hmm! — lay him out.'

'Okay, Maria, but what are we lookin' for in here?'

'I am looking for a photographic negative — which might explain the metol quinol drops on that sheet. It may be well concealed, too. If we can't find it then let me know if you discover anything that seems even remotely interesting.'

Pulp began a systematic search with all the care his training as an ex-thief and confidence-man had given him. With bits of wire he had drawers and cupboards open magically and when he had finished there was not a thing to prove that he had been anywhere near them.

Nor did there seem to be anything in the room that should not rightly belong to a science master — until Pulp gave a whistle of excitement and lifted something up from the lowest cupboard of the small dresser in the corner.

'Ultra-violet lamp!' he exclaimed. 'Bet you this is the one that burned that kid's arm!'

Maria hurried over and examined it eagerly. 'Definitely possible,' she agreed. 'And still in use, apparently — the element is in good working order. Put it back exactly as you found it, Mr. Martin . . . we are making progress.'

Pulp returned it to the cupboard, relocked the door, and went on with his search. At length the centre drawer of the desk was unlocked and open under Pulp's hands.

'Well, whadda ya know!' he breathed finally. 'Take a gander at this, Maria — '

He handed over a photograph. 'I reckon the kid in this photograph looks exactly like Frances Hasleigh!'

Together he and Maria studied the photograph under the desk lamp. It was fairly creased, but clear enough. It showed a laughing, fair-haired girl, undoubtedly the late Frances Hasleigh — but apparently many years younger to judge from her short frocks and white socks. Her arm was linked through that of a young man — a smiling fellow with upright bearing and tousled dark hair. Behind the two, dim, but more or less distinct, was part of an open-air café with big sunshades on the tables, and more remotely still the outlines of the Eiffel Tower.

'Definitely one of the prize exhibits of this case, Mr. Martin! This man here is two people in one — he is Major Hasleigh, Frances's alleged father, and he is also our science master, Mr. Whittaker!'

'But this guy here looks a real strong piece of work — and Whittaker is as bent as an old shoe. I don't get it.'

'Neither do I — entirely,' Maria reflected. 'Major Hasleigh was upright and strong in appearance, like this young fellow here — but as I have told you he was wearing a very indifferent disguise. It is the same man, beyond a shadow of doubt.'

'Then what in heck's the connection?' Pulp demanded. 'Can't be husband and wife, surely?'

'I think the most likely relationship is brother and sister. No doubt we will soon find out . . . Put this back where you found it, Mr. Martin.'

He obeyed her, though puzzled. 'I don't get it. I rather thought you'd confront him with it.

'As you become more versed in the analysis of crime, Mr. Martin, you will find that you never confront anybody with anything until all the *other* facts fit into place. For the moment this piece of information is exclusively ours. Superintendent Vaxley had the same chance to investigate the matter: if he missed the point that is his — er — funeral . . . As for that negative which was the prime reason of our visit, it does not seem to be here. I hardly expected it would be lying about for us to pick up. Best move we can make now is to go along to the laboratory and see if those chemicals Whittaker was using this afternoon are still there. Come — '

She switched off the light before opening the door. The corridor was still deserted. They glided out of the study silently, relocked it, then by devious routes finally reached the laboratory and peered inside. It was dark and empty.

'Evidently Mr. Whittaker has retired to bed,' Maria remarked, after she had closed the shutters and put the light on. 'But at any rate we can see if — '

She stopped with the bench drawer open in front of her. The various small chemical bottles which she and Pulp had both seen Whittaker place there in the afternoon were now gone.

Pulp shrugged. 'All kinds of folks use this lab if they want, don't they? Why should he leave his stuff around for other people to monkey with?'

'If it were ordinary material it wouldn't

matter,' Maria answered. 'Obviously it is extraordinary — a secret of his own which he does not wish anybody to find. Presumably as soon as we left here this afternoon he came and reclaimed his various chemical bottles . . . Some of ours are missing, too, I see — those that are college property. Hmmm! Most interesting!'

'I don't see the point,' Pulp argued. 'If he trusted you and me with them — and he did because he left us alone — why not everybody else?'

'He obviously thinks he has nothing to fear from us — but he has from other persons, or perhaps one other person. In which case,' Maria finished thoughtfully, 'there is only one other likely place to find anything — and that is his bedroom.'

'With him in it maybe,' Pulp said dubiously.

Maria smiled gravely. 'I warned you that we might need the pan handle, did I not? Come.'

Pulp followed as she set off through the wilderness of the college. She detoured to her study, to emerge again — much to

Pulp's astonishment — with a tin of cocoa and a small box of white talcum powder. Then without any explanation she continued the trip until they both arrived outside the science master's bedroom door. They stood listening and were rewarded by the sound of deep breathing.

'Getting his shut-eye all right,' Pulp nodded. 'Open up.'

Maria slid the key in the lock and turned it gently; then like phantoms they glided into the darkness beyond, closed the door, then stood accustoming themselves to the gloom. After a while they could descry the dim figure of a man in bed.

'Pan handle,' Maria whispered in Pulp's ear. 'Can you do it?'

'A cinch,' he whispered, moving forward.

He was wrong, for the moment his hand touched the man his arms came up protectively and locked themselves round Pulp's back. For a moment or two he needed all his strength to resist, then his fingers and thumbs crept behind the man's head and pressed inexorably. Gradually the grip around his body weakened — until with a little gasp the man relaxed and became still.

'Okay,' Pulp panted. 'He's out cold. Put the light on.' The bedside lamp snapped into being and Maria moved silently forward, stood looking down at the man.

'How long will he remain unconscious?' she asked uneasily.

'With the strength he seems to have it might be about ten minutes. I'll stick around and give him another two cents worth if he comes to — '

'Did you say the 'strength' he's got?' Maria asked sharply.

'Yeah, sure. But this guy ought to be weak, oughtn't he? Stoop-shouldered, washed-out looking — '

Maria put down her cocoa and talcum powder on the table, shook some of the cocoa on to her handkerchief. 'The stooped shoulders could easily be simulated by leaning his body forward, and there are many excellent preparations for making the skin look pale. In other words — a phony! We were looking for a strong man, remember, and I think we've found one. And his amazing alertness in attacking you straight from sleep shows that he rests on the edge of danger, expecting attack at any moment . . . Now for Heaven's sake keep him quiet while I try this experiment.'

Maria first sprinkled her white powder on the dark hair, then applied the cocoa powder to the face. She studied it critically and then looked about her. Going over to the washbowl she searched about until she found a white bristled toothbrush. She came back and placed it under the unconscious man's nose.

'When in doubt, Mr. Martin, use the tools at hand. So says Jameson in his *True Faces and False* . . . Despite this very rough-and-ready make-up I can plainly see now the face of Major Hasleigh, satisfying me once and for all that this is the same person. That point proved we can restore him to normal — '

She put the toothbrush back in its place, brushed the hair until all the powder was away from it, then carefully washed his face with her own dampened handkerchief, taking care none of the powder scattered on the bedclothes. The mysterious Mr. Whittaker was then back to his usual appearance and showing signs of coming round until Pulp's fingers and thumbs administered a gentle squeeze.

'Might as well look around while we are about it,' Maria decided, and thereupon began a systematic search while Pulp stayed at the bedside. But for all her searching she found no trace of what she wanted.

'I am looking for a negative, but I don't seem able to find it. A man who wishes to keep a secret does not leave it lying about. We'll have to think of some other way of getting at it — '

Maria broke off, her eyes gleaming suddenly.

'I have it! Sherlock Holmes, in the case of Irene Adler — *Scandal in Bohemia*, to be exact — apparently set fire to Irene Adler's house in the belief that with sudden danger she would fly to the thing she valued most. Brilliant psychology on the part of the late Conan Doyle, Mr. Martin. Brilliant! We might follow in the footsteps of that marvellous fictional character for a moment and try the same — er — stunt.'

'Set fire to the place?' Pulp asked in alarm.

'No, no — just consider: he will awake with the realisation that he was attacked. If he has a secret what is the first thing he'll do?'

'See if it's still safe?' Pulp hazarded.

'Exactly! Which means that one or other of us has got to be here to see what he does when he wakes up. Hmm — how do we do that?'

They looked around them, then finally Pulp went to the window and opened it, closing the curtains behind him to conform with the blackout. After a while he reappeared.

'There's this ledge out here,' he said. 'I could get on it and watch through the curtain crack just what he does. If he dives for the window first I'll have to clock him one. That's the only chance if it rates being worth it.'

Maria thought swiftly. 'Do that, Mr. Martin — and I will go back to my own quarters. There is a chance that Mr. Whittaker may report his attack to me. Advise me the moment you have any information.'

'Okay, Maria. You beat it.'

She picked up the powder box and cocoa tin, then went out and locked him in. Smiling triumphantly to herself she retraced her way down the empty corridors.

When she got back to her study it was thirty minutes after midnight. The need for sleep was upon her, but she had to wait until Pulp had something or other to say, so she pulled out her record book and brought her discoveries up to date.

Have definitely established the fact that the peculiar Major Hasleigh and Clive Whittaker (new science master) are the same person. Am wondering if the Identity Card and Ration Book of Whittaker are forgeries as Frances Hasleigh's were.

From a photograph Mr. Martin and I have discovered I lean to the view that Whittaker and Frances were brother

190

and sister. Have yet to prove it. <u>Certainly they were in Paris together some years ago.</u> Tie up: Frances's shoes and Whittaker's alleged studies in Paris and Europe. I have established beyond doubt that it was Whittaker who removed the girl's body to the mausoleum. I have found the ultra-violet lamp that I think caused such burns on her arm. Whether he did the original murder or not I do not yet know. I am sure of one thing — Whittaker is a very strong young man posing as a delicate one.

The police have arrested Robert Lever for Frances's murder because of the circumstantial evidence of his fountain pen being found in the death clearing. I do not believe there was a pen in the clearing to start with. I think it was put there after my examination. Must look into this. Inquest and funeral are ahead of me . . . Would like to know what it was on Frances Hasleigh's forearm that was so impor-tant it had to be burned away. Would like to know, too, what sort of a research Whittaker is engaged upon — why he uses explosives and particularly where he has taken quite a few chemicals that are college property. Do not think I could gain much by outright questioning of him, however. He might take fright. Shall bide my time. Certainly there is a definitely French flavour about all this that must be cleared up — even the name of Frances. This was obviously assumed — so why the 'France' in it? To keep in mind some poignant memory perhaps?

Hope to get results soon through Mr. Martin's excellent aid . . .

P.S.: Whom did I see in the quadrangle? Too small a figure, I think, for Whitaker.

The time is 12.45 a.m.

Maria stifled a yawn as she locked her book away, and settled herself back in her chair to wait. She realised that she must have fallen asleep when a hand began to shake her shoulders.

With a start she awoke to find the excited face of Pulp bending over her.

'Shake off them cobwebs, Maria! I've got something!'

'Oh! Excuse me gaping, Mr. Martin — I've been asleep.'

'Yeah — it's quarter to three now and I'm as stiff as a cell door after being stuck out on that ledge. But I got results — look here!'

Proudly he laid a glass photographic negative — half-plate size — on her blotting pad. She gave a start and looked at it fixedly.

Pulp sat down and rubbed his chilled hands before the radiator. 'I got on that ledge like you told me, and after about ten minutes Whittaker wakes up, see? Well, like you figured from that Sherlock Holmes racket, he threw a monkey fit and started looking himself over, like he was plumb scared some injury had been done him. He felt his face a lot, too — maybe it was sticky from what you'd done to him. When he found he was all in one piece he skipped out of bed and went over to the dressing table. He unscrewed the wood back of the mirror and there, stuck by suction to the back of the glass, was this thing! Say, did that guy look relieved!

'Anyway, he left it where it was, screwed the thing up again, then went back to bed. So I figured I'd better wait until he got to sleep again, and I didn't feel too safe with him havin' a revolver under his pillow. I saw him examine it and then put it back. I got back into the room at last, though, and it took me half an hour to get the back off the mirror without making a sound. I had to work in the dark with my penknife as a screwdriver. The screws were fairly easy with him havin' taken them in and out a few times. I put the mirror back then and skipped pronto.'

'You shall have double pay for this night's work,' Maria said, pulling forth her strongest lens from the drawer and peering at the plate.

The scene on it was microscopically small and from the background it was clearly the girl's forearm that was showing. Imbedded in it, however, perhaps two inches from the wrist, was a circle, and within it lay symbols and figures only just visible even under such high magnification.

'Mr. Martin, take these notes down,' Maria ordered briefly, the lens close to her eye. '7 — F.M.; 15-A.M.L.; 4-Sil-Nr; 4-Carbo-Tet; 6 — Ammonia . . . And 3 — L.M.G.; 11 — K.F.L . . . Got that?'

'Sure. But hanged if I know what it means.'

'Nor I, Mr. Martin, but we'll do our best to find out. It's definitely a formula of some kind, related to explosives. The silver nitrate and F.M. — fulminate of mercury — tells us that . . . And for some reason this formula was imprinted on that girl's arm. Evidently invisible to the eye in the ordinary way unless the skin surrounding it became brown — as it would under ultra-violet radiation. A most brilliant precaution and yet at the same time most mystifying . . . And apparently Mr. Whittaker is responsible for most of it.'

Maria paused and stifled another yawn.

'I'm afraid I can't concentrate when sleep is so necessary. I'll look further into this tomorrow. Your best move is to return this plate immediately so that Whittaker will not know what we've been up to — then tomorrow, if the time taken up by the inquest permits, we can examine the matter thoroughly. For tonight, Mr. Martin, that is all . . . And here is the double pay I promised you.'

'That's what I like about you, Maria — always pay on the nose. Okay, I'll return this plate and then skip off back to the Fox. Call me again when you want me. Be seeing you.'

After Pulp left she folded the formula he'd written down into a small square and put it in the back of her watch before preparing for bed.

8

The following morning before departing from the School to attend the inquest, Maria had two important things to do. Since Miss Tanby was to be with her to give evidenee, she handed temporary authority to the head monitor; and second, she had a brief interview with the undertakers who arrived to prepare the dead girl — now back again in Room 10 — for the funeral.

By ten-thirty Maria found herself sitting with Miss Tanby in the train, studying the summonses to the inquest which had arrived in that morning's mail . . .

To either side of them, looking very humbled and very neat were Joan Dawson and Beryl Mather; and Vera Randal, Molly Webster, and Cynthla Vane. These three girls in fact were unusually quiet and obviously not at all easy in their minds . . .

After lunching in Lexham they proceeded to the Coroner's court. Maria found it was a tedious affair, time in which she was itching to be off and follow up her own peculiar line of reasoning.

When it came to Robert Lever's turn, however, she began to take more interest.

'You have heard the evidence of Superintendent Vaxley in regard to yourself, Mr. Lever,' the Coroner said, glancing up from his notes. 'Have you anything to say to confirm or deny the evidence?'

'I deny everything!' Lever retorted hotly. 'I only had a passing acquaintance with the deceased.'

'Do you mean by that your association with her was limited to the occasion when she asked you the position of the star Sirius?'

'That's right. I had never paid any attention to her before then. In fact she had only arrived at the school that very day. The next thing I knew was that she had been murdered.'

'Why, in your opinion, did the deceased go to such extraordinary lengths to determine the position of a certain star?'

Lever shrugged. 'I have no idea, sir. I have no complaint to make about losing my position: I was fully aware of the strict rules concerning pupils and teachers. I do think, though, that the thing was deliberately engineered, otherwise the Housemistress would not have turned up so conveniently.'

'You have heard in the evidence of the Housemistress that she was informed of the girl Hasleigh's infraction by another girl in the dormitory who had seen her leave. Do you suggest that the deceased deliberately made her departure noisy so that the news of it would travel rapidly to the ears of a teacher?'

'Frankly, yes. But I can't imagine why — '

'Yes, indeed,' Maria muttered. 'My view exactly — '

'Mr. Lever,' the Coroner resumed, 'you do not deny that you were near the scene of the tragedy on the day in question, do you?'

'No, sir. I was in a boat on the River Bollin — as I have already admitted to

Superintendent Vaxley. But I had no connection whatever with the tragedy.'

'Just why did you take rooms in the village instead of going further afield?'

'Chiefly because I thought it would be less expensive than in London. My idea was to take a short holiday while looking for a fresh job — or else await my calling-up papers. If you think I stayed near at hand because of Frances Hasleigh you're dead wrong!'

The Coroner looked at him coldly. 'I would warn you to be a little more respectful in your tone, Mr. Lever . . . Now, just what did you do on the afternoon of the tragedy? Be very explicit.'

'Why, I went down to the river about half-past four with the intention of doing a little study; then I thought I might get the sunshine better if I went out on the river. So I hired out a rowing boat and took it into mid-stream. Reaching a pleasant spot, I tied the boat to a tree, and there I stopped, reading.'

'You imply then that the footprints on the soft mud of the river bank, found by the superintendent, were made when you tied up the boat? And not because you went on to the clearing where the tragedy was enacted?'

'I do, sir — yes. My footprints could not have gone beyond the bank because I didn't go any further.'

'Since grass begins very near the bank edge your footprints would not have shown anyway,' the Coroner answered coldly. 'Perhaps, though, you will tell us how your fountain pen got into the clearing?'

A shade of worry crept over Lever's face. 'I just don't know the answer to that, sir. I had it last in the Sixth Form, before I left. In fact I was going to use it on the night Frances Hasleigh came to see me, then I found I had not got it. In my hurried departure from the school I forgot all about it . . . I was always leaving it lying about somewhere. The clip being loose I didn't often carry it in my pocket.'

The Coroner made some more notes, then Lever was told to stand down and the first of the girls — Vera Randal — was called to the stand.

Maria listened keenly to everything the girl had to say, and her story was identical in every respect to the one she had told so far. In fact each of the girls, when not too nervous, clung in essence to her original tale. Then Maria found herself called to the stand.

'Miss Black, you are the Headmistress of Roseway College, are you not?' the Coroner asked.

'I am.'

'You have heard from Superintendent Vaxley's evidence that the deceased's remaining living parent — Major Hasleigh — cannot be traced, and that even his bank does not seem to know where he is . . . Why did you agree to take into your school a pupil with such hazy family connections?'

'They were not hazy then,' Maria replied. 'I fail to see what bearing it has on the matter.'

'Hmm . . . Er — during the deceased's brief career as a pupil with you did you suspect her of having any ulterior motive for being in the school? Did she seem, for instance, like a girl hiding from the law, or anything of that nature?'

Maria shook her head. 'I suspected only one thing about her — that she was older than sixteen, and later on medical evidence corroborated my belief. Outside of this she was a quiet, highly intelligent girl, and except for her two infractions in breaking bounds after lights-out I detected nothing wrong with her.'

'The first time she broke bounds she went to keep her rendezvous with Mr. Lever, but where do you imagine she went the second time after Lever had been dismissed? The evidence of Miss Randal has led us to believe that she went to see Lever again. Do you share that view?'

'I definitely do not,' Maria replied curtly. 'Miss Randal is in no position to make such a guess. Nobody knows where the girl Hasleigh went the second time, and I least of all.'

'Can you imagine why she again went at night instead of by day when she would not have been breaking bounds?'

'By day or night she would have broken bounds,' Maria declared. 'She was under detention. But I imagine she went by night so that there would be less chance of attracting everybody's attention And I also believe that only a motive of the utmost urgency could have so impelled her to take a second risk . . . Beyond that, sir, I have very little to say — except I think that instead of pouncing on Mr. Lever because of circumstantial evidence it would be more fitting if the law tied up the loose ends in this case.'

The Coroner blinked. 'After all, Miss Black,' he said mildly, 'this is an inquest, not a murder trial. We do not imply that every detail has yet been cleared up: we are here merely for the purpose of assembling the evidence relevant to the death of Frances Hasleigh. However perhaps you will elaborate your 'loose ends' assertion?'

'With pleasure!' Maria smiled grimly. 'I do not think it would be entirely out of place to discover who moved the body of the dead girl from the room I had assigned for it to the college mausoleum. And why was it done? A vital point which I feel somehow cannot be relegated to Mr. Lever!'

'You may rest assured, Miss Black that that point, and all others, will be thoroughly examined . . . For the moment that is all, thank you. Call Henry Tompkins.'

Tompkins proved to be the Bollin boatman who duly verified Lever's actions on the day of the crime. Maria was not very interested. She remained apparently lost in thought until the proceedings were over, with the jury summing up the business as wilful murder and Robert Lever finding himself referred to the next Assizes. Here, for the moment, the matter rested.

'Can we go home now, Miss Black?' Beryl Mather asked anxiously.

'We are all at perfect liberty to do so, yes,' Maria nodded, getting to her feet. Then she turned to the Housemistress. 'Miss Tanby, I will leave the girls in your care and follow you later. I must speak with Superintendent Vaxley.'

Tanby nodded and Maria made her way across the court to where Vaxley was putting his records away in his brief case.

'Oh, hello, Miss Black,' he greeted as she came up to him.

'I just wanted a word with you, Superintendent. Have you arrived at any fresh conclusions?'

He gave her a quick look. 'I might ask you the same question. What have you found out?'

'Mere theories,' she shrugged. 'Nothing that you yourself could not have found . . . However, it is this business of young Lever which interests me. I'd like to discuss him with you — or even better have a word with him myself if that could be done?'

'I'm afraid it can't,' Vaxley sighed. 'I am only engaged in the case professionally and I cannot allow an — er — unqualified outsider to enter into it. But I will try and tell you whatever it is you wish to know. Maybe I can have that pleasure over tea in the Temple café?'

'Splendid!' Maria beamed, suddenly aware of the fact that it was time for her afternoon refresher; so she accompanied the superintendent out to his car and before long was seated with him in a quiet corner of the café with tea and cakes before her.

'As I told you over the phone,' Vaxley said, stirring his tea, 'I have to follow out the obvious in my capacity — therefore I had to issue a warrant for young Lever's arrest. I have revenge as the motive, as you know, but somehow — Well, in my heart I do not believe he would even speak offensively to a girl, let alone murder one. Yet everything seems clear cut: him near the clearing on the river; his footprints on the bank — and last of all his fountain pen. That is definitely the most damning piece of evidence.'

'Superintendent,' Maria said quietly, 'I give you my word that when I went over that clearing before you, not two hours after the tragedy, even as Inspector Morgan had done before me, there was no sign of a fountain pen! I believe it was put their afterwards.'

'By the murderer, you mean?'

'Naturally. Somebody knew that Lever was most opportunely on the river at that time and used the idea to switch the blame on to him. We have Lever's sworn statement that he left his pen in the Sixth Form room, from where I believe it was taken later and used as 'evidence'.'

'But, Miss Black, doesn't that implicate one of your own pupils?'

'That is the first impression, yes,' Maria admitted. 'Let us look at it this way: One of the pupils saw the pen, knew that it was Lever's, and appropriated it — not as an act of theft, but to take it away for safety until it should be asked for. Now, if one of the girls involved in this crime knew that they were likely to be implicated what is the first thing they'd do? Look for a cat's paw! If one of the girls knew that Lever had been near the spot in the afternoon, what easier than to shift the blame by going back to the clearing at the earliest moment and throwing down the fountain pen there?'

'Could any of those three girls who performed the joke have seen the river from where they sat on the bank in the lane?'

Maria did not answer: she was staring ahead of her.

'How foolish I am! On the night of the tragedy, some hours after it had happened, I saw a dim figure in the school quadrangle, heading into the School House. It seemed to me too small to be a full-grown person. It could have been a schoolgirl returning from putting that pen in the clearing.'

'It could!' Vaxley gave a start. 'About what time was it?'

'After lights out anyway,' Maria said, musing. 'It may mean something — or nothing. But I believe you asked me a question, Superintendent?'

Vaxley repeated it.

'Certainly they could. It is in full view from there. You must have seen that for yourself surely when conducting your search?'

'My mind was on other things,' Vaxley shrugged. 'Which seems to make Vera Randal, Molly Webster, and that Vane girl directly responsible in more ways than one. Vera, I should say is just the type who would confiscate a tempting fountain pen, and she knew who might be in for it when the tragedy was discovered. She could also have seen Lever on the river . . . Yes, it is possible that it was her you saw in the quadrangle returning from the clearing. In point of fact, there are only three girls for it because the others were bound and gagged. True, the river could be seen from the clearing, too, but with those girls all tied up — No, I think we can discount that. But, Miss Black if it should happen that Lever is disproved as the murderer whom have we to look for?'

Maria sighed. 'There, Super, I face an impasse. I am more concerned at the moment, seeing an innocent man freed than in putting my finger on the guilty party.'

'And if Lever didn't do it we've also to discover some other motive than revenge,' Vaxley mused. 'Of course, the fresh motive *could* be whatever it was on that girl's arm, but since we have no idea what it was we have nothing to go on. I do know that it was ultra-violet, anyway, or something very like it. There is power laid on in the mausoleum, you know.'

'Yes,' Maria murmured, 'I found the bared wires, too . . . Super, what is your interpretation of the second scoring on the end of that tree branch?'

'I think the murderer tied a rope round

it to drag the branch down lower so it could be seized — or else so that he could tie it like that for the time being and then fasten the girl to the centre part.'

'Which seems to prove she was definitely unconscious,' Maria reflected. 'Presumably from that pressure behind her ears. If she were not unconscious can you imagine the hard job it would have been for the killer to lift a struggling girl, bound though she was — who probably knew her life was in danger — to the tree branch and then knot the rope three times as well? No mean feat!'

'I believe she was definitely unconscious all the time,' Vaxley replied. 'And the other girls as well. All the murderer had to do was fasten the rope round Frances's neck, drag her under the tree branch, trail the rope up the tree as he climbed up, fasten the rope to the branch then come down and cut the other rope which was holding the branch down. Up would go Frances, and there it is.'

'Not altogether,' Maria smiled. 'The terrific jerk of the branch jumping back into position would have dislocated her neck. But it was not dislocated! She died from strangulation through hanging — so says the medical evidence . . . Which also cuts out my earlier theory of suicide. I thought maybe she had tied herself to the tree and then cut the cord holding the branch down — but many things are against it. The dislocation angle for one; the absence of the rope which held the branch down for another, and no sign of the knife with which she might have slashed at it.'

'Then the only explanation is that she must have been hanged slowly!'

'Yes, but why?' Maria demanded. 'If she were conscious there would have been real reason for it — torture! And, remember, not a sign of a footprint anywhere, though we both assumed, and probably correctly, from the dead girl's torn stockings, that she *was* dragged to that tree.'

Vaxley was silent, his brows knitted, so finally Maria got to her feet.

'Well Super, I must be getting back to the school. My normal duties await me.'

He gave a start and rose, too. 'Then I

am coming with you, Miss Black, to have a word with that girl Vera Randal. And I shall take another look at that clearing before long. You have given me fresh field for thought — and I'd like to repay it by driving you home. I have to return to my temporary headquarters there, anyway.'

★ ★ ★

Vaxley tackled Vera Randal the moment they arrived back at Roseway. The bullying head girl was clearly nervous when she found herself — and nobody else — called for an interview with the Superintendent and Maria, and her fear took shelter behind an unconvincing arrogance.

'Miss Randal, when did you see Mr. Lever's fountain pen in the Sixth Form room?' Vaxley asked bluntly.

'His fountain pen? I never saw it at any time!'

'You are the head girl of the Sixth, Miss Randal; you heard Mr. Lever say at the inquest today that he had left his pen in the Sixth Form room. You must have been near the teacher desk at some time in your capacity as a keeper of order. Come, come, you can do better than that! We are not dealing with a school prank, remember, but with cold-blooded murder.'

'I still say I haven't seen it,' Vera retorted stubbornly.

'Another question, then,' Vaxley said. 'Do you remember if, on the night of the tragedy — after lights out — anybody broke bounds in your dormitory?'

'Not that I know of,' the girl replied, thinking. 'I had a bad attack of nerves after that horrible event in the afternoon and I took some sleeping tablets so I could be sure I'd rest. If anybody broke bounds I'd never have known about it — and I don't think any of the others are very light sleepers — '

Vaxley tried yet another angle.

'You say that you sat on the bank of the lane while the tragedy in the wood must have been enacted. Could you see the river from where you were?'

'Yes, sir — easily.'

'Then you must have seen Mr. Lever in his rowing boat?'

Vera shrugged. 'I don't remember. I wasn't much concerned with the river: my main interest was on the wood and waiting for Frances and her two cronies to reappear.'

Vaxley gave a sigh. 'All right, young lady, you may go — ' Then as the door closed he looked at Maria.

'Well, Miss Black, any reactions to that?'

'Hard to say. She may be lying, of course — but on the other hand it may be truth. For the moment I'm prepared to leave the point in abeyance in the hope that it may explain itself. I never flog my mind for a solution, Super.'

Vaxley smiled and got to his feet.

'Well, for my part I'm going to Bollin's Wood again before the light starts to fade. I have the feeling I may have missed something even yet. I'll be seeing you again before long — '

After he'd gone, Maria left her study and made her way to Room 10 in the visitors' wing. Frances Hasleigh's body was there all right this time, and as Maria had expected the undertakers had been busy. The girl lay in her coffin now, garbed in a single white shroud, her hands folded on to her breast, her eyes closed and chin bound into place. The burned forearm was still strikingly noticeable.

Maria frowned as she gazed down on the dead young face.

'Pity you had to die so early, my dear,' she muttered. 'Was it because of your courage or your foolhardiness? That is what I have got to find out. Rest assured that whoever killed you will be brought to justice!'

Her next call was at the laboratory, and to her satisfaction it was deserted. She had half expected to find the inevitable Mr. Whittaker there, but evidently he had not the time at the moment to spare for his activities.

She locked the door, then went over to the bench and took out the formula from the back of her watch, studied it carefully. She took down some of the ingredients from the shelves and then paused.

'Up the wrong tree, Maria,' she muttered. 'No chemical formula can be complete at fifty per cent, which is just what these percentages total up to. You have only half a formula — not a complete one! Dear me, most annoying! In any event, not all these ingredients are familiar. What, for instance, are L.M.G. and K.F.L.? Secret symbols.'

And since the arm of Frances Hasleigh only contained half a formula it seemed logical that the other half must be in the possession of Clive Whittaker. Possible, too, that the private chemical symbols were known only to him — or to the dead girl. Maria felt prompted for a moment to seek him out and confront him with everything she knew — then she thought better of it.

'No, Maria, to explode your theories now with only half the mystery solved — even if that — would be a fatal mistake. It might even bring the police in again to arrest Whittaker and your most valuable clue-piece would be snatched away. Better bide your time and try a fresh angle.'

She put the bottles back, then returned her copy formula to her watch. She had hardly done it before a slight sound made her glance up sharply. It seemed to have come from the window. As yet the evening light was fairly good and she had not closed the shutters.

She clambered up slowly and laboriously on to the bench. By the time she was peering through the glass on to the deserted quadrangle there was not a sign of anybody.

Quite convinced in her own mind that somebody had been there, she left the laboratory and returned to her study. For an hour or more afterwards she was busily occupied with her normal school routine, checking up with the head monitor on the day's education and arranging details for the morrow . . . Then as the summer night began to settle down she felt free again to think and plan.

She browsed over the notes she had made in her record book.

'An electrician bared those two wires in the mausoleum,' she mused, 'and a triple knot is used by the electrical profession . . . Which brings me to Whittaker. I can confront him with the truth at any moment that suits me, but first let us see where his activities lead him. There are so many loose ends . . . '

She jotted down the unexplained points one by one: Triple knots, French shoes, fountain pen, parcel of stockings for Joan Dawson, figure in quadrangle, reason for the Major Hasleigh deception, and the mystery of Sirius. Did it mean anything? Every one of them puzzling strands in the web and demanding an exclusive attention if they were to be fitted into the pattern.

Turning the pages of her book, Maria came to that isolated earlier note she had made:

Blue eyes — blue eyes — brown eyes? Is this physically possible? Check.

Going over to her bookcase she took down Sullivan's *Limitations of Science*. Soon she was absorbed in the chapter on biology and before long found what she wanted. She wrote down word for word from the book: '*Biologically, according to Mendel's famous theory of the recessive unit, it is impossible for two parents with blue eyes to produce anything but a blue-eyed child. A brown-eyed child from blue-eyed parents is impossible because the child has no brown units from which to select.'*

★ ★ ★

'Marvellous!' she breathed. 'And no doubt it is a point which the law would overlook.'

She crossed it off the list of posers and transferred her attention to the puzzle of Sirius.

'You cannot afford to leave any point unsettled, Maria,' she decided, getting up and donning her overcoat and beret — with umbrella and torch for good measure.

In a few minutes she was out in the quadrangle. The dusk had fallen now, diffused by the rising moon, and the stars were gleaming mistily through a warm haze. In a moment or two she had picked out Sirius in his masked, blue-white splendour.

'I don't know what you have to do with it,' she commented, 'but I will try anything once.'

Keeping her eye on it she advanced in its direction, and took note of where it led her. First she arrived at the school wall. She went beyond it by way of the little lattice gate and found herself on the playing fields with open country before her. She went on resolutely, tripping here and there over the roughness of the ground where the girls had ploughed it up with their hockey matches.

Still she continued, then she paused and checked her watch in the moonlight. She had been on her way for about fifteen minutes.

'And Frances was away for an hour and would go far faster than I,' she reflected.

She left the playing fields presently and, still keeping Sirius right in front of her, went past the far end of Bollin's Wood and so came to the river. She detoured to the little wooden bridge spanning it and found herself once more facing rugged countryside. If she went on much further, she knew, she would arrive at the old disused tin mines with which the district was riddled. In fact she could see their outer works looming ahead of her in bare skeletal towers.

She was still directly in line with Sirius — so on she went, and after another twenty minutes plodding, she arrived at the first of the tin mines. Had she not known this derelict spot intimately from daytime association, and over many years, she would have been utterly confused. Old paths were twisted and ran into dead ends; artificial hills of excavation loomed; deep shafts were only roughly fenced off. It was like a ghost town all on its own, and as she knew a most exciting — not to say out of bounds and dangerous — haunt of some of her younger pupils in search of adventure.

Maria sat down to rest on a big stone. 'I deem it wisest to stop at the first place in a direct line with Sirius. Though what on earth tin mines have to do with it I have no idea — '

She broke off, aware of a slight sound from somewhere. Instantly she got up from her rock and crouched behind it, peering intently over the top. The sound came again, much nearer, and echoing. She realised that it was coming from down the nearest mineshaft — the sound of feet on one of the old iron ladders.

Tensely she waited as a head and shoulders presently appeared. The figure proved to be Clive Whittaker. He paused at the top of the shaft, dusting himself down and looking keenly about him, then he turned and began to walk away towards the distant river bridge.

Maria watched him out of sight, then she got up slowly.

'So Sirius *meant* something: far more than a pretext to talk to young Lever . . . Now, do I risk going down here or do I call on Mr. Martin for assistance?'

The thought of a few more miles to the Fox Hotel and back again decided her against it. She would work on her own and take the risk — so, gingerly, she climbed over the shaft edge and felt for the ladder's rungs with her feet. Once she found them she began to go down slowly. The circle of stars at the top of the shaft had become an apparent six-inch width before she reached the bottom.

Breathing hard, she felt for her fountain pen torch, switched it on. It shone its little circumscribed beam on to glistening walls, and into a mine tunnel with the old half-obliterated wagon tracks.

Maria went forward resolutely with umbrella in one hand and torch in the other.

The tunnel went for perhaps a hundred yards, turned a corner, and then came to an end in a big door. Probably at some time it had led to a storage room. Now, however, it was fastened with a very new and up-to-date padlock and hasp.

'I should have summoned Mr. Martin,' she muttered. 'He could have undone this lock in a moment. As it is — '

She snatched a hairpin from out of her bun of hair and thrust it into the lock gently.

For all her determination she had set herself a hard task. For ten minutes she wriggled and poked with the wire, bending it into all kinds of shapes — then to her delighted astonishment, just as she was about to give up, there was a click and the lock sprang open.

'Definitely luck, not judgment,' she told herself, and took the padlock off with her handkerchief to prevent fingerprints. The door squeaked as she pulled it to one side, then she eagerly flashed her torch beyond.

The light settled on a goodish-sized space that was obviously being used as a habitat of some kind — even to the candles stuck in two bottle-necks and the matches beside them. Maria soon had the two tallows spluttering and then looked about her.

There was no furniture: heavy stones were so arranged that they made chairs, a table, and a kind of bed — with straw and old newspapers for covering. On the rough, stony floor were crumbs by the thousand, some empty meat tins, and in a far corner empty bottles that had once contained lemonade, lime-juice, and orange cordial. And to judge from the lightness of the dust upon them they had not been there very long.

Maria prowled round — then she gave a little whoop of delight as in one corner she came upon an assembly of bottles, tightly corked, and marked respectively — L.M.G., K.F.L., and Z B Z. Two of them anyway were the identical private symbols she had in the formula. And there were not only these present, but also small quantities of fulminate of mercury, nitro-glycerine, and so forth, together with a few test tubes, retorts, and one complete beaker. She gave a grim smile as she studied the apparatus more closely and saw the little tab-plate on the bottom — *Roseway College*.

'Apparently our Mr. Whittaker has done a nice lot of pilfering from the college lab,' she commented. 'Hmm! What have we here?'

More small bottles apparently, inscribed with symbols she had not encountered so far — M.L.X., V.G.R., and P.L.I. Presumably they appertained to the half of the formula she had not so far discovered.

'A laboratory away from everybody, hastily made and well hidden,' she reflected. 'But what on earth is it all *for*? I just don't credit Mr. Whittaker's tale of being interested in the analysis of explosives. There is more in it than that . . . Great Heavens, I wonder if he is a saboteur or a German spy?'

Improbable: the man had no trace of European accent, and neither had Frances had either. Besides, Roseway College was a good thirty miles away from anything of military value. A spy or saboteur would hardly choose a select college for young ladies as his base of operations. No; it was not that — but definitely something very mysterious was going on and Whittaker was up to his neck in it — as Frances had no doubt been until death had overtaken her.

Further searching revealed nothing more to Maria, so she blew out the candles, switched on her torch again and left, taking care to snap the padlock shut behind her — and once again holding it in her handkerchief. She began to retrace her way up the tunnel — then a sound behind her made her glance round.

Her heart began to race a little, for she could not see anybody. She went on again hurriedly, stumbling in her anxiety — then all of a sudden there was a racing of feet from behind her and before she had a chance to turn round an arm was under her jaw and a knee in the small of her back. She went over helplessly into the dust. Somehow though she still retained a grip on her umbrella. Her torch had gone and it was impossible for her to see her attacker, so she lashed out savagely with all her strength.

Evidently she landed home, too, for there was a little gasp of pain, then a figure loomed dimly before her vision and gave her a resounding crack on the jaw. Simultaneously she felt a jerk from somewhere near her chest, then the noise of running feet dying away into silence — to be followed a few moments later by the sound of somebody hastily ascending the iron ladder as her attacker escaped.

Dazed, her head singing, Maria got to her feet again and felt for her torch. Apparently it was nowhere within reach, so she had to feel her way forward in the pitch darkness. As she became slowly accustomed to it the going was easier and she found the upward shaft without mishap. Naturally her attacker had long since vanished from sight.

At the bottom of the shaft she paused for a moment, collecting her scattered wits. Then as she pulled her coat more firmly about her she discovered something — her watch and chain had gone!

'Somebody anxious to get that half-formula and knew just where it was. Of course! The laboratory window!'

Somebody had obviously been watching her every move, had deduced from her studying the formula and taking the bottles down from the shelves that she had the formula. Whittaker? She was prepared to swear that he had not seen her at the mine — unless he had deliberately made it look that way and had come back after seeing her go down the shaft.

Taking a deep breath, Maria began to mount up the steps to the top of the shaft.

She was panting and dirty by the time she reached the top, her jaw aching less furiously and her general feelings grim. Apart from the loss of the half formula she was none too happy about losing the valuable watch that had been her mother's.

'Whoever came after me had to leave footprints,' she mused, straightening up in the moonlight and looking about her. 'It's just possible that this night's work may have proved the undoing of somebody. Now, what have we before anybody else starts to upset things by walking about here?'

The loss of her torch was a big drawback, but the moonlight was strong enough for her now accustomed eyes. Besides, the soft soil about the mine top was lightish in colour from excavation dust and none too difficult to see. By going on her hands and knees Maria could faintly descry the impressions her attacker had left in the dirt. They were not the marks of a man's boots or shoes, but of a woman's, and a small woman at that. A neat high heel imprint and a small sole. There they were — coming and going.

Maria felt in her pocket, took out a piece of old string, and measured the exact width and length of the print, and marked the string. Then she hurried from the mine as rapidly as her tiring legs would allow, to arrive back at the college just after midnight.

Pausing only to tidy herself up, she marched upstairs to the Sixth Form dormitory and switched on the lights.

There was a general stirring in the beds and surprised faces looked towards her. Her eyes swept down the line of beds. Not a single girl was absent.

'I am disturbing you at this late hour, girls, for a grave reason,' she said grimly. 'I have reason to suspect that one of you broke bounds tonight.'

Nobody spoke, then Vera Randal seemed to think she ought to say something.

'Nobody has been out of here tonight, Miss Black. I know because I haven't been to sleep yet — '

'Why haven't you?' Maria interrupted curtly.

Vera turned her face slightly and revealed a bulge down one side of it.

'Toothache,' she moaned. 'The draught in the train today, I think.'

Maria hesitated a moment, then: 'I am not doubting your statement, Randal, that no girl has left here tonight, but I require proof. Each of you girls will go to your locker immediately and produce your shoes.'

There was an immediate though grudging response and the shoes were laid before her in neat rows.

'Put these outside the door,' she ordered. 'If any of you feel like a further little jaunt you will not get far without shoes. Quickly!'

Within five minutes her order had been obeyed, and each girl sent back to bed. The locker doors she closed herself after a glance in each one, then she paused as she came to the closed one belonging to the late Frances Hasleigh. Frowning over a thought she took out her duplicate key and unfastened the door. Inside were the dead girl's clothes and belongings, waiting until it should be decided what must be done with them.

But on the floor was one pair of shoes — amidst half a dozen pairs or so — powdered with grey dust!

Maria stared fixedly at them, then lifted them out. She relocked every door, then went out of the dormitory without a word.

In the corridor, undisturbed, she measured all the shoes with her marked piece of string, but only one pair fitted exactly to the length and breadth — and they were Frances Hasleigh's. And the grey dust on the uppers and still wet soft mud in the instep seemed to make it conclusive.

'Amazing!' Maria whispered. 'None of the other girls could have worn them — not with any comfort, anyhow . . . Good Lord, unless I can throw some light on this very soon I shall begin to think I was attacked by a ghost or else none other than Frances Hasleigh herself!'

9

Brought to something of a standstill by her latest discoveries, Maria did not attempt to probe any further during the night. She went to bed trying to puzzle things out, but, tired out, she soon fell asleep.

The following morning the funeral of Frances Hasleigh was the main thing on her mind.

She satisfied herself that the girl was certainly quite dead anyhow, for she took one last look at her before the coffin lid was screwed down — as also did Sir Kenneth Gadshaw, head of the Board of Governors, who had evidently considered it his duty to be present at such an unusually sober occasion.

'I have made the best arrangements possible in the circumstances, Sir Kenneth,' Maria said, as they returned together towards her study. 'Having no traceable relatives or parents I made arrangements for the girl to be buried in the village cemetery. Later, if her true relationship is properly established, we can give her relatives the full facts . . . As to the school mourning, I did not consider it expedient, considering the nature of her death, to order a general closing down for the morning. It will be a quiet affair with half an hour interval at ten-thirty in respect to her memory.'

'Yes — quite good,' Sir Kenneth agreed, reflecting. 'And — er — this unexpected funeral does not cost the school anything?' he asked rather heartlessly.

'No. The fees paid by Major Hasleigh have amply covered the expenses and left a small surplus . . . As to mourners, I have permitted Joan Dawson and Beryl Mather, as the dead girl's study-mates, to attend the funeral at their own wish. And, of course I shall go, too. There will be nobody else.'

'A most tragic and mysterious affair altogether, Miss Black, which I feel — on behalf of the Board — you have handled well.'

As they reached Maria's study door, Sir

Kenneth held out his hand.

'I am sure I can leave everything with you, Miss Black.'

'You may rest assured,' she nodded, and with that he took his departure.

Entering her study she found Joan Dawson and Beryl Mather awaiting her, both in the darkest clothes they could find and with a wreath standing on the floor between them.

'You are here early, girls,' Maria commented, surprised.

'I sort of anticipated things, Miss Black,' Joan explained. 'If you hadn't let us go to the funeral we were going to ask you to take this wreath and put it on Frances's coffin. I just wanted to know if it would do and if we're dressed properly for the occasion?'

Maria looked at them both critically.

'Raise your arm a moment, Joan — I believe you have burst a seam at the back here — '

The girl half raised her arm then let it fall back again. She gave a wry smile.

'I'm young to start with rheumatism,' she sighed.

Maria gave a faint smile and pulled the costume into place.

'No need to worry, my dear, it isn't a tear; only a bit of white cotton. Yes, I think you will both do admirably. You had better wait here for me while I get ready. By that time the hearse and coach should have arrived.'

Maria left the study, returning ten minutes later in her black mannish costume, the inevitable umbrella on her arm, and her keen, good-looking face set in the appropriate dignified expression.

'Come, girls,' she ordered briefly, and they followed with the wreath between them.

The hearse and coach had just arrived in the quadrangle. Many eyes were watching from the various classrooms as the coffin was brought out on the shoulders of the pallbearers. Maria watched it silently, then motioned the girls to put their wreath on the coffin as it was slid into the hearse. Along with a large one from the school itself it comprised the only intimation of remembrance.

'Into the coach, girls,' Maria said briefly, and followed them.

During the journey to the cemetery she observed the two young faces constantly. On the face of Beryl, round and rosy-cheeked, she detected a genuine light of sorrow. On Joan's face there was an expression of reserved calm, as though she had a tight rein over her emotions.

The burial itself differed in no way from other burials, the brief service led by a rather laconic vicar . . . Maria was glad when it was over.

Then as she turned from the open grave with the two girls at her side she gave a little start.

Not far away a figure dodged out of her sight behind a tall burial colonnade — Clive Whittaker beyond doubt! Evidently he was absent without leave from his college duties.

'Go on to the coach, girls, and wait for me,' Maria ordered. 'I have a little matter to attend to.'

She waited until they were out of sight behind the trees lining the drive, then she turned towards the colonnade where she knew Whittaker must still be concealed. As she reached it he emerged rather shamefacedly.

'I — I know I shouldn't be here, Miss Black,' he said hesitantly, and it struck her that his face was nearly grey with genuine concern and sorrow. 'There is half an hour's break from lessons, though, and at the last moment I decided to risk coming. I wanted to pay my last respects to that poor girl.'

'My dear young man, you should have mentioned it to me. I didn't know you were even interested in the funeral.'

'No, of course, you couldn't — but I had a great admiration for that girl in the brief time I was acquainted with her. She was brilliantly clever, and it is so rare in these days to find a young woman with keen scientific knowledge that I — Well, despite her age, I am afraid I fell in love with her.'

'Despite her age?' Maria repeated. 'Didn't you read the papers in which it was clearly stated that she was twenty-three?'

'Yes, but it was no use to me after she

was dead, was it? Had I known her real age I might have done many things to show that I cared for her.'

'Would you care to take a last look at the coffin before it is covered?'

'You're very kind, Miss Black. I would — yes.'

She returned with him to the grave, and watched his face as he stared down into the cavity. No man could have expressed such grief over a girl he had just fancied because of her abilities. In every line of his face, in the tears he fought to keep out of his eyes, was grief of the uttermost . . .

'Funerals always have a strange effect on me,' he said quickly, as though he felt Maria's eyes were reading into his very soul.

'I suppose there is a psychological reason for it,' she shrugged. 'However, we cannot delay here much longer, Mr. Whittaker. We have the school and daily routine to remember. Would you care to accompany the two girls and me back to the college?'

He nodded gratefully and walked

beside her to the coach where Joan and
Beryl were already seated. They both
looked surprised at the sight of Whittaker,
then they relapsed into a kind of
interested attention as they watched the
sight of a man trying to prevent tears. In
fact, Beryl looked once as though she
wanted to giggle — until she caught
Maria's cold eyes. There was no such
levity from Joan: she simply stared with
puzzled dark brown eyes, and her teeth
biting into her lower lip as though she
were trying to think something out for
herself.

Arriving at the school, Whittaker
uttered a few words of thanks then
hurried off to resume his duties. Beryl
Mather turned, too, towards the School
House where lessons were in progress,
but Joan remained behind.

'I'd — I'd like to speak to you, Miss
Black — privately,' the girl said.

'Oh? Come with me, then.'

Maria led the way to her study, seated
herself at her desk, and waited expectantly.

Joan felt inside the pocket of her blouse

and suddenly whipped a yellow object into view, laid it on the desk. Maria found herself looking at her own gold watch and chain.

'I know it's yours, Miss Black. It has the name of Louise Black inscribed on the back. I suppose she is — or was — a relative. It's the one you wear, isn't it?'

'The name,' Maria's eyes narrowed, 'was my mother's. Joan, where did you get this watch?'

The girl hesitated, her face colouring. 'I — I found it in Vera Randal's blazer pocket!'

Maria said nothing, and with infinite calm studied the watch. Then she finally laid it on one side, and fixed Joan with her most piercing stare.

'I know that I'm being a sneak,' Joan said, 'but after you coming last night and asking if any of us had been out of bounds I felt I had to speak. Vera broke bounds last night — and that lump in her face wasn't toothache. It was toffee!'

'Indeed! And where exactly did Vera get toffee from at that hour of night, and in these days of rationing?'

'Well, about an hour after lights out Vera started bragging about some food and toffee she'd received from home, which she said she'd hidden in the pavilion on the hockey field. We dared her to go and get it — and she said she would. But she was afraid of her footprints being found near the pavilion, so she put on Frances's shoes instead of her own. They didn't fit properly and they must have hurt her terribly, but she did it. She got them by using a safety pin to unfasten Frances's locker . . . '

'Go on!' Maria snapped.

'She put the shoes in her pocket and slid down the drainpipe in her stockinged feet. She was away for nearly an hour, and said she'd been delayed by trying to get into the pavilion. The window had jammed or something. We had just about started on the food when you arrived. There was only time to dodge the stuff under our beds when the lights went up. Vera, in fact, had only just taken her clothes off and started on the toffee — '

'And had returned Frances's shoes to the locker?' Maria asked curtly.

'Yes, ma'm. Then after you had gone we had our feast, but Vera got her face sticky with toffee and couldn't get to sleep for it. She had no handkerchief handy so borrowed mine. I asked her for it this morning. She said she'd put it in her blazer pocket — which was hanging on the bedrail — and to get it for myself. I did — and found this watch at the same time. I knew it was yours right away, so I kept it. I've been trying to tell you about it all this morning, but I didn't have the nerve — until now.'

'Frankly, I consider the conduct of all you young ladies deserving of the most severe censure,' Maria said grimly. 'And I shall visit the Sixth Form room in a moment and learn the full facts for myself before deciding the punishment . . . For the moment, Joan, you are dismissed.'

Joan rose, then hesitated. 'What I don't see,' she said, frowning, 'is how Vera ever managed to get hold of your watch anyway.'

'That issue is best left with me, Joan. You may go.'

The moment the door had closed

Maria snapped open the back of the watch. Just as she had expected the formula copy had gone. She closed it up again, held it by the winding stem and breathed on it gently. A variety of blurry fingerprints came into view, but so confused that they amounted to nothing.

Maria left her study and swept into the Sixth Form room just as Miss Tanby was wrapped up in one of her pet algebraical treatises. She waited in surprise as Maria moved to the desk and gazed steadily over the array of girls. Joan Dawson was in her usual place, she noticed, looking very discomfited.

'Girls, it has come to my knowledge that last night you indulged in a — er — beanfeast after lights out. That is utterly against regulations, as you all know. Before I give the name of the ringleader I am giving the chance of a confession. Now, what took place in the dormitory last night after lights out?'

There was a long, tense silence — then in the front row of desks Vera Randal stood up.

'I went out after lights out, Miss Black

245

— to the pavilion for some food and toffee. In fact we all of us wanted a beanfeast, so I risked it.'

'Then when I asked for somebody to come forward because I had suspected one of you had broken bounds you told a deliberate lie?' Maria demanded.

'Not altogether, ma'm — I just didn't admit it. That lump in my face wasn't toothache. It was toffee.'

Maria took out her watch for all to see. 'Vera, while you were on your excursion last night you found my gold watch. Why didn't you speak when I asked, and return it to me?'

Vera's jaw dropped. 'Your — your watch, Miss Black?'

'I am not going to mention names because I do not wish anybody to be victimised. But this watch of mine was found in your blazer, Vera. I'm waiting for your explanation!'

Vera looked about her with narrowed eyes. Her gaze settled on Joan Dawson, who averted her face quickly.

'I don't know anything about it, Miss Black,' Vera declared. 'And I'll bet it was that little sneak Joan who gave the whole thing away!'

'Do you infer that this watch just walked away from me and put itself in your pocket?' Maria snapped.

'I don't know — I didn't do it!' Vera shouted.

Maria switched the topic abruptly. 'I have proof that you used the shoes of the late Frances for your escapade, to cover up your involvement in breaking regulations. The mystery of that girl's death has by no means been cleared up yet. If this is reported to the police they may place a very different construction on your actions . . . You might even be arrested!'

Vera suddenly wheeled round and dived over her desk, caught Joan Dawson by her collar and yanked her to her feet.

'You lying swine!' she yelled. 'I'll finish you for this! I'll — '

She struck Joan a stinging blow across the face. She stumbled backwards and crashed on to the floor. In blind rage, Vera dived for her, tore at her hair, kicked her legs, then drove her bunched fist into the girl's jaw.

'Try and get me mixed up in a theft, will you?' she screeched. 'Blabbing all that stuff about me — ! Take that! And that!'

Gasping, helpless, Joan lay flat on the floor and protected herself as best she could — then Maria swept into the scrum with Tanby behind her.

'Girls! *Girls!*' With one sweep of her arm Maria drove Vera on one side and held her tightly. Tanby hauled the dazed and shaken Joan to her feet. Blood was trickling from a cut in her lower lip and the venom that glinted in her dark eyes was startling for a moment.

'You dirty bully!' she whispered viciously. 'One day I'll get you for this, Vera! I'll make you scream for mercy before I'm finished with you! And when you scream I'll hurt you all the more! You cheap — '

'Silence!' Maria commanded. 'Never in my life have I witnessed such a revolting affray between two so-called young ladies! I am disgusted! Shocked! And I am blaming you, Randal, for starting it!'

'Me! Look here, Miss Black, I'm not having this little beast telling lies about me and getting me involved in — '

'Be *quiet*! I saw everything that happened. Joan did not hit back; she had no chance. For this, Randal, you will spend one week in the punishment room with every privilege cancelled. Miss Tanby, see that she is allowed to wash and tidy up and then take her to the punishment room and bring me the key.'

'I tell you Joan is telling lies about me! I never saw your old watch — !' Vera stormed, as Tanby seized her arm.

Maria waited in icy calm as the girl was led away — then she looked at the pale, quivering Joan as she dabbed her bleeding lip.

'All right, Joan?' she asked quietly.

'Yes, ma'm — thanks. I'm sorry I said all those things, but I couldn't help it. My nerves go to pieces when I'm attacked. I — I just can't bear pain . . . Vera has a terrible temper when she starts.'

'Go to the matron and have your bruises and cuts fixed up,' Maria ordered.

'I'd rather not, Miss Black. I don't like being fussed over: it makes me irritable. I'll be all right.'

'As you wish, Joan,' Maria shrugged. 'I

can't compel you — '

Joan nodded and went back to her desk. Maria looked round on the excited girls and they quieted under her imperious gaze.

'Last night's infraction of the rules has been brought to a head of its own accord, and for that reason I shall say nothing more about it. I shall find out from Vera herself the exact circumstances concerning my watch, and in the meantime let her punishment be a lesson to you. When Miss Tanby returns you will proceed with your lesson.'

With that she turned and left, closed the form-room door sharply behind her, then stood listening for a moment.

'What a rotten sneak you are, Joan!'

'Vera wasn't entirely responsible — !'

Maria smiled pensively to herself as she made her way back to her study.

10

After dinner Maria felt conscious of the fact that she was in danger of getting enmeshed in her own investigative web. She felt the need of pulling out the unwanted strands and following the remainder to the source. As usual she turned to her record book. After reflecting, she wrote down her thoughts as they came to her:

Frances Hasleigh had a real reason for asking where Sirius was. Following this star's direction last night I came to an old tin mine, which has become a rendezvous for Clive Whittaker. There are chemicals there, some pilfered from the school, which explains why he so rarely frequents the laboratory now. I need to find the other half of the formula before I can decide what he is driving at. My original copy of the other half-formula (from Frances's forearm) has been snatched from me last night while I was down the mine. This leads me to the queer affair of my attacker using the shoes of the late Frances Hasleigh. Vera Randal has admitted that she wore these shoes last night when she broke bounds. I have the impression that she is lying — and I am not at all convinced but what Joan Dawson was mixed up in it. This girl Joan interests me — though I can't yet determine where she fits into the puzzle. Last night I hit my attacker a crack on the shoulder with my umbrella: this morning Joan complained of rheumatism in that self-same shoulder. Another point: she refused to go to the Matron after a fight with Vera Randal. Was it because matron might have inquired about the bruised shoulder?

I find it all very peculiar. And why was Joan uncomfortable on her feet for so long after the clearing tragedy when — as far as we all know — she only trod on some thorns? This should not have made her limp for so long a time.

But if for a moment I considered that she killed Frances Hasleigh, what possible motive could she have? No — I cannot credit this. Clive Whittaker showed genuine concern at the funeral of Frances today. Is he a relative of hers?

Matter of triple knots, silk in rope, and the exact fashion of Frances's death not yet cleared up.

The time is 2.45 p.m.

Maria read the notes through, then picked up the telephone. After a short interval she was speaking through to Vera Randal's father in London.

'Oh, Miss Black? Yes? Anything wrong?'

'Not exactly, Mr. Randal — though it does concern an infraction of the rules,' Maria said. 'What I would like you to tell me is this: Have you recently sent a parcel of food and toffee to your daughter?'

'Have I *what*? Why, of course not! As if I could in these days! Why, isn't she getting proper nourishment or something?'

'No, no nothing like that,' Maria

answered calmly. 'I just needed to know first-hand before passing an opinion. Thanks, Mr. Randal. I'm sorry I had to bother you.' Maria replaced the receiver thoughtfully.

'Ellison, in his treatise *Side Angles on the Obvious*, says that the hardened criminal, in a corner, will put out an obvious story in order to confuse the issue,' she mused. 'Here we have a milder form of a similar case. Vera Randal either got scared and invented that story of food and toffee — or else she was *forced* to tell it! Hmm — all the girls swear food and toffee was there all right. Where from? Why not the tin mine?' She sat back in her chair, her eyes narrowed with concentration

'Let us assume that Whittaker used that mine as a kind of habitat before he came to this school. He would have food and drink. Now, any surplus he had he would probably move away from there, perhaps to augment his school rations. Likely place? School pavilion! Yet how did anybody else know it was there? Hmm — all the girls have used that pavilion recently during their hockey matches. All or any might have known it was there . . . It's very likely that the beanfeast was composed of Whittaker's surplus food — and Vera Randal knew it was there.

'If I exclude her from my calculations, it leaves only Joan Dawson. A mere schoolgirl and probably a better friend than even Beryl Mather. And yet there is that other point: Joan is brown-eyed, yet her parents are both blue-eyed. Which proves what? That Joan Dawson is *not* their child? Even if so, what help is it to me?'

Her suspicion was one that could be either proved or disproved, so she wrote a letter there and then to the Registrar General of the Births, Marriages and Deaths Department at Somerset House, enclosed the appropriate fee for a search, then went out and posted the letter in the school mail box.

Just about to re-enter the School House she caught sight of Superintendent Vaxley's car coming through the gates, so she turned towards it as he stepped out into the quadrangle.

'Were you expecting me, Miss Black?' he smiled, raising his hat and shaking hands.

'No, though I am glad to see you, Super,' Maria responded. 'I am hoping that you may have something interesting to report. Come along to my study.'

Within a few minutes he was facing her across the desk.

'I've been pretty busy recently,' he said, 'and I've found out some things which serve to bear out your original belief in the innocence of Robert Lever.'

Maria smiled warmly. 'Such as?'

'Well, I've been busy tracing the exact identity of Frances Hasleigh. It has not been an easy job because France is under German occupation, but we did manage to glean one or two facts through the Protecting Power . . . To cut the story short, Frances Hasleigh was an assumed name, and her identity card — as you know already — was a forgery. She was not even registered as a British subject under that name. Her real name was Edith Lillian Brownhill.'

'Very interesting, Super. But how does

it affect the case of Robert Lever?'

'I'm coming to that. Edith Brownhill was twenty-four years of age, and there is a brother — Thomas Edward Brownhill, four years her senior. I've spent a lot of time tracing this relationship — or at least the Yard has — and we covered several counties in order to do it. Once I found the right name I looked for the names of relatives and found the name of the brother, mother, and father. The mother and father are both dead, but the complete family used to live in Acton some ten years ago. I went personally to Acton early this morning and managed to find two inhabitants in the neighbourhood of the Brownhill family who remembered them quite well. From description there was little doubt to me that Frances Hasleigh and Edith Brownhill were one and the same person, whereas the description of the brother fits this science master you have here — if he had a neat moustache. That is a trifle though.'

'Whittaker, eh?' Maria reflected.

'Exactly. While in Acton I went to the local newspaper office and asked for a photograph, if possible, of the Brownhill family. Finally I was given a photograph of all four of them at a fancy dress ball for the local chemists, and it established the identity of the two younger ones once and for all. But it started another train of thought. Why chemists? I made further inquiry and found that old man Brownhill had been a chemist — and a good one, too, with a shop in the high street. But apparently he had also been a research chemist and inventor.

'At one time, in 1929, he offered a new type of explosive to the Government, but they wouldn't consider it at any price — chiefly because in those days war was not a thing to be taken seriously. Anyhow I have not been able to trace any further evidence of him offering his explosive to anybody else. He seemed to lead a quiet life until 1932, then he died just one week before his wife. After that the two children apparently disappeared from the district.'

'At which time they would be twenty and sixteen respectively?' Maria said thoughtfully.

'Just so. That definitely would have been the end of the trail for me had I not already got the wheels moving at the Yard. The French angle began to tie up with the Acton angle. The Yard found out from the French authorities in London that the names of the two children were registered in the French records for late 1932 as émigrés from Britain, that they had come to live with an aunt and uncle who — though British — were domiciled just outside Paris for business reasons. Further than that I have not got, but considering everything I think it was a pretty good distance, and it opens up a new set of hypotheses.'

'Definitely,' Maria agreed, thinking. 'But how does this affect Lever?'

'The moment I saw the resemblance to this Whittaker fellow, and recalled that he was a new arrival here at the school, I realised he had to fit in somewhere — especially so since I found he, too, was not registered with the rest of people when the war began. It is certain that his identity card and ration book are also forgeries.

'I have had men toothcombing the district around here for information concerning him and Lever ever since this business started and from the post-office-cum-grocery shop a clue did emerge. It seems that the shopkeeper remembers the spasmodic visits of a young man to buy bread, minerals, and unrationed cooked meats — in other words stuff which did not need a ration book. Obviously he was keeping the book back until he landed somewhere with an address. From the description Whittaker fits exactly. I found this information waiting for me when I left you yesterday afternoon. I had then to think of a place where he might have been living, and, going over the details in my mind I recalled Sirius. So I — '

'Followed the direction of Sirius, went down the tin mine, and found Whittaker's rendezvous, eh?' Maria asked drily. 'A gratifying example of parallel reasoning Superintendent! It shows that my own ingenuity works in the same way as an accepted master of the profession.'

'You mean that you, too, know about his hideout near Bollin's Wood?'

'Yes, I know of it. I was there last night.'

'I see. Well, Miss Black, it puts us on common ground. What did you find?'

She told him briefly and he nodded.

'Yes, that's what I found, too. You went last night, you say? I was there in the small hours of this morning, just before the stars faded — and I came to this college, outside the gates, so I could get my direction, following the line taken by Frances Hasleigh — '

Vaxley paused and fumbled in his coat pocket, laid a small fountain pen torch on the desk.

'This is yours, then?' he asked, rather disappointedly.

Maria smiled, picking it up and pocketing it. 'I dropped it in my travels last night.'

'I thought it might have been a valuable clue,' he sighed; then he brisked up again. 'However, if any proof were needed that the mine had been — and still is — Whittaker's hiding-place the footprints around the top provided it. I found shoe-prints that exactly match the shoe casts we made of Frances Hasleigh. The prints can still be found in the soft soil round the mine-head top. Fortunately we've had no rain for a fortnight. I also found a man's prints — Whittaker's no doubt — and those of — er — '

'Myself?' Maria suggested.

'I know that now . . . Here is a point, though. That mine head directly faces Bollin's Wood, only half a mile away. The clearing where the girl met her death is some twenty-five feet from the river's edge — then across the river is the brief stretch of soft soil ground leading to the mines. Now, on the river side of the clearing the trees are sparse. It is easily possible to see into the clearing from the mine with a pair of field glasses.'

'Yes?' Maria murmured, her thoughts elsewhere.

'What was to prevent Whittaker having seen — perhaps accidentally — what was going on in the wood? He might have been at the mine then, just arriving perhaps after afternoon lessons, and with the aid of glasses he brought into clear relief the girls in the clearing. He recognised his sister among them and could see that she and her two friends were bound and gagged. He could have reached the clearing in five minutes over the bridge.'

'And hanged his own sister!' Maria exclaimed. 'My dear Superintendent, you're way off the mark.'

'Close relatives have murdered each other many a time before now,' he said grimly. 'It *could* have happened this time.'

'And the motive?'

'Whatever it was on her arm. It all ties up with him being the one who moved her dead body, too.'

'You cannot arrest a man on that evidence, can you?'

'Not yet. Evidence has to be very complete before you can issue a warrant. But I am certainly going to find out what he was doing and where he was on that particular afternoon at the fated time.'

'And if he gets the least suspicion that you are wondering about him, he may disappear as mysteriously as he came,' Maria pointed out. 'It is your misfortune, Super, that you will be compelled to give yourself away. On the other hand I could worm it out of him without giving him any cause to suspect.'

Vaxley nodded slowly. 'Yes, you could. And we might save ourselves a lot of trouble that way . . . Anyway you can see now how Robert Lever's conduct is rendered far less guilty by this new factor. Yes, Miss Black, I'll leave Whittaker's movements on that afternoon in your hands to investigate.'

'I'll find out everything I can. But don't expect immediate results.'

'We can wait — for the right kind of evidence,' Vaxley smiled. 'And if you don't succeed we can arrest him for misrepresentation, suspicion of maintaining a private arsenal in contravention of the Defence regulations — and other things. We've a case against him all right, but we want the facts.'

'Quite so, but tell me something, Superintendent. What theory have you about the bogus Major Hasleigh, and his so-called daughter? What was the purpose behind it?'

Vaxley reflected. 'Well, I have a theory — of sorts. These two young people fled from France just before it was invaded. Between them they had a secret — which might have been their father's original explosive formula for all we know. They got into England by some means and evaded detection. They could not live long as fugitives so had to think of something quickly. They had some money with them. The brother created the character of Major Hasleigh and disguised himself, as he thought, to look like such a personage, lodging his money in the Elmington Bank, near which place they must have been at the time. His sister became his daughter and he put her here in a safe place. Then as Major Hasleigh he vanished again and set himself up at the tin mine. So the girl could find the spot easily he perhaps suggested that she had only to follow Sirius from the college and she'd come straight to it.'

'Excellent,' Maria beamed. 'My own thesis exactly — except that I think that these two young fugitives were in need of chemicals to make an explosive and they chose a college as the most likely source, without exciting any suspicions. I think then that Frances hit on the two-edged idea of finding out about Sirus and firing the science master simultaneously. She made a noise in the dormitory knowing somebody would tell on her. By getting rid of Lever she left a vacancy. Then, when she knew the advertisement would be in the paper for another one, she went to the mine and told her brother — which accounts for her second breaking of bounds. She did it at night, of course, because of day detention. Her brother applied, no doubt with forged references — which I had no reason to suspect at the time — and the Board of Governors accepted him. Being a capable scientist it was easy for him to live up to his job. Thanks to Frances's strategy, brother and sister were together under one roof, and he used the mine as a kind of repository for the chemicals he had appropriated . . . I think the chemicals that we cannot identify may be combination chemicals — that is, a formula of percentages of many chemicals made up as one ingredient. In the complex science of chemistry it is often done for simplicity.'

Vaxley smiled and got to his feet.

'You certainly know your textbooks Miss Black, to derive such deductions. I often wonder why you spend your time in a college. We could use a mind like yours to great advantage. However — '

'I am purely an experimenter,' Maria shrugged, rising to her feet. 'I'm glad if I can help the law. I could even tell you a lot more than I have done so far, but I have my own angles remember. Rest assured that I will get into touch with you the moment I have anything new to report on Whittaker.'

Vaxley nodded and shook hands, then as he was about to depart Maria stayed him.

'By the way, Super, I think it might prove advantageous if you had a thorough check up made on the parents of all the girls concerned in the tragedy — except the mythical Hasleigh, of course.'

'Easily done, Miss Black. I'll let you know results — '

'And one last thing, Super. I wonder how Whittaker did the murder without leaving footprints?'

'There'll be a way round that. There are ten different ways of preventing footprints, you know — from wearing boards on your shoes to covering in the earth after you. It'll fit in.'

After Vaxley went out. Maria reflected that it would help the mystery a good deal if she could find out where her half of the formula had gone to, or else find out who had the complete formula. Whittaker, perhaps?

That same evening, in response to a telephone summons Pulp Martin presented himself in Maria's study. It was about seven-thirty.

'Bit nearer, Maria?' he inquired eagerly, settling opposite her desk.

'Many angles, Mr. Martin, little proof,' she shrugged. 'At the moment I have a number of missing links, you see.'

'Yeah? Sling them at me and I'll see if I get bubbles in my think-tank.'

'Only, Mr. Martin, if what I say goes no further. It was given to me confidentially by Superintendent Vaxley.'

'You know me, Maria. Give!'

So Maria gave — in detail — relating everything Vaxley had told her and adding her own impressions on the beanfeast and the tin mine, together with the news of her attacker and the theft of watch and formula.

'It's kinda sticky all right,' Pulp admitted. 'But as I see things, you've got three possible culprits for the death of that kid — this Whittaker guy, Robert Lever, or Joan Dawson — or even Vera Randal. But you can eliminate Joan Dawson because she's a schoolgirl with no muscles strong enough to shift that mausoleum paving stone; Lever because his pen makes him too obvious; and what do we get? Whittaker!'

'Excellent conclusions, Mr. Martin,' Maria agreed, nodding. 'Whittaker is using that tin mine as a sort of rendezvous for some secret activity — but it was a woman, or perhaps a girl, who attacked me last night and stole that formula. Whittaker would not have had the time to get back to the college, steal Frances Hasleigh's shoes — even granting he could ever manage it with a room full of girls — and use them for faking footprints. So the only girl I can see fitting into the pattern is — Joan Dawson.'

'But I thought you said that it were this Vera Randal kid?'

'I've a theory, Mr. Martin . . . Vera Randal said she went for the food and toffee, yes — but there are lots of ways in which she could be forced to say that. Girls are very unmerciful to one another when they wish. I know that. Again, I have the assurance of Vera's father that no such toffee or food was ever sent to her. On the other hand, if it was Joan who attacked me in the mine last night we may be sure that it was not her first visit there — that at some previous time she had probably seen Whittaker leave with his food and put it in the pavilion — '

'You mean,' Pulp mused, 'that last night she used that as an excuse to get outside and follow you? And later forced this Vera kid to say that *she* had been out?'

'It's the only possible explanation. Somebody was watching me at the laboratory window when I put my formula away in my watch. If it was Joan she would keep herself in touch with my movements somehow. The moment she knew I was going out — an easy job since her bed is directly under the window overlooking the moonlit quadrangle — she thought up this idea to get out as well.'

'Then you think she may have killed Frances?'

'I have no proof, Mr. Martin, but she's certainly mixed up in the business somewhere. Suppose she *did* take the formula from my watch — and I believe it was she because of her bungled excuse about finding it in Vera's coat — what would she do with the formula?'

'Destroy it, I guess.'

'No, Mr. Martin — it's only *half* the formula, remember. If she wants all of it she will keep that stolen portion some-where and strain every nerve afterwards to find the other half. I am quite sure that Whittaker has it in its entirety, so if an attack should be made on him I think we can guess who the culprit is.'

Pulp frowned over a thought. 'Look,

Maria, why did this kid deliberately come and tell you about finding your watch?'

'Because she knew — or at least guessed — that I would make inquiries, that I would probably demand to know if any of the girls had broken bounds, which I did. She was prepared for all that, and once she had got Vera Randal to admit that she went out she felt on safer ground. The next morning she produced the watch, saying she had found it in Vera's blazer. In that way she believed she could stop any further inquiry about it and blame it all on to Vera — but from the way things went in the classroom this morning I still think Joan had more to do with things than Vera.'

Pulp sighed. 'I just can't figger what a kid of her age has to do with it.'

'That, Mr. Martin, is beside the point . . . We have got to act. If she took that formula she has it somewhere, and very possibly here in the school. Perhaps in the study she shares with Beryl Mather or else in the locker in her dormitory, or on her person.'

'It might be buried in the hockey field,'

Pulp suggested, rather sarcastically.

'No,' Maria mused, 'I don't think so. I imagine she will keep it somewhere near at hand for immediate reference if need be. First, I think her study should be searched — ' She looked at her watch. 'Hmm — an hour and a half before supper-bell. The coast will not be clear until then — but I could have a look through her locker before they all set off for bed.'

'Don't want me for that, do you?' Pulp asked uneasily.

Maria smiled. 'I would not think of embarrassing you, Mr. Martin. I sent for you because I want your opinions on progress so far and because later on I shall probably go to the mine again for a further check up, and this time I do not intend to take any more chances. No, I shall examine this girl's locker and then we will discuss further. Just make yourself comfortable until I get back. If any of my staff should call just tell them I will return shortly . . . '

'Okay,' Pulp nodded.

Maria paused for a moment as she

stepped out into the corridor. She could not be sure, but she thought she heard the sound of fast-retreating footsteps down the angle corridor that led to the studies.

'Easy, Maria,' she muttered, closing her study door sharply. 'Probably just one of your young ladies in a hurry. No need to add to your complexities.'

She went down the corridor, across the main hall, and up the staircase. She passed one or two girls on the way who inclined their heads respectfully . . . Then as she reached the Sixth Form dormitory corridor she went more slowly in case any girls appeared from the opposite staircase — the shorter and usual way from their studies below. But nothing happened by the time she reached the dormitory door.

She knocked sharply. 'Miss Tanby, are you in there?'

Since there was no response and she knew full well that Tanby would be swotting over preparations for tomorrow's lessons, she stepped into the long cool room —

Then she got the shock of her life as

her eyes were automatically drawn to the open door of Joan Dawson's locker. Hanging in the centre of the tall steel cupboard, her face nearly purple and her eyes starting, was Joan! Apparently she was still conscious, for her feet, three inches from the floor, and tightly bound together, kicked desperately.

Momentarily, Maria was paralysed with horrified amazement, then she dived for the cupboard and supported the girl's weight against her own body. As she struggled with the cord holding her up she half realised that there were three knots — just as in the case of the rope that had hanged Frances Hasleigh.

At last she had it undone and the half fainting girl fell heavily across her shoulder, unable to speak for the gag jammed and tied in her mouth. Staggering a little under the weight Maria carried her across to the appropriate bed and laid her upon it, tore the gag away and opened the collar of her blouse.

Joan's face had gone ashy white now and her breathing rasped.

About her throat the rope had left an

ugly red weal. A dozen new thoughts were chasing through Maria's brain now as she dashed to the nearest washbowl and hurried back with a glass of water and a soaked sponge. Under the influence of both the girl began to recover a little. Then Maria turned her over and unfastened her wrists — again triple knots. Then her ankles — again triple knots. With a little sigh and a deep breath Joan relaxed and lay looking up at Maria's pale, stern face.

'Th-thank God you happened to come, Miss Black,' she whispered, fingering her bruised throat. 'Another few seconds and I think I might have died — '

'You *would* have died!' Maria assured her grimly. 'That was the obvious intention. Who attacked you?'

'I — I can't be sure,' the girl muttered. 'And I don't know why, either. I came in here to get a book — you'll find it under my pillow here. I was going to take it down to the study to read — then just as I reached the bed here somebody came up from behind me and tied a gag in my mouth. I couldn't see behind me. My hands were jerked behind me and tied, too — then I was thrown on my face on the floor so I still couldn't see who it was. Next thing I knew my ankles were fastened. Not a word was spoken — whoever it was didn't want to give anything away. He — or she — must have been hiding in here. Perhaps I was seen on my way up here and my attacker came in silently behind me . . . I don't know.' The girl paused, breathing hard.

'What happened then?' Maria demanded.

'I was left flat on my face for a while. Then whoever it was hauled me along, face down, to the locker. The key had been in the lock all day as a matter of fact. I was supported inside, my back still to my attacker. I saw a cord with a wide noose hanging from the centre peg — a noose just big enough for my head to go through. I struggled, but it wasn't any use. I was lifted up and my head was pushed through the noose, then I was released and swung about by my neck. I was slowly strangling and was pretty close to passing out when you came . . . Did you know what had happened, ma'm?'

'No, Joan, I didn't know. It was simply Providential chance. I came in here to look for Miss Tanby as a matter of fact.'

'Yes — I seem to remember hearing you call her name.'

Maria sat on the bed beside the girl. 'How do you feel now, Joan?'

'Oh, I'll be all right in a few minutes. Honestly, Miss Black, I begin to think there is a homicidal maniac loose somewhere. First it was Frances — now me, her friend. I wonder if Beryl will be next?' she went on anxiously. 'Maybe some kind of order to it — three girls, all friends, have got to die for some strange reason . . . '

Maria smiled faintly. 'You have been reading too many detective stories, my dear. I think the issue goes much deeper than that. Suppose we see what we can find to help us apprehend your attacker? You say you were *lifted* up to the noose? Did it seem to you that there was only one person involved in that?'

'I'm sure of it, Miss Black.'

'Hmm. Then it wasn't a schoolgirl lifting you. You are no inconsiderable weight. Isn't it rather odd that when you were lifted you did not glimpse your attacker's face, or at least some part of the figure?'

The girl shook her dark head. 'My back was to whoever it was and I couldn't move with my feet bound. Two hands gripped me under the arms, lifted me up, and there I was left dangling. By the time I'd twirled round to the front whoever it was had gone. I think he went towards the window.'

'He?' Maria repeated, and Joan shrugged.

'Only assumption, Miss Black. I don't know — '

'You are probably right in your assumption.' Maria was thinking of the slab in the mausoleum. Then she got to her feet. 'Just you rest a few moments, Joan, while I look round.'

She examined the window first. It was open, as all of them had been throughout the day, but there was no evidence of anybody having scraped across the woodwork. Of course, the attacker had probably worn rubber-soled shoes, since the girl had been caught so unawares.

Maria next picked up the three lengths of rope that had been used and studied them. No silken cord this time, but ordinary clothes rope cut into lengths.

She laid them aside finally and looked into the locker, studying it intently. There did not seem to be anything different about it.

Round its base, perhaps a foot from the floor, was the shoe ledge with its assortment of footwear, and on the floor a number of them had been tossed down carelessly. Maria looked at them and the floor itself and the steel walls. No sign of anything abnormal. Thoughtfully she withdrew and closed and locked the door.

'Anything, Miss Black?' the girl asked anxiously.

'I'm afraid not.' Maria returned to the bedside, then said: 'Can you get off the bed a moment, Joan?'

The girl nodded and stood waiting. Maria went behind her.

'Just let me see what weight you are, Joan.'

She slipped her hands under the girl's armpits and strained to lift her from the floor, without success.

'Hmm — most interesting,' she commented, 'It would take a man all his time — '

'Miss Black, do you think I should tell the police what happened, or my parents?' the girl asked anxiously, turning. 'Another attempt may be made on my life and I've got to have protection. I'm scared!'

'I realise that your position is most unpleasant, Joan,' Maria said quietly, 'but the police are already busy on the job, trying to find the murderer of Frances — obviously the same person. If you want police protection you would probably have to go into custody and be protected in that way until the murderer is found. I don't suppose you will want to do that. But what you *can* do is never go anywhere without company — say two girls at least. That will act as a deterrent to anybody who might make a second attempt on you.'

'It didn't when Frances got hanged,' Joan said worriedly.

'You were all bound beforehand then,'

Maria pointed out. 'No, Joan, you can best help your own case, the name of the school, and the search for Frances's murderer by doing as I have said . . . '

'All right, Miss Black. I'll try and behave as though nothing has happened, and if I find anything out I'll let you know right away.'

'Good!' Maria smiled. 'Now you had better get back to your study before Beryl wonders about you.'

The girl nodded, buttoned up her collar, took the book from under her pillow and departed. Maria picked up the ropes again, then opening Joan's locker she searched for the missing half formula, but she found nothing.

'Extraordinary,' she muttered, compressing her lips.

Picking up the cords she left the dormitory and returned to her study — to find it blue with cigarette smoke as Pulp sat with his tawny-yellow boots perched on her desk and his chair tilted back.

He withdrew his feet hurriedly and sat up, stubbing out his cigarette. He looked at Maria expectantly.

'Mr. Martin, we have a new turn of events. I found Joan Dawson nearly dead in her locker, hanged in the identical fashion of Frances Hasleigh — only the noose was larger and there was no — er — pan handle grip behind her ears. If I had not arrived when I did she would have died.'

Maria sat down at her desk and laid the three lengths of cord before her 'Clothes rope Mr. Martin, which does not tell us a thing since it can be purchased anywhere and — Hmm, this is not new rope. It has been tied round something — and for some time. See the natural kink that has been imparted to it? Anyway the interesting point is that the ropes were knotted in the same fashion as in Frances Hasleigh's case. Triple knots. So it was the self-same person again.'

'Or else somebody imitated the knots to throw blame on somebody else?'

'A smart thought, Mr. Martin, but incorrect. I believe that this job with Joan was done in a hurry: there would be no time to make an imitation of knots. It was that person's natural way of tying a cord

— and that being so it is going to lead us straight to the murderer in the end. Yes, everything was hastily done . . . The gag was none too tight, the wrists and ankles were by no means secure. Had she not been hanging by her neck I don't doubt but what Joan could have got free fairly easily.'

Pulp scratched his red head.

'Look, Maria, don't the kid know who done it? She weren't blindfolded nor nothin'?'

'She was held so that she had no chance to see her attacker. But her attacker was strong enough to raise her bodily in front of him, a good three inches from the floor, and keep on supporting her until he had her head in the noosed cord. Holding her under the arms it would take some doing, especially since she must have struggled. When I tried to raise her — with her connivance — I could not move her from the floor.'

'Whittaker!' Pulp yelped, sitting up with a jerk. 'Remember how he hauled Frances's dead-weight about and shifted that flag-stone? Look here, Maria, that guy is a public menace. He wants shovin' in the pen.'

'First, Mr. Martin, I want to be sure what he is up to, even though there is enough evidence even now to get him arrested.'

'I get it — you want him red-handed? The mine, for instance?'

'Exactly.' For a while Maria was lost in thought, staring at the cords in front of her. 'Everything ties up so neatly,' she muttered. 'That triple knot, as I told you, is the standby of an electrical engineer, the marine service, and the emblem of many girls' and boys' forestry organisations — hmm, I wonder?'

'Wonder what?' Pulp asked.

'Just a thought, Mr. Martin, which I may test later.'

'Seems to me,' he said, 'that this Whittaker guy easily fits into the electrical engineer racket. He's a scientist, ain't he, and that means electricity, too. He'd be the most likely to use a knot that way.'

'Perhaps,' Maria admitted, 'but there is another angle to it which I may examine later — '

'Doesn't this attack on the Joan dame put her out of the runnin' as the killer of Frances?'

'I never said she was the killer, Mr. Martin — and this attack on her makes it seem more unlikely than ever — but I still do think that she was in some way involved in that attack on me. I've looked in her locker for some sign of that formula, by the way, but there is no trace. Next — in about thirty minutes — I'll try her study. In the meantime I have an important matter to attend to.'

Maria pressed the house phone switch and summoned Miss Tanby. On arrival she regarded Pulp doubtfully as he reclined in the choking haze.

'Hi'ya, Toots!' he greeted, waving his hand.

Tanby stiffened and looked down her long, thin nose, then she glanced at Maria appealingly.

'Mr. Martin has his own individual way of greeting people,' Maria said calmly. 'Don't feel offended, Miss Tanby . . . I sent for you because I want Vera Randal released from the punishment room immediately. Here is the key.'

'So soon, Miss Black? But she has only been in since this morning. Hardly sufficient punishment for her behavior, surely?'

'Perhaps not, but things have happened since that seem to show that the life of Joan Dawson may be in jeopardy. I am going to appoint Vera Randal as her keeper — her jailer if you like — and it will be her own definite responsibility to see that Joan does not go out of school alone until further notice. She must always have company, for her own safety. If at any time Joan *does* go out alone I am to be informed immediately. You, too, Miss Tanby, will have an eye to the girl.'

'I will do all I can, of course,' Tanby agreed, 'but why is such a precaution necessary? You say her life is in jeopardy — ?'

'I believe so, but more than that I cannot tell you. Just see that my instructions are carried out, please. I've chosen Vera Randal to act as keeper because she is head girl and has a bitter dislike of Joan. She will come running quickly enough if she finds her wandering off by herself, in the hope of getting her into trouble . . . That is all, Miss Tanby.'

She nodded, rather puzzled — then as she turned to leave Pulp added:

'Be seeing you, sugar.' But he made a wry face as the door closed. 'Sugar! That dame's puss is as sour as last week's hash. Say, Maria, why do you have such a lemon-squeezer for a teacher?'

Maria coughed a little. 'We have no time to discuss Miss Tanby. We have more vital matters to attend to — '

11

'There is, for instance, the silk rope with which the original crime was committed,' Maria said musingly.

Pulp nodded and waited as she drew the short length of silk rope from the desk drawer.

'With my limited facilities for investigation it is not going to be an easy task, but never let it be said that Black Maria is not a trier. Now, what have we here?'

She went over to the book. From the goodly array of volumes she possessed she finally laid an assortment on the desk.

'Dry stuff, Maria,' Pulp commented, picking one up and glancing through the pages. 'When I get a book I like one with pitchers in it. You know — dames!'

'Please reserve the baser side of your nature for your off-time, Mr. Martin,' Maria responded. 'Study that book you've got and see if you can find any plates or context relating to a rope similar to this one on the desk here. I will do likewise. If you find anything, no matter how small, mention it.'

He nodded rather wearily and began to study the pages. So did Maria, and in this wise half an hour passed before she gave a sudden exclamation and looked up sharply.

'I believe I have it! Just listen to this — in Wilcox's *Enough Rope*: 'Of the three best known types of rope on criminal record we have the single garrotting twine, very thin and very tough, by which cutting as well as strangulation is produced; the cabular four-stranded hemp rope which will hold the heaviest body or object; and the toughened silk cord, so slender that it will push into a small pocket or wrap round a body without being noticeable, and yet will take a tremendous strain. In its less villainous aspect it is the favourite rope of a stage magician because of ease in working. The garrotting twine originates in Barbados, the four-stranded hemp rope in Southern England, and the silk cord in South France, being in reality the surplus material remaining from the weaving of silk fabrics for the Parisian market'.'

'But are you sure it is the same sort of rope?' Pulp asked.

'Not entirely, but it is a product of France, and, as I have told you, France figures quite a lot in this case. I think we may take it as more or less correct.'

'Meaning that the killer came from France?' Pulp hazarded.

'It's possible — and the rope certainly did . . . Hmm — 'Push into a small pocket or wrap round a body . . . ' That is most interesting. It does not get us any nearer the killer perhaps, but at least it explains away what was a loose end — in more senses than one. Now I think I have time to write a short letter before we start our little investigation.'

'Letter?' Pulp repeated. 'What about?'

'It has every bearing on the case, I assure you.' Maria drew a sheet of notepaper to her and wrote busily for several minutes. Finishing it, she caught Pulp's inquiring look.

'Just a shot in the dark,' she explained.

'I'm applying to the London headquarters of the Boys' and Girls' Forestry Organisation for a list of members over the last few years. By that I might find out if our friend Whittaker was ever in one. It might explain the queer way of tying knots, too.'

'Knots is right,' Pulp growled. 'We're tied up in 'em!'

Maria sealed the envelope, stamped it, then got to her feet. 'I think we're ready to leave, Mr. Martin. We can post this in the school box later. Come — '

She got into her coat and beret, then together they came out into the corridor.

'The study first,' Maria said, and tried the door of letter F. It was unlocked, for no pupil was supposed to keep her study as private property. Walking in, Maria switched on the light, and locked the door with her master key.

'Now, Mr. Martin, you know what we are looking for?'

'Sure — your half of the formula which somebody frisked.'

Together they began the search. With his former training in petty larceny and

Maria's reputation for thoroughness they made a pretty good job of the study between them, but they found no trace of the thing they sought.

About to give up, Maria's attention became riveted upon a dress trunk in the corner alcove.

'Look!' she exclaimed. 'There are the distinct marks of where a cord has been round that — and it belongs to Beryl Mather. See the initials — B.M?'

Pulp hurried over to her side. 'Say,' he breathed, 'that cord that hanged Joan tonight — '

'Could have come from here, yes,' Maria acknowledged, her eyes narrowing. 'This is really most unexpected. I wonder if — '

She broke off as she looked at the shelf above the dress trunk.

'Joan's bags are missing, Mr. Martin! See?'

He saw what she meant. In a recess in the wall, above the trunk, was a shelf clearly meant for small luggage. A travelling case marked B. M. was there all right, but beside it was an empty cavity.

Maria swung round hurriedly and pulled aside the curtain over the clothes pegs. There were a few coats there, each one with an identity tag.

'All Beryl's,' she said worriedly. 'Everything of Joan's has gone. Good Heavens, I wonder if that attack tonight scared her so much she bolted from the school? Quick — come with me!'

As they left the study, headed for the staircase, en route for the Sixth Form dormitory, Tanby came speeding into view.

'Oh, Miss Black!' She was nearly out of breath. 'I have been trying to find you. Joan has disappeared! She isn't anywhere in the school, and the lodge-keeper never saw her go out. I only found it out when I told Vera Randal to look after her. She came back in about ten minutes and said she couldn't find her . . . Sup-suppose she's been kidnapped?'

'I doubt that,' Maria answered grimly. 'I have just discovered that her bags and outdoor clothes are missing, so she has gone of her own accord. Send Beryl Mather to me right away, will you?'

Tanby hurried off again. In a few minutes she returned with the startled girl, a dressing gown hugged round her corpulent figure.

'Beryl, when did you last see Joan?' Maria asked briefly.

'Not since just after tea-time, Miss Black. I went in the common room after tea to make arrangements with Madge Tarrant about our next hockey match. I was there all the evening. When I went into the dining hall at suppertime Joan was not there. I thought she'd perhaps got another of her nervous fits and was off her food . . . I'm never off mine, of course.'

'So from just after tea until supper-bell you never were in your study?' Maria asked, frowning.

'No, ma'm.'

'Very well, Beryl — you can go back to bed. Thank you for your information.'

Beryl went off and Tanby waited inquiringly, a vague surprise in her pale eyes as she studied Maria's coat and beret.

'Shall — shall I order the girls to dress

and form a search party?' she asked presently.

'Later perhaps, Miss Tanby, but not now.'

'Can't say I blame that kid for takin' a powder, you know,' Pulp remarked. 'To be half strangled and then be told not to worry because you'll have protection — '

'Mr. Martin, I was afraid Joan would do this: that was why I appointed Vera as her watchdog. She acted right away evidently, but I don't see that she can have got very far yet. We might at least be in time to save her walking into trouble. Come, Mr. Martin.'

They left Tanby staring dazedly after them and hurried out into the quadrangle. On the way to the school gates Maria posted the letter she had written, then out in the lane she looked left and right.

'Railway station?' Pulp suggested.

'It seems the only likely place,' Maria admitted. 'The buses are not running at this hour, but there are trains for London up to 1.30 in the morning. Yes, it's our best chance — and we've got to hurry.'

'Suppose she went in the opposite direction, towards Langhorn?' Pulp said, as they hurried along in the starlight.

'She might have,' Maria nodded, breathing hard, 'but I cannot imagine why she should want to.'

So on they went, a good fifteen minutes' walk, arriving at last at the blacked-out little office of the stationmaster. They found him reading a magazine.

'Why, hallo, Miss Black! Late hour for you, ma'm.'

'I am looking for a runaway pupil, Mr. Shaw. Have you seen one about here?'

He shook his grey head. 'No — I ain't seen any girls all this evening. Only two travellers I know pretty well, but nobody else.'

'Well, thank you anyway, Mr. Shaw. If you *do* happen to see a dark-haired, dark-eyed schoolgirl with bags marked J. D. just try and delay her and ring up the school immediately.'

'Aye — I will.'

Baffled, Maria led the way outside again and looked at Pulp in the dim light of the rising moon.

'Well, if she did go to Langhorn,' he said, 'we can kiss her goodbye. Why not ring up her ma and pop and see if she's gotten home?'

'She couldn't have done so that rapidly, Mr. Martin. Dear me, this is a most unpleasant turn of events. If anything happens to that girl I'll never forgive myself.'

'Look, Maria, you afraid that Whittaker might bump her off?'

'Yes, that is exactly what does haunt me! You see, I — ' She broke off suddenly. 'Mr. Martin, we are going to take a long chance! I believe it was Joan who attacked me down in the mine, therefore she knows where it is. Did she go *there*, I wonder? Come on — we can take the short cut through Bollin's Wood.'

She started off immediately and five minutes brought them both to the stile in the lane, opposite where Vera Randal and her cronies had sat on the fateful day. They climbed over it and headed through the dark underbrush towards the fated clearing. Then as they were halfway through it towards the bank of the river

Pulp caught Maria's arm suddenly.

'Say, I hear something!' he breathed.

The sound came again, more distinctly — a low, sobbing note of distress that rose suddenly into a shriek of pain.

'Over here!' Pulp yelled, and vaulted the bush in front of him. He went diving forward through the undergrowth with Maria stumbling after him,

The gloom of the wood, despite the moonlight, made it impossible to see anything beyond two dim figures. Pulp chose the taller one and landed out with all his mighty strength. The man went crashing backwards and reeled against a tree, brought up his fist to save himself, then got a second punch in the jaw for his trouble. Weakly he sagged, but he didn't altogether collapse.

'Stand on your feet, you snivellin' heel!' Pulp snapped.

But instead a revolver blazed in the dark and Pulp doubled sharply as searing pain sliced through his shoulder. Gasping, he staggered against the bushes, lost his balance and fell over. For a moment Maria thought of chasing the already departing unknown with her umbrella, but realising it was useless she turned back.

Pulp was getting slowly to his feet, holding his shoulder tightly. Nearby, dazed but apparently unhurt, Joan Dawson was standing. Near her lay the dark outline of her travelling case.

'What happened, Joan?' Maria put a supporting arm round the trembling girl.

The girl suddenly buried her face in her hands and burst into violent sobs and laughter alternately.

'Stop it, Joan!' Maria commanded.

The girl went on sobbing and laughing by turns until a sound slap across the face stopped her hysteria.

'I — I was attacked again! It must be the same man. And it is a man — I saw that much, but I don't know who he is. I was just leaving the school — '

'Why?' Maria interrupted. 'Why didn't you stay in the college and have protection?'

'I was too frightened! I wanted to dash off home: my nerves were gone. I had to get out! I'd only got a little way down the lane when I was overtaken by this man and I must have been knocked senseless. Anyway, I fainted — '

'Just a moment,' Maria said. 'Were you hit on the head, or what?'

'All I felt was a hand on the back of my neck and then things went swimmy. Miss Black, how did you get here for the second time and save my life? How do you know? And I'm not going back to the school, I tell you! When I left you in the dormitory I came down to the study, found Beryl wasn't there, so I packed my things and left them ready to leave when it was dark. I've thought it all out. I won't come back!'

'I can understand your reluctance, Joan, but you *must* return . . . As to my finding you here it was quite by chance whilst trying to trace you — '

'Say, Maria,' Pulp said hoarsely, 'what this kid got was the pan handle at the back of her noodle. And I've got to get to a doctor quick, too. I've parked a slug in my shoulder.'

'Yes, of course,' Maria agreed hastily. 'Pick up your bag, Joan, and come with us . . . We have a doctor at the school, Mr. Martin. You are sure you can walk?'

'Just about,' he panted. 'And when I get the guy that plugged me I'll tear his heart out, so help me!'

Very reluctantly, Joan picked up her bag and followed the two out of the wood into the lane, Maria supporting Pulp as best she could.

'What were you screaming for, Joan, when we arrived?' she asked presently.

'He was twisting my arm. I'd only just recovered consciousness and the first thing I knew he pounced on me, seized my arm and bent it up my back.'

'Nobody would go to all that trouble just to twist your arm, Joan. What did the man want? Information?'

'No — all he said was, 'You escaped the last time, but you won't this!' Or something like that. Then I thought my arm was going to break — '

'And you didn't recognise his voice?'

'No — unless it was disguised so that I couldn't.'

'Hmmm — ' Maria relapsed into thought until they reached the college.

Then she concerned herself with Pulp Martin's injury first and hurried him straight to the school sanatorium. There she left him in charge of Dr. Wood and then proceeded to her study, still with the silent Joan at her side.

Maria could now see how deathly pale the girl was, how a haunted light gleamed in her dark, expressive eyes.

Maria motioned for her to sit down. 'Joan, are you quite sure you are telling me the truth? Are you convinced you did not recognise your attacker?'

'I swear, Miss Black, that I don't know who he is, and I never saw him before. As I said before, I think he must be a maniac with a weakness for killing schoolgirls.'

Maria sat down at her desk and switched on the telephone to the lodge. She was answered by the voice of Andrews, the night watchman.

'Andrews, find Mr. Whittaker and have him come to my study right away. Impress upon him it is extremely urgent.'

'Yes, ma'm. Right away.'

She switched off and sank back into thought. Joan, too, remained silent. Then after a long interval there came a knock and Whittaker entered, a silk dressing gown over his shirt and trousers.

'Forgive the attire, Miss Black,' he apologised, smiling. His puzzled glance went from the pale-faced girl and back to Maria. 'Is there anything wrong?'

'Quite a deal is wrong, Mr. Whittaker,' Maria answered gravely. 'Have you been out at all this evening, or perhaps seen anything of a tall, strange man lurking about?'

'Why, no!' Whittaker shook his head. 'As a matter of fact I have just finished playing chess with Professor Chalfont, the botany master. You can have a word with him if you wish to check up . . . Though I can't imagine why.'

Maria showed no sign of the surprise she felt.

'Thank you for being so explicit, Mr. Whittaker. I am sorry I had to disturb you.'

Whittaker shrugged and went out. Puzzled, Maria glanced back to Joan again.

'I want to be allowed to return home,

Miss Black! Under escort if it can be arranged. My life is not safe in or near this school, and you know it!'

Maria said nothing immediately.

'Did you send for Mr. Whittaker because you thought that he attacked me?' the girl persisted.

'I sent for him,' Maria answered, 'because he is the youngest teacher in the college and as such probably the most alert. You heard me ask him if he had seen a man prowling about. There is the chance that after all we may be dealing with a homicidal maniac.'

Joan nodded slowly. 'I still think you did it because you believe he attacked me. But it wasn't he. I'd have recognised him in a moment.'

Maria got to her feet. 'Joan, I have come to a decision. The only way you can be kept safe until matters are straightened out is by going into protective custody. Obviously I do not intend to hand you over to the police in order to accomplish it, so I shall assume responsibility. Henceforth, until this maniac is appre- hended, you will be confined to the punishment room — not as a transgressor, but for protection. I will see to it that you have every attention and will delegate Miss Tanby to set you your studies for as long as need be.'

'I'm not going to do it!' Joan stated flatly. 'What is there to prevent me being attacked even then? The punishment room is not a sure guarantee of my safety!'

'It's the nearest thing to it,' Maria answered, 'and I wish to keep you under my eye for the moment. With barred windows and somebody watching the locked door you will be safe enough.'

'But — but I want to ask my father to take me away! You can't keep me here! I've got certain individual rights!'

'I will of course get in touch with your father immediately,' Maria promised. 'But for the moment surely you would rather have detention in the punishment room than perhaps — death, if you remain free and unwatched?'

Joan gave a reluctant nod. 'All right, ma'm, perhaps you're right — but please do ask my father to come and take me away as soon as possible.'

'I will,' Maria nodded. 'Now pick up your bag and come with me.'

Joan obeyed and in five minutes she found herself in the rather drear confines of the sparsely furnished punishment room, with its plain bed.

'I will have somebody to stay on guard,' Maria said. 'Anything you may need will be brought immediately. We'll have a further chat in the morning. Good night, Joan.'

The girl said nothing so Maria went out, locking the door. She reflected, then added the heavy padlock to its hasp and locked that, too. Satisfied, she went downstairs again, outside, and to the watchman's lodge. In a few moments she was talking to Andrews, the night watchman.

'Andrews, your duties will be inside tonight. Take up a position outside the punishment room on Floor Three, and if Dawson — who is inside the room — should ask for anything see that she has it. But in no circumstances is she to be allowed to leave, even if you have to use force to prevent her.'

Andrews nodded his grey head. 'Okay, Miss Black. Do I stay until morning?'

'Until eight-thirty. I'll see that you are relieved then. Here are the keys to the door — lock and padlock. Now be off right away.'

Maria saw him out of the lodge and heading towards the School House in the moonlight, then she went over to the sanatorium to find Dr. Wood, and check on Pulp.

'He'll be all right in a day or so, Miss Black,' he said. 'Nothing very serious. The bullet lodged in the fleshy part of his shoulder. Here it is — if you're interested.'

Maria nodded, and took it from him as he handed it over from his desk.

'Point thirty-two,' he said. 'Fired from an automatic.'

Maria studied it in silence, then said: 'You don't mind if I take charge of it? I'll need it for the police.'

'By all means take it. And I suppose you'll want to see Mr. Martin?'

She nodded, so Wood directed her

through the sanatorium to a private room where Pulp was lying in bed in a rather vivid pyjama suit, bulging on one shoulder with bandages.

'Maria!' he exclaimed, as she came in. 'I was just gettin' the jitters lookin' at these walls.'

Wood raised his eyebrows, then went out as Maria glanced at him briefly. She drew a chair to the bedside and seated herself.

'You are my last call tonight, Mr. Martin,' she said. 'I wanted to be sure that you are comfortable . . . I shall make it up to you for getting shot on my account, believe me.'

'Aw, it ain't the first time I've parked a slug. Only thing that's been worryin' me, Maria, is did you find out anythin' about who done it?'

'Frankly, Mr. Martin, I have no means of being certain — yet. I certainly suspected Whittaker as the culprit, but he has an alibi — namely, that he was playing chess with our botany master until quite a late hour this evening. I'll be checking it tomorrow — or rather later this morning. However, your being shot at may help me a good deal. You see, a point thirty-two automatic was fired at you: I have the bullet in my hand here . . . What I have to do now is draw the fire of the one I suspect — Whittaker, of course — and see if the same type of bullet is fired again.'

'Say, take it easy, Maria! If you get lead in your brains or your heart you're just a pushover for a florist. You can't do it, not while I'm around to take the belly-punches — '

'Please don't excite yourself,' Maria interrupted, smiling. 'I shall do it in such a way that the bullet will be aimed at me but I shall be nowhere near it. There are many decoys I can devise by simple reference to Brown's *The Art of Artifice*. However if I do succeed and get a second bullet from a man I *know* to be Whittaker, you see how much ties up? We have Joan's attacker, my own attacker, the flagstone-mover, the body snatcher, the man who shot you — all resolved into one person!'

'Swell idea,' Pulp admitted. 'And it sort

of makes him the murderer of Frances Hasleigh, too!'

'Not entirely Mr. Martin. Though it lays the onus of responsibility heavily upon him.'

'The what? Okay, skip it . . . What about that kid Joan? She in here too?'

'No. I have locked her in the punishment room to ensure her safety.'

'What! I thought you was fond of kids, Maria. She must have been hurt plenty after that arm-twistin' act, to say nothin' of being scared. Yet you lock her up! I thought you'd rush her to the doctor, see what was missin' and damaged, and then shut her up in the care of a nurse.'

'I have simply done what I think best, Mr. Martin,' Maria shrugged. 'And now I really must be going; I'm very tired. I'll call and see you again.'

'While you're about it,' Pulp said, 'get this sawbones to speed things up a bit. I don't want to be stuck here when I should be helpin' you.'

'I'll see what I can do,' Maria promised. 'Good night, Mr. Martin.'

She went out quietly and paused only

long enough to ask Dr. Wood to speed Pulp's discharge all he could, then she returned to her study.

Here, her notes had to be made whilst events were fresh in her mind..

Steadily she began to write:

Is there a maniac abroad in the region of this college, or is this attack on schoolgirls part of a deliberate plan? I believe the latter — and that I have the first threads of the solution in my hands. I suspect Clive Whittaker of being a prime factor in the case in spite of the fact that he seems to have an alibi during the attack on Joan Dawson tonight, i.e., playing chess with Professor Chalfont, the botany master. Twice within a few hours Joan has been involved in alarming happenings — once nearly hanged, and the second time attacked in Bollin's Wood. I am afraid that Chalfont, being exceptionally absent-minded, will not be much help in checking Whittaker's alibi (a fact of which Whittaker may be well aware).

There are certain differences between

the hanging of Frances Hasleigh and that of Joan Dawson which interest me . . . Have locked Joan in the punishment room for safety, and have been assured that Mr. Martin (who was shot tonight), will soon be well again . . .

Maria stifled a yawn, then added a few more lines:

When I come to reflect on what is probably the real answer to this riddle I am definitely revolted — yet in view of the many psychological treatises I have read, explaining in detail the working of the abnormal mind, I cannot help but think it is the only answer. Soon, I believe, I shall know.
The time is 1.15 a.m.

12

Next morning, Maria had Andrews relieved by the day porter, then looked in on Joan — still in bed and urgently demanding to know if her parents had been notified. This question Maria sidetracked, unwilling to admit that she had been too busy or too tired to attend to it so far. Finally she left with the assurance that breakfast would be sent in — then Joan was to dress and prepare for lessons Miss Tanby would bring.

Finally, after breakfast and chapel and instructions to Miss Tanby, she was free to pursue the matter that obsessed her. She sent for Professor Chalfont and, looking as vague and elderly as usual, he presently arrived in the study and sat blinking over his glasses across the desk.

'Can you tell me,' Maria asked, 'if you played chess with Mr. Whittaker, the science master, last night?'

'Last night? Chess?' The old man

frowned. 'Oh, yes, I played chess.'

'With Mr. Whittaker?'

'I think so, yes. I have been thinking such a lot about my address to the young ladies on the inner corolla of the *phacelia campanularia* that I do not recall much else.'

Maria gave an indulgent smile to hide her irritation.

'Please try and be more exact. *Did Mr. Whittaker play chess with you last night?*'

'Yes — he did,' Chalfont said, recollection dawning on his seamed face. 'We played one game, but I hardly remember anything about it, except that I took his rook. I don't remember many things outside my work, you know.'

'At what *time* last night did you play chess?'

'I'm afraid I don't know, Miss Black. I never know what time it is. I hardly remember to draw the blackout curtains at my study window until somebody tells me.'

'Was the game after blackout?' Maria asked quickly. 'Did you play by daylight or electric light?'

'Oh, it was electric light. I remember that . . . But what time it was I don't know. I rely on the chapel clock — when I hear it.'

'Thank you, Professor,' Maria sighed. 'I won't take up any more of your time.'

He went out, muttering to himself, and Maria tightened her lips.

'If he were not so brilliant a botanist I would consider asking the Board to pension him off,' she mused. 'I think he did have at least one game with Whittaker from what he says — but it is just as I suspected. Whittaker knew that Chalfont would never know the exact times and so he made it his alibi. Perhaps he played one game with him, either before or after he came back from that attack on Joan . . . More probably after. Hmmm — that reminds me. Whittaker showed no signs of Mr. Martin's punches — but a punch on the jaw does not always show. I fancy that the time has come for a 'showdown' with Mr. Whittaker.'

She took up the house phone and asked for Whittaker to be sent to her study immediately. A long time passed and nothing happened, then the instrument buzzed sharply and Miss Tanby's voice came floating through.

'We can't any of us find Mr. Whittaker anywhere, Miss Black! I'm certain he is nowhere in the building. I found his Fourth Form biochemistry lesson in uproar and no sign of Mr. Whittaker!'

Maria started. 'But he ought to be taking that lesson in the Fourth this hour! Very well, I'll look for myself,' Maria finished grimly, and switched off.

She left the study, starting on a tour of discovery that lasted for thirty minutes. In this time she covered every possible spot in the college, finishing up in Whittaker's study. She blamed herself, too, for not having come here in the first place, for she found it denuded of all Whittaker' belongings — just as his bedroom had been. In a word — the bird had flown!

'Evidently took fright,' Maria frowned. 'Hmm — now what? Just what is it that Bilton says in his incomparable *Crisis to a Case*? Ah, yes! 'Should your suspect become afraid of you and disappear on that account, follow him or her to the most likely hiding-place you have found in the course of your research . . . ' Dear me — excellent! Accordingly, the logical inference is that he *may* have gone to his tin mine rendezvous. As far as I know he is not yet aware that I know of the place.'

Quickly she donned her coat and beret, grabbed her umbrella and a large-sized torch, and marched resolutely towards the school gates. Recalling a treatise on tracking she took good care not to show herself any more than necessary when she had at last crossed the bridge over the Bollin which gave direct access to the grey soil land immediately facing the tin mines.

She proceeded by a series of dodging movements, hiding at intervals behind the higher rising of ground and peering over the top of them. Not that there was any sign of life. She reached the first tin mine without mishap and peered down into the depths.

No sounds came, so after a quick glance about her at the deserted land-scape, she climbed over the top of the stonework and felt for the iron ladder, began to go down gently, trying make as little noise as possible.

She reached the base of the shaft, breathing hard. Cautiously she peered into the gloom. Only it was not all gloom! There was a distinct big rectangle of yellow light in the near distance. She realized it must be the open door of Whittaker's rendezvous with the candles casting their light into the tunnel.

Her umbrella tightly gripped in her hand in readiness, she edged her way along. It occurred to her once to question why the door should be open, but she was so filled with the excitement of the chase she did not dwell on it too deeply. She finally gained the edge of the doorway and peered round it —

Then something happened! There was a sudden rush of movement in the tunnel and somebody seized her violently by the shoulders and gave her a mighty shove. She went stumbling forward helplessly into the underground room, brought up sharp against an old packing-case doing duty as a table and twirled round.

The door slammed. The tall figure of

Clive Whittaker was standing with his back to it, the yellow candlelight dancing on his harshly set face. And for the first time he was standing erect, without the stoop he evidently adopted as a disguise.

'I apologise for bundling you in here,' he said. 'I heard sounds out in the tunnel and so I left the door open to attract the intruder. I had no idea that it was you . . . But I am not totally surprised. I've long suspected that you were keeping tabs on my movements. And I resent it!' he finished bitterly. 'Can't a man go about his business without being watched?'

Maria looked about her, saw another upturned crate, and sat on it decisively. Then with her hands resting on the crook of her umbrella she regarded Whittaker with her cold blue eyes.

'He can, Mr. Whittaker — providing he does not break the law. That you have done — quite a few times. For one thing you are a thief. You have consistently stolen chemicals from the college laboratory and brought them here. I've seen them here, with the college tabs on the bottles.'

'What are a few chemicals to a college of that size?' he asked contemptuously.

'Of itself it is perhaps a trifling matter — However, there are other matters.' Maria sat back on the box as he stood waiting tensely. 'You see, I am not just a headmistress. I am an investigator. With the death of Frances Hasleigh in such terrible circumstances it became my duty to try and find out who killed her. I am a long way towards the solution — and in the course of my researches I was automatically led to you, and your connection with that girl.'

'I had no connections with her!' Whittaker said stonily.

'You are lying, Mr. Whittaker — or should I start calling you by your real name of Brownhill?'

He looked at her sharply.

'I see I touch a sore spot, Mr. Brownhill! For simplicity, however, I'll go on calling you Whittaker. You were not a stranger to Frances — you were her brother!'

He said nothing. Sinking his hand deeper in his coat pocket he waited.

'Your father was an inventor of explosives,' Maria proceeded. 'He invented a very powerful one and it was rejected by a then war-unconscious Government. He realised, however, that one day war would perhaps come and then would be the time for his secret to be used. In case of his death he handed on the formula to his children — yourself and your sister, Edith Lillian Brownhill, otherwise Frances Hasleigh. I believe that he divided his formula into two sections, half to you and half to your sister. Why I do not know, unless it was to be sure that you would always work together — or that without both of you the formula could never be used. He had the formula tattooed on Frances's and probably on your own forearms, no doubt with a chemical of his own choosing — invisible on the normal skin, but perfectly clear if sunburning occurred. In other words, that part of the skin containing the written symbols of the formula was so drained of its pigment that it could not tan. Any scientific laboratory can produce the effect. Thereby, when the surrounding skin is tanned, the untanned

322

part leaps into relief . . . you follow me, Mr. Whittaker?'

'Yes,' he breathed, clenching his fist. 'With what you know you can ruin everything I've worked for. You probably know plenty more, but you're not going to tell it! If you get me arrested now, just at the most vital part of my work, I'll never succeed. No, you are not going to tell anything, even if I have to kill you!'

'I do not doubt,' Maria said, watching him narrowly, 'that you would do as you say — '

She suddenly broke off, whizzed her umbrella round and struck Whittaker a resounding crack on the right pocket of his coat. His hand was plunged inside it and he gave a gasp of pain, jerked his hand out and an automatic with it. Again he got the umbrella upon him — on his shoulder this time — then right across his face. Dazed, the pain of the blows staggering him for a moment, he reeled back against the door. In those seconds Maria dived for it, pushed him on one side — but she got no further. He clutched her arm and whirled her back.

Simultaneously he fired his automatic and the bullet only just missed her, thudding into the table-crate.

Desperately, she twirled round. Whittaker was clearly prepared to kill her if he could — or at least find some violent way to silence her if only for a time. She watched him fixedly as he levelled the automatic again.

But the second shot never came. From somewhere outside there was a sudden commotion. The door shot open and as Whittaker swung round a truncheon came down on his wrist with resounding impact. With a yelp he dropped his gun and held his arm, gazing helplessly at a police officer, quickly followed by another constable, and then Superintendent Vaxley.

He entered as calmly as ever, tall and gangling. Her confidence returning, Maria noticed that he did not appear in the least surprised to see her,

'You are under arrest, Thomas Brownhill, for misrepresentation, assault, and trespass. Other charges will be enumerated at the station. Here's the warrant . . . All right, boys, take him out.'

'A moment,' Maria interrupted, coming forward. 'I was just in the middle of a most interesting exposé. I was just telling him his real life story. I'm sure he would like me to finish.'

'You can go to hell!' Whittaker retorted.

The superintendent nodded and glanced at him. 'You may as well hear the rest of it, Brownhill . . . You can help yourself by coming into the open, you know . . . Why did you pose as Major Hasleigh, a non-existent character? We know exactly what happened. A fortnight prior to your appearance at Roseway College you and your sister — alias Frances Hasleigh — were in a fisherman's cottage on the Dover coast, near the village of Milhaysham. You were both exhausted and had apparently been swimming for some hours. From that point we traced your movements. You came up to this part of the country and attacked a military major by the name of Ballam. You knocked him unconscious and stole his uniform. Next you were seen in this district for about ten days not as a major but as a civilian . . . From a chemist in Lexham you purchased a carton of dark tan powder and one of white talcum. You tried to get lotion and stain, but there was none to be had, and evidently you did not dare to seem too pressing. You said it was for a birthday present, no doubt to allay the suspicions of the chemist, for it was an odd purchase for a man to make. Your sister could have done it much better, but evidently you chose to do it yourself — '

'Been busy, haven't you?' Whittaker asked drily. 'All right, Edith — Frances — was my sister, and she didn't get the powder because I only happened to think of it on the spur of the moment while I was making food purchases.'

Vaxley glanced at Maria as she stood listening with a grim face.

'Disguised as a major with a red face and grey-white hair and moustache,' Vaxley resumed, 'you lodged just enough money, with a small surplus, in the Elmington branch bank — Elmington being the next spot where you appeared. You left no address with the bank, simply stating that you would forward an address once you had joined your unit abroad . . . Following this we have it on good authority that you had two forged ration books and identity cards made by a man in the East End of London. We've picked him up, by the way, and his description satisfies us. Undoubtedly he made out two books and cards in the names of Frances Hasleigh and Clive Whittaker — and on checking up we've proved that neither of you are registered in the census or at the food department. You gambled that your own — and your sister's — work would be done before the forgery was found out . . .

'Well, you next appeared at Roseway College with your bogus daughter. In the meantime you had no doubt been using this mine as your rendezvous. Those facts we know, Brownhill, and we've gone to a lot of trouble to make sure.'

He shrugged. 'All right — I admit it all. So what? I had my reasons!'

'There is much more than this, though,' Maria said eagerly — then glancing at Vaxley: 'I have already told him what I believe to be the true story of the formula, Super.'

'You have? I'd like to hear it.'

Maria repeated her theory and Vaxley nodded slowly at the end of it. Then he gave Whittaker a sharp look of inquiry. 'Is that correct?'

He shrugged. 'You have a talent for nosing into my affairs, Miss Black. Anything else?'

'Plenty!' she retorted. 'I suspected something queer from the moment the tan began to trickle on your face on the day you brought Frances to the school. I realized you were in disguise — but at that time I did not know why. In fact I still don't, unless it was all arranged to keep your identities hidden from somebody who was pursuing you for the sake of the formula. I believe that you selected Roseway College as a good hideout, and at first you went on living in this tin mine here while Frances studied the layout of the school. By a double-edged trick she got rid of the science master and you took his place. She had not a good knowledge of the district, so you told her she could find this mine easily enough from Roseway by following Sirius in a straight line. Right?'

Whittaker began to look less insolent and more surprised. Almost unconsciously he nodded.

'You wanted to get into the college because of the chemicals you needed for your formula,' Maria went on. 'Chemicals you could not get from any chemist without the necessity of signing for them: and that you might have found difficult. Your plan, as I see it, was for you and your sister to work together in the execution of the formula, but before it could be done she was murdered . . . You found out where the body was — a not very difficult matter considering that all the girls started talking about it in spite of my order — and to get the formula from your sister's arm you sunburned it with ultra-violet rays, photographed it, and then left the arm so burned as to be useless to anybody else looking for the formula . . .

'After I had surprised you once or twice in the laboratory with your chemicals you felt you needed somewhere safer and so you moved your stuff to the mine here. Last night you realised that the law was likely to close in on you quickly — that I knew too much — so, after your attack on Joan Dawson, you invented the alibi of playing chess with Professor Chalfont, knowing full well that his absent-mindedness would probably save you. Maybe you did play chess — '

'Yes, I played chess with him,' Whittaker said. He hesitated, then: 'Well, since most of what you have said is more or less correct I suppose I've nothing to gain by denying it.'

'Your gain will come in telling the truth,' Vaxley snapped out. 'What is all this chemicals business? What are you driving at?'

'It goes back rather a long way,' Whittaker answered quietly. 'Many years ago, our father tried to interest a then peace-loving Government in an explosive he had invented, but they wouldn't hear of it. My father was not bitter, but being a pretty keen student of history, and of Germany in particular, he was reasonably sure that one day war would come again, and when it did he wanted the Government to have his explosive, not in theory or formula but ready made up . . . He realised his children might be the ones to do the job, but he did not want only one of us to get the credit — or the brickbats. So, for safety in case other people tried to get hold of it, and to make sure that my sister and I would be more or less inseparable, he hit on an ingenious plan . . .

'He had fifty per cent of the formula tattooed on each of our forearms, doing it himself and using a bleaching acid which destroyed the pigment of the flesh everywhere the needle touched. The result was that the formula could only appear if the surrounding skin area were sunburned, or otherwise rendered brown. But not by stain, for that would blot out the formula as well. It had to be a natural brownness created by the action of the skin pigment itself. Obviously the solution to producing the formula at will was ultra-violet radiation . . . On top of this he made us swear that we would always remain as close as possible to each other, and neither of us would attempt to complete the formula single-handed.'

Whittaker paused for a moment, considering. Then:

'Well, dad died — and mother, too. Edith and I were not very old at that time and so we went to live with relations in Paris. But it seemed that the news of the valuable formula we possessed between us had somehow leaked out, for there were several occasions when we were in danger from European agents trying to get the truth out of us. We managed to escape these troubles, but when war approached things began to get really hot. One German agent in particular was determined to learn where the formula was and what it was about, so we decided — upon this advance warning — to get out of France right away, come to England again, and seek the protection of the Government once we had handed the completed explosive sample over. You see, without this we could not approach the authorities — for we had elected to sneak into England and because of that we had no identification, very few credentials to show we were British — and anyway, after spending so many years abroad, we stood the chance of even being locked up as doubtful to the country's interests while inquiry was made concerning us. That would have meant our being separated and the explosive could not be made. So we decided on another plan that might hold up long enough for us to get an explosive sample finished.

'We managed to commandeer a motor-boat from the French coast and it brought us to within a mile of the Dover coast. It was a dim, misty summer night. Turning it adrift we dived overboard and swam the rest of the distance, landing finally near the fisherman's cottage, which our French guide had arranged for us. We stayed only one night, then we were on our way again. We were in England, and that was all that counted . . . Now what?'

Whittaker looked from Maria to Vaxley, then shrugged.

'I don't need to go into the details because you have them already, Superintendent. I changed what French money we had into English currency and lodged it in a quiet, out of the way bank. I had the name of a man able to arrange ration books and identity cards, and this, too, I fixed — once we had our plan clearly set out. It was to come to the college, mainly for the possibility of getting chemicals. To this end I stole a military uniform from a major, and it was after this that I went to London to fix the ration and identity cards because Edith and I knew now what we were going to do. We had it all fixed that somehow she would rid the school of the resident science master and let me take his place, so I had my cards fixed for that possibility to begin with . . . Until she accomplished this job she was to take what chemicals she could from the college laboratory and bring them down here to me, for we naturally realised that down here we had a fine rendezvous . . .

'Then, out of a clear sky, she was murdered!' Whittaker's jaw set viciously. 'Somebody, obviously in league with the European end who had traced our movements, was still after us and had struck! But I felt reasonably sure they had not got the secret. Edith was not the kind of girl to ever betray a secret trust, even if she died for it — which she did . . .

'It was not a time for tears and sorrow. I had to get the rest of that formula before she was buried. You guessed how I did it, Miss Black, but when I had just finished my job in the mausoleum something disturbed me. I thought I heard somebody in the crypt above. I decided to get out quick . . . Afterwards I worked at the formula all I could and in the meantime tried to imagine who had killed my sister. I didn't get very far, though . . .

'Then, yesterday — about an hour or so before supper-bell — I returned to my study unexpectedly from the laboratory — where I had been doing some genuine experiments connected with my school work — to find Joan Dawson waiting for me. She said she had come to ask about a point in biochemistry, and when I had answered it she left. Half an hour later I discovered that my formula, which I had written on a piece of paper and hidden behind a picture, had gone! I felt sure that she had taken it — and even more sure when after dark I saw her in the quadrangle while I was out taking a stroll before bedtime. She had a travelling bag with her and was obviously leaving the school. I followed her, convinced by now that she was somehow responsible for my sister's death, and my intention was to force the truth out of her. I seized her by the back of the neck and by thumb and finger pressure forced her into unconsciousness. When she recovered I was trying to find out if she had taken my formula or not when you came up, Miss Black, and that hefty thug with you. I always carry a gun, so I fired at him — and then ran for it . . .

'I realised things were getting too hot, so I decided to get out. I had intended finishing my work down here and perhaps tackling Joan Dawson later on, for I couldn't leave the secret in her hands. I had a copy of the formula, of course — Frances's half anyway, on a photographic plate — and my own half is on my arm here. So — well, I haven't finished my job after all, and now it looks as though I never shall!'

There was a silence as Whittaker looked

from one to the other of them. Then Maria asked a question:

'I notice, Mr Whittaker, that you do not refer to your earlier attack on Joan when you tried to strangle her in the same way as your sister was strangled.'

'I don't understand. The only time I attacked Joan was yesterday when she was escaping. I was even prepared to kill her to avenge my sister, for I'm sure she's connected with it.'

'What other attack is this, Miss Black?' Vaxley asked, puzzled.

'Joan Dawson was hanged in her locker yesterday evening by an unknown, and I rescued her,' Maria shrugged. 'From her description it seems to have been a man, and a strong one — '

'I don't know anything about it!' Whittaker declared flatly.

'Or did you just conveniently forget it?' Vaxley asked. 'You have no proof that the girl took the formula: if she could get into your study, then so could anyone else! Was the door locked?'

'Well, no. I had only intended being away a few minutes, but my laboratory

337

work interested me so much I forgot the lapse of time.'

Vaxley smiled unbelievingly. 'So anybody could have gone into your study besides Joan Dawson. Why pick on her?'

Whittaker's face became sullen. 'It was the obvious conclusion — especially when I saw her leaving the school with her bag packed.'

'Are you quite sure you were not waiting to see if she *did* leave the school?' Vaxley demanded.

'All right, I was,' Whittaker admitted. 'I expected that she would if she had got the formula. When she did I felt that it was conclusive.'

Vaxley resumed his questioning. 'What makes you so sure that the Government would not have given you protection and facilities to work had you only presented yourself with your sister in the proper way?'

'After the way they kicked out my father — '

'I suggest,' Vaxley interrupted, his eyes narrowing, 'that you deliberately *avoided* presenting yourself to the Government, went through all this subterfuge for one purpose only — to have the secret entirely to yourself and cash in on it!'

Whittaker gave a start. 'Are you insinuating that I killed my own sister?'

'I am merely making a suggestion: even from your own confession you were amazingly callous in the way you hauled your sister's dead body about to get the secret from her — '

'I had to! I could easily have been discovered in the room where she was lying — '

'Nor,' Vaxley interrupted, 'did you apparently blink an eyelash when it came to desecrating her corpse by burning her forearm. To you I suggest that she was less than nothing, that she had a secret on her dead body that you wanted.'

'This is absurd!' Whittaker exclaimed bitterly. 'If, as you undoubtedly are suggesting, I hanged her, why did I not get the formula then instead of waiting until she was brought back to the school?'

'For obvious reasons — you had no way of sunburning her arm in the clearing, and for another thing I believe that Joan Dawson was showing signs of recovering consciouness. You were not sure whether she saw you or not and thereafter were wary of her. It is most extraordinary that your sister was first rendered unconscious by a hand grip behind the ears, and then you use the same method on Joan Dawson — '

'Rubbish!' Whittaker snapped. 'Anybody with a knowledge of self-defence can use that grip.'

Vaxley did not seem to hear. He went on deliberately:

'I believe that Joan Dawson kept a watch on you and the formula and that she perhaps stole it finally in order to hand it over to the law. That is accepting your theory that she did steal it from your study. You knew that it was the proof of your guilt and so you tried to stop her getting away. As to that other attempt in the locker, I imagine that you tried that, too, but it did not quite come off.'

Maria cleared her throat gently. 'Perhaps I should mention, Super, that I was attacked in this mine on the night I found it. And it was not Mr. Whittaker who did it. I am almost certain that it was probably Joan Dawson, wearing Frances Hasleigh's shoes. From my watch locket was stolen the half of the formula which I had obtained from the photographic plate hidden behind Mr. Whittaker's dressing table mirror.'

'You mean that it was you who attacked me that night in my bedroom!' Whittaker exclaimed.

'It was my assistant, Mr. Martin.'

'I thought that that was Joan Dawson's work, too,' Whittaker muttered, frowning.

'You thought too many things,' Vaxley said. 'As for Joan attacking you, Miss Black, she probably mistook you in the dark for Whittaker — '

'Hardly,' Maria said quietly. 'She knew my locket so she must have known it was me.'

'Well, then, the only explanation is that she was trying to get the whole formula together in order to indict Whittaker here, and she tackled even you to do it knowing that you had part of it. Possibly she even thought you had all of it . . . How did she explain her breaking bounds in order to come here?'

'She told a most extraordinary story.' Maria sighed. 'Tell me, Mr. Whittaker, have you at any time moved any food from here and placed it in the school pavilion?'

He looked vaguely surprised. 'Yes I did — at one time. It struck me as a good place to hide what I had stored up. Tinned stuff mostly and some toffee. I had planned to use it if ever I needed to move on in a hurry. Far quicker to the pavilion than to come here.'

'Thank you,' Maria murmured, pondering.

Vaxley resumed his hostile questioning. 'Mr. Whittaker, where were you between four-thirty and six on the day your sister was murdered?' He glanced at Maria. 'I rather thought you were going to get this information, Miss Black.'

She shrugged and smiled. 'The police are so much more efficient,' she murmured, but she waited with obvious interest for Whittaker's answer.

'Between four-thirty and six? I went out to the village to do some shopping.'

'Correct — and at approximately

four-forty-five you bought a set of six photographic half-plate panchromatic plates from Baxter's, the chemists.'

'Yes, I did,' Whittaker admitted. 'Then I went for a stroll — '

'And got back to the school at six-thirty. We know all that. Yet from the village to the school it is no more than twenty minutes' walk at the outside. Where were you in the intervening time? Can you prove you went for a walk?'

'How the devil can I? I don't know anybody about here — but I went for a walk!'

'Through Bollin's Wood perhaps?' Vaxley asked.

'I did not! Anyway, supposing I did how could I know that my sister would be there then?'

'*Then!*' Vaxley cried. 'That little word 'then!' You knew that she was going to Bollin's Wood! Come on, Whittaker — out with it!'

'Yes, I knew it,' he muttered. 'I heard them talking it over in the quadrangle as I passed them — those six girls, my sister among them.'

'You then purchased panchromatic

343

plates because you knew just what you intended doing,' Vaxley stated grimly. 'You were ready to take a photograph of your sister's arm even before she was dead — '

'No, no!' Whittaker shouted. 'I got the plates so that I could photograph her arm the moment we could get together.'

'I don't believe you,' Vaxley said. 'You knew just what you were going to do from the moment you heard the girls talking in the quadrangle! You got the silk rope and then went out to buy your plates — with murder in your heart!'

'Lies!' Whittaker shouted hoarsely. 'Why the devil don't you use your smart tricks on Joan Dawson and see what she had to do with it? I'll swear it was she — or, if not, Robert Lever. I suppose you have conveniently forgotten that piece of evidence?'

'No,' Vaxley retorted. 'If anything, that fountain pen makes things all the blacker for you. By his own statement Lever forgot that he had left it on his desk in the Sixth Form room. Quite shortly afterwards you took the form in science, saw the inscribed pen, and realized what a useful thing it might prove when you wanted to deflect evidence. You made it your business to find out if Lever was still in the district — which he was.'

Whittaker's face had gone pale. 'You're right off the track! I loved my sister, I tell you!'

'I am not going to argue any more,' Vaxley said briefly 'The rest can be thrashed out in court . . . All right, boys, take him out.'

Whittaker was led from the underground room. Then Vaxley walked over to the chemical bottles and studied them. Finally he picked up the formula lying beside them and studied it.

'Our own chemists had better have a look at this lot before we move them,' he commented. 'If there *is* a new explosive here something will have to be done about it . . . You are very quiet, Miss Black. Is the finding of the killer, even though he is not officially charged yet, something of a shock to you?'

'Sorry, Super; I was just thinking something out to myself . . . You certainly have built up a case against Whittaker. Well, you followed your angle all right — and I am following mine.'

'But, Miss Black, there is nothing more to follow! Whittaker has as good as admitted the whole thing.'

'I am afraid,' Maria said, 'I do not agree with you . . . However, for the moment I have nothing more to say. I still think I can throw some light on this business from my own viewpoint. If this should be so, where can I reach you?'

'I shall be in this district for a day or two yet until these chemicals are analysed . . . And now, perhaps I may see you safely to the outer world?'

'Thank you, Super — if you will pardon me a moment.'

Maria turned to the table-crate, took out her small penknife. In a moment or two she had dislodged the bullet Whittaker had fired at her and tossed it up and down in her palm.

'I'd like to keep this, if I may?'

Vaxley picked up Whittaker's gun from where it had fallen on the floor.

'If you wish, Miss Black — but I must

have that bullet and the one which hit your henchman when this case is prepared for trial. No more than two days' grace, I'm afraid.'

'That will be ample,' Maria smiled. 'Now I am ready to return above.'

The two constables and Whittaker were at the top of the shaft, waiting. One of them Vaxley detailed to stay on the spot, then with Whittaker handcuffed to the remaining man the party set off towards the Bollin River bridge.

'Tell me, Super,' Maria remarked presently, 'how did you arrive so opportunely to save me from Whittaker?'

'Simple. We've had our eye on the mine for some time now. We saw him come this morning, and shortly afterwards we followed. I felt we had better see what was going on.'

Maria nodded, slowed her walk until the constable and Whittaker were out of earshot, then she asked another question.

'Did you by any chance find time to look into the records of the parents of the various girls involved? You remember that I said it might prove of use in this case.'

'Yes, we looked into it, but nothing came out of it — nothing vital anyway. All the parents are quite respectable members of the community and have been domiciled in Britain for many years, most of them all their lives. They all seem pretty moneyed, with Herbert Dawson topping the list.'

'Being an industrialist, and in these days, that is hardly surprising,' Maria murmured, thinking.

'Seems to control quite a lot of organizations,' Vaxley reflected. 'But he seemed to only achieve real power after his second marriage.'

'So — twice married,' Maria said, looking up sharply.

'Yes. His first wife died five years ago, by whom he had the girl Joan. Then his second wife came on the scene and her influence seemed to have a big effect on him. He rose to real greatness. I imagine she must be a woman who wields a lot of the power behind the throne.'

'Her name being Clara, I believe?'

'Clara Maude Dawson, née Einhart,' Vaxley replied. 'Sounds kind of foreign to me. Frankly, Miss Black, I can't understand what in the world such information is worth.'

'Later, perhaps, I will repay your courtesy for giving it,' Maria smiled. 'I suppose you don't know where Mr. Dawson met his present wife?'

'He could have met her anywhere, I suppose. He travelled extensively before the war.'

Maria relapsed into silence. It was clear some deep thought was in her mind.

13

It was dinner-time when Maria arrived back at Roseway and she found an official letter waiting for her stamped Somerset House and relayed from its evacuation address in North-West England. She tore the envelope quickly and smiled over the form she pulled out.

Joan Dawson — sex, female — born 1924 — London. Parents, Herbert Dawson (Steel Exporter) and Evelyn Beatrice Dawson, née Montrose (Housewife).

'Excellent, Maria' she murmured, 'There are times when you astonish even yourself!'

She folded the copy certificate away carefully then brought out her record book and began writing:

I must confess to an admiration for Superintendent Vaxley for the way in which he has painstakingly built up a case against Whittaker — alias Brownhill — though I feel there must still be a doubt in the Super's mind because he has not yet issued a murder warrant for Whittaker, but has arrested him on charges of misrepresentation, assault, etc.

Everything he cites against Whittaker apparently ties up, and were it not for other angles I would also be inclined to think that Whittaker did murder his sister. I cannot, however, forget his genuine grief at the graveside. No man, no matter how good an actor, could have simulated grief so convincingly.

I feel interested in the fact that Whittaker bought his photographic plates before the death of his sister, and I believe his story that he had intended to photograph her arm so he and she could work together. Why not? It would be the quickest way to get the formula in its entirety and there was little time for them to be together for long periods without exciting suspicion. To have written it all down on a piece of paper might have been too risky — though obviously Whittaker was forced into this in the end for simplicity. Clearly, the plans he had in mind to ensure safety all fell to pieces upon the girl's death. I have discovered that Joan Dawson's mother died five years ago, a point that intrigues me, more particularly so as the second wife seems to have boosted Herbert Dawson, the girl's father, to amazing industrial eminence since the marriage. There, I think, lies the root cause of this very intricate but fascinating crime puzzle.

Superintendent Vaxley is going to be very surprised if I solve it after all!

The time is 12.55 p.m. and I am feeling in need of a most hearty repast.

Five minutes later she entered the teachers' dining-hall, and from her frozen countenance it was plain that she was not intending to respond to the curious looks cast at her. By this time, of course, her spasmodic appearances and disappearances had been noticed by everybody

. . . Miss Tanby, however, did not lack courage even if she was without sex appeal.

'Miss Black, did you find Mr. Whittaker?' she whispered, leaning sideways.

Maria ate for a moment in silence, then: 'Yes, I found him — and we shall have to advertise once again for a science master. Mr. Whittaker will not be able to continue his duties.'

Tanby waited for some further explanation. Since none followed she asked another question.

'Do you believe it is safe yet for Joan Dawson to be released from the punishment room?'

'No,' Maria replied calmly.

'No? You mean that she is still in danger of being killed? After all, Miss Black, you can be frank with me, surely? Or even with us,' she went on, raising her voice and looking round. 'Every one of us knows that Frances Hasleigh was murdered, that the police have been — and presumably still are — investigating, so — Was Mr. Whittaker arrested for the murder?'

Maria sighed. 'Since you force the issue, Miss Tanby, he was arrested, yes — on suspicion.'

'And it was he who attacked Joan in the Bollin Wood last night?' Tanby asked eagerly.

'It was — but it was not he who attacked her earlier in the evening when she was nearly hanged in her locker. So, you see, there is still a need for precaution.'

'You mean that — that the police may have made a mistake in arresting Whittaker?'

'Let us just say that they have taken the obvious course whereas I have — er — hmm! After all,' Maria broke off, looking round on the attentive faces, 'this is neither the time nor the place to discuss the problem of Frances Hasleigh's murder. I would prefer to let the matter drop — for the moment.'

'Joan Dawson is getting most fractious,' Tanby said worriedly. 'I had to talk to her severely this morning.'

'You did? Why?'

'She seems to resent being locked up. I set her studies as you ordered, but she never even troubled to open the books — then when I went along to inquire how she was getting on she as good as threw the books at me, demanded to know why you had not sent for her people, and — well, I never saw a girl so furious! I had always thought of her as so quiet. Of course, she blazed up a bit that day in the classroom when she and Vera Randal fought — '

Maria reflected. 'In a way I can understand the girl's emotions. Just the same, she must stay where she is, at least for a while. I shall be sending for her parents very shortly.'

Tanby hesitated over a further question, then seeing the firm set of Maria's lips, she thought better of it. The rest of the meal passed routinely, with Maria confining her remarks to matters essential to the school's curriculum.

'And this afternoon,' she observed, 'I shall follow out my normal school procedure and take the Fourth Form in mathematics, Miss Tanby.'

Maria got up from the table and glanced at her watch. There was a full thirty minutes yet before class-time, so after a call in her study she went across to the sanatorium and found Pulp Martin just at the end of his dinner and surrounded by a haze of strong cigarette smoke.

'Hi-ya!' he greeted, waving an arm. He studied Maria's face keenly. 'Say, I know that look! You've found somethin'!'

Maria drew up a chair and sat down. 'Yes, I have found something — in fact almost everything — but I can't fit things into place until you are up and about again. Then I have an assignment for you, in London. I am going to play a hunch, and there is no other person who can help me do it.'

'Yeah?' His big face lighted. 'Somethin' tough?'

'I need somebody to go to London because there are two questions I want answering. First, I want you to find out all you can about Herbert Dawson, the industrialist. He is the father of the girl Joan Dawson who is so involved in this whole business. I'd suggest that you begin inquiry with his firm — Herbert Dawson

Limited, who have their headquarters in Great Shandon Street, near Trafalgar Square. I cannot advise you what to do then — whether to strike up an acquaintance with one of his employees or something, but I must find out all about him. Is that asking too much?'

Pulp grinned. 'I've got ways of finding out things — especially in a pint-sized country like this — which would get a high-class dame like you stymied. I'll find out everything double quick — or else . . . What's the other point?'

'I have just learned that Joan's present mother is her stepmother and that her own mother died five years ago. Her name was Evelyn Beatrice Dawson, formerly Montrose. I wish to establish, beyond a shadow of doubt, where she died.'

'But look, Maria, couldn't you get that from the death record people?'

'Yes, I could — but I fancy it would not tell me all that I want to know. I think this final piece of information will clear up the whole mystery and Frances Hasleigh's killer will be there for all to see, convicted 'beyond all disproving!'

'I've followed you this far, Maria,' Pulp sighed, 'but this slug sort of got me stopped for a bit. What's been happenin' in the meantime?'

'Whittaker has been arrested on various charges, and a strong hint that he murdered Frances was thrown in.'

'Well, that ain't a surprise. Do things sort of check up on it being him?'

'Most accurately. He has admitted practically everything that we deduced — namely, that the girl was his sister, that she had a formula tattooed on her forearm, that he shot you last night — ' Maria paused and fished two bullets from the pocket of her dress. 'Which reminds me,' she added. 'I thought I had better check up. I drew his fire, you see. This bullet here was fired at me this morning by him, and as you can see it is identical to the one fired at you last night.'

'Right enough, but what does it prove?'

'That Whittaker is speaking the truth! Since he freely admits to attacking Joan Dawson and firing a gun at you — both serious charges — I am prepared to believe that everything else he said was true also. Few people, if you know psychology, tell a story that is half lies and half truth. Definitely one or the other, especially so when life itself is at stake.'

'Maybe you're right,' Pulp admitted. 'But things look bad for him. That Vaxley guy has sure got everything wrapped up with neat bows on it.'

'Which I may untie with one pull on the ribbon,' Maria smiled. 'That is what I am aiming at, Mr. Martin — not so much to prove the identity of the real killer — though that is important enough — but to feel the drama of that glorious moment when I shall have proved myself the equal — if not superior — of the police! To me that will be a foretaste of heaven!'

Pulp was wide-eyed at her unexpected emotion; then she gave a prim cough and got to her feet.

'To return to the matter at issue. You understand exactly what I require of you?'

'Right on the nose. I'm ready to go the moment you can shake the sleeping draught out of that sawbones . . . Be sorry

359

in one way, though — I get a kick out of watching that blonde nurse I've gotten myself. She's got a swell pair of hips — the swinging kind. Yum-yum!'

Maria coughed slightly. 'I shall make it well worth your while to forsake the pleasure of your nurse's — er — hips, Mr. Martin, believe me . . . And now I'll have a word with Dr. Wood, and if I can get him to release you please come along to my study and see me. If I am not there inform one of the staff so I can be located.'

Maria went on to the surgery and found Dr. Wood busily writing at his desk.

'I am not a doctor, Dr. Wood,' she said calmly, 'but I am quite convinced that my friend Mr. Martin is no longer a candidate for this sanatorium. I want him released.'

Wood reflected. 'Well, I think a few more days — '

'I believe,' Maria interrupted, 'he is malingering! As for his arm, there is nothing to fear. As I entered this morning to note his progress he raised his hand over his head in greeting. I do not think his arm can be so very bad if he can do that.'

'You're right,' Wood agreed grimly. 'I'll see that he is discharged immediately.'

Smiling to herself, Maria departed. Her watch told her she had just three minutes to reach the Fourth Form room and relax over the brain-stunning mysteries of square roots.

★　★　★

Maria felt much better when she had finished tormenting her young ladies with the horrors of advanced mathematics.

It was three o'clock now and she had about fifteen minutes before her next departure — biochemistry for the Sixth instead of the arrested Whittaker. Since it was not Maria's way to waste fifteen minutes she went up to the punishment room, gave Mason a brief interval for a walk then entered the little room to find Joan lying on the bed with her hands locked behind her head

'My people here?' she asked eagerly, her eyes bright.

'Not yet.' Maria answered quietly. 'But they will be — I promise you that.'

'Why do you keep putting it off, ma'm?' the girl asked in bewilderment. 'What have I done that you won't let me see them?'

Maria found a chair and seated herself. 'There have been many things to do, and I have not had much chance to inform your parents. But I am going to do so — later this afternoon. However, I came here for a little chat. Why did you throw your textbooks at Miss Tanby?'

Joan sighed. 'I don't like her! She snoops about and is so beastly cocky with her orders. Here was I cooped up; then she came in and said you've got to study this and that — so I threw the books at her!'

Maria saw that the books still lay by the door with their covers bent back. There was also an ink bottle that had upset on the woodwork. Across the door was a great blue stain where it had struck.

'While I can understand your being resentful, Joan, I will not have this sort of behaviour,' Maria said. 'Next time Miss

362

Tanby brings you your work you will obey her.'

'I'm sorry,' the girl muttered. 'It's just that I get like that at times. Nerves, I suppose.'

'At your age!' Maria exclaimed. 'Absurd!'

'It isn't!' Joan insisted, her dark eyes shining. 'I get fits like this at times, when everybody seems to become unbearable to me. I want to clear them out of my way, throw things at them ... I don't know why,' she finished simply. 'It just is, that's all.'

'It is a weakness you must try and master, Joan,' Maria said quietly. 'I have heard you refer to your nervous fits before. You see, you are not much more than a child yet, and if you do not overcome this trouble it will overcome you ... Tell me, are there any things you particularly hate? I know I have my own private dislikes — such as the — er — effluvium from a wet dog!'

The girl looked rather surprised for a moment, then said slowly: 'I don't like teachers like Miss Tanby. I detest history and mathematics — and sunshine, and days when there is no wind blowing.'

Maria gave a start and glanced through the barred window.

'You mean you don't like a beautiful sunny day like this?'

'Yes!' Joan was so emphatic she sounded rude. 'I like the wind, the rain, the confusion . . . I even like this war,' she went on eagerly. 'It's exciting! Death everywhere and no peace. No deadly calm where nothing ever happens.'

'Are you fond of your parents, Joan?'

'Of dad yes. I love him dearly — but I don't like my stepmother! She's hard, cruel, and domineering. I'm afraid of her! It was she who suddenly sent me to Roseway here, as though she had decided on it on the spur of the moment. I didn't want to come!'

For some reason tears started suddenly into Joan's eyes, then she threw herself full length on the bed, her face buried in the pillow and her shoulders heaving convulsively.

Maria watched her for a moment, then she put her arm about the girl.

'Come, come, my dear! Whatever is the

matter? You can tell me. I am your foster-mother while you are in this school, remember. For Heaven's sake, child, what is it?'

'I can't tell you exactly,' Joan's chin quivered. 'You would think me a crybaby. I try and look tough just so that I can get by — but I'm not tough really. I'm frightened! Scared to death of everybody and everything! Just that nobody really likes me, I suppose. I'm only happy when I'm alone. Oh, Miss Black, don't you understand? I haven't a soul in the world outside dad who cares a hoot for me. My stepmother hates me and foisted me into this school so I could be removed from home, where we got on each other's nerves. And dad is too busy to care where I am. I've no brothers or sisters . . . When I lost mum I lost everything. Oh — I wish I were dead!'

Maria patted her arm gently.

'You pretty nearly were on two occasions, my dear . . . Now you just try and keep a hold over these emotions of yours and I'll have you out of this room as quickly as possible. Promise me?'

Joan gave a slow nod, her face white and drawn.

Maria got up quietly and left the room, then when she had locked the door her face set harshly. There was a light of naked cruelty in her blue eyes.

She turned as Mason reappeared to take up his position as guard once again.

'Between you and me, Miss Black,' he said candidly, 'that lass in there is a rum 'un. She spends half her time dead quiet, then she comes bangin' on this 'ere door fair fit to bring the place down.'

Maria nodded absently. Then Mason seemed to remember something.

'Oh, there's a man in your study to see you — a fellow with red hair and an American accent. I met him as I went out into the quad for a smoke. He asked to see you.'

'Thank you,' Maria acknowledged briefly, and went on her way. When she got to her study Pulp Martin was there ready and waiting and apparently as Herculean as ever.

'Trouble, Maria?' he asked quickly, as he noticed her unusually stern expression.

She gave a little sigh. 'You might call it that, Mr. Martin. Sometimes it is bitter to have one's inner suspicion realised. However — ' She broke off and went to her cashbox, handed some money over. 'Here you are, Mr. Martin. Double pay, and report back to me at the earliest moment. By telephone if need be.'

'Rely on me,' he nodded. 'And look after yourself!'

She shook his big paw and then moved over to her desk as he went striding out. For a while she gazed fixedly in front of her.

'That anyone could be so diabolical!' she whispered. 'I was not far wrong when I recorded in my book that the psychological implications appalled me. Now it is more than an implication: I am convinced of it. I *have* the answer, but so sombre a one I find it hard to believe. My nose for investigation has definitely led me into the mind of a fiend!'

She glanced at her watch: it was more than time for her lesson to the Sixth on biochemistry. She was not in such great form this time and the girls got away with their mistakes fairly easily. Maria seemed to spend most of her time glancing through the window, and when she evidently saw whom she was waiting for she brought the lesson to an abrupt close and departed — to hurry out to the postman as he entered the quadrangle.

He had one letter for her, the envelope headed in the left-hand corner — *Boys' and Girls' Forestry Organisations*.

Entering her study she ripped the flap and intently read the letter she withdrew from the envelope:

Dear Madam: June 18th, 1940
In answer to your inquiry our files show no trace of a Clive Whittaker having been enrolled with us; but we have information on the other party you mention. A Joan Dawson of London was a member of our organisation three years ago, and rose to the position of patrol leader.

She is recorded as having been a girl with notable talent for guide-work and leadership of younger members. She passed the necessary examinations to gain this promotion, i.e. self-defence, tracking, fire-making, knot-tying, analysis of flora and fauna, and so forth.

Answering your further inquiry, the triple knot is indeed our emblem, as you will note on the top of our memorandum herewith.

Hoping to have been of service,
Truly yours,
(Capt.) Robert Desmond,
Chief Forester.

Maria lowered the letter slowly, and smiled in relief. 'Last links in the chain, Maria,' she murmured. 'There remains only Mr. Martin, and a good deal of typing on your part if Superintendent Vaxley is to have a complete dossier of this most interesting but rather horrible case. However, first thing first.'

The first thing was a pot of strong tea brewed by her own hand: the next thing after it was to take out her black book and commence a long and difficult sifting of the various pointers she had written down. But it was interesting now because everything fitted automatically into place.

She began the work at a quarter-past four and it was nearly half-past seven in the evening when she had finished. She clipped the numbered sheets of typing together, read them through, then an hour later went in search of a rather belated tea.

This done she had to possess herself in patience until she heard from Pulp Martin. Not until then could she launch that onslaught of facts that she had tested, proved, and cross-checked . . .

Two days went by for Maria, days in which she chafed bitterly at the delay . . . In another chat with Joan she told her that her parents would soon be arriving, but did not add that she had not yet sent for them. Joan herself merely accepted the information with a kind of silent bitterness.

Then, just after tea-time on the third day, Maria received a telephone call from London. She snatched up the receiver.

'Yes — yes? Miss Black speaking.'

'Hi-ya, Maria! This is Pulp shootin' his face off!'

She pulled a scratch pad to her and

wrote busily as his voice began to chatter in the receiver. For several minutes he talked with hardly a break and Maria's hand executed shorthand at lightning speed. At the end of it she was smiling triumphantly.

'Magnificent, Mr. Martin! I have it all down. You have done wonders . . . The moment you get back here I shall see that you have the highest remuneration.'

'Okay,' his voice replied cheerfully. 'I'll be back some time tomorrow. Be seein' you.'

Maria hung up the receiver, waited a moment or two, then dialled the operator. In a few minutes she was speaking to Herbert Dawson.

'Something really important has come up which I am afraid only a personal visit by yourself and your wife can resolve.'

'But just what is it, Miss Black? In regard to Joan, do you mean?'

'Yes, I'm afraid so. I'd like you both to come over here tomorrow. It is an urgent matter I cannot decide for myself and I'd much rather talk to you and Mrs. Dawson personally than over the telephone.'

'Oh, very well, Miss Black, if that is the way you want it. I cannot imagine why both of us should be needed, but we'll be there. Will about eleven tomorrow morning suit you?'

'Admirably!' Maria agreed. 'And thank you so much.'

She rang off, ran her fingers up and down her watch-chain, then again she picked up the telephone and rang up Vaxley at the local police headquarters. He had to be fetched from his room in the hotel opposite.

'This is very unexpected, Miss Black. Anything wrong?'

'That depends on the point of view, Super. But I have most certainly got some information which I think will interest you, particularly if you have it before the approaching trial.'

'Connected with Whittaker?'

'Definitely so — and Lever, too, if it comes to that. I am sure you would like to be saved from putting your foot in it, wouldn't you?'

'Look here, Miss Black, what information *have* you got? Can't you tell it me now? My work in this district is over now: the chemists have been and analysed those chemicals. They do constitute a mighty explosive, by the way, and the Government has taken over the formula pending the law's decision in regard to Whittaker ... I'm leaving for London again tomorrow.'

'Then delay it, for your own good,' Maria insisted. 'Be here at eleven tomorrow morning, and bring a couple of constables with you. You might leave them in the lodge where they won't be seen: I'll make the necessary arrangements. Then if need arises they can be reached by the house phone straight away. Understand?'

'Frankly, I don't — and if it were anybody else but you, Miss Black, I'd think twice before complying. However — '

'I'll expect you at eleven then, Super,' she said calmly, and put the receiver back.

Turning to her shorthand notes she began to type them out, adding them finally to the typed dossier she had already made. Then with a flourish, in green ink, she wrote across the front sheet:

The Case of Frances Hasleigh. Maria Black's Conclusions.

'Maybe I am wasted as a Headmistress?' she reflected. 'And yet, somehow, life here is so very interesting. Sometimes in a college for young ladies one can find crime and peril more rampant than in the darkest alleys of a great city . . . '

She clenched her fist on the desk for a moment, then set about her preparations for retirement . . .

14

Maria was not in the least interested in the college routine the following morning. After breakfast she hurried through the chapel prayers in record time. Then she went straight to her study and sat down with the air of a judge facing an empty court.

She had an hour to wait, and she spent it thinking deeply — then at a minute to eleven Superintendent Vaxley arrived. He greeted her cordially enough, but it was clear from his expression that he had his doubts even yet as to what was afoot.

'You are a most extraordinary woman, Miss Black,' he said, 'but I hope that all this business is not just to try out some theory or other. Time is very valuable to me.'

'And to me,' Maria said composedly, sitting back in her chair 'Everything that will happen this morning will be absolutely vital — to you, to me, and to the interests of the law in general. You brought your two constables?'

'And put them in the porter's lodge, yes. Naturally I don't understand the reason for the request.'

'You will,' Maria smiled. 'Any moment now I am expecting Mr. and Mrs. Dawson here. I shall take the liberty of introducing you as Mr. Shaw, if you don't mind. I wish to avoid all hint of the fact, at first, that you are connected with the law.'

Vaxley looked his astonishment. 'Well, all right — Look here, are you trying to prove that they are mixed up in this business?'

'First things first, Superintendent. As an officer of the law you should know the danger of words without proof. Ah! There are Mr. and Mrs. Dawson coming in at the gates now.'

Maria half rose and looked through the window. Then she sat back and waited, her lips tight.

Before long there was a knock at the door and Mr. and Mrs. Dawson were admitted, neither of them looking particularly cordial.

'So good of you to come,' Maria greeted them, getting to her feet and shaking hands. 'May I introduce Mr. Shaw, a great friend of mine.'

They shook hands all round and then settled themselves in the chairs Maria had already provided. Herbert Dawson glanced doubtfully at Vaxley. Maria made a brief excuse and pressed her house phone switch.

'Have Joan Dawson released from the punishment room and sent in to me, will you, please?'

'Yes, Miss Black.'

Mrs. Dawson gave Maria a rather acid look. 'I don't wish to seem discourteous, Miss Black,' she said briefly, 'but if our conversation is to be concerned with Joan I feel sure that Mr. Shaw here will be — er — well, redundant.'

Maria's smile quickly faded. 'The law is never redundant, Mrs. Dawson,' she replied. 'I made a slight error in introducing Mr. Shaw here. I should have said Superintendent Vaxley of Scotland

Yard. As you will undoubtedly be aware from the newspapers he has been engaged on the case of Frances Hasleigh . . . Forgive my little deception, but I did not wish to alarm you too soon. Better that you be comfortable first.'

'What are you talking about, Miss Black?' Dawson himself asked bluntly. 'Has Joan got herself into trouble with the law after all? Good Lord, it hasn't something to with that murder?'

'I'm afraid,' Maria replied coldly. 'it has quite a lot to do with it.' Then at a knock at the door she got to her feet and admitted Joan, pale-faced and troubled. She went over to her father, kissed him gently, then sat down without a word . . .

Maria surreptitiously locked the door, put the key in her pocket, and looked round with that air of drama she could never resist in moments of triumph. Slowly she moved back to her desk, every pair of eyes fixed on her.

'Superintendent,' she said simply, 'I have solved the murder of Frances Hasleigh! I have followed out my own angles to inescapable conclusions, and while I know you have done a fine job of work by following the obvious facts, I dare to think that I have done a better by finding the real killer.'

The Dawson family were all gazing at Maria as though petrified,

'Confound it all, Miss Black, what do you mean?' Dawson burst out abruptly. 'How dare you stand there and waste our time with such statements? What have we to do with it?'

'Everything!' Maria retorted, and the sting in her voice silenced the industrialist for a moment. With his wife and daughter he watched as Maria lifted her bulky typed dossier from her desk.

'For you, Super — in detail,' she said gravely, handing it over. 'This is the black-and-white record for you to read and check in any way you wish. You will find it watertight and dovetailed. For my own part I shall limit myself to a brief résumé of my research.'

Silence. Joan had gone so pale she looked about to faint, while in the eyes of Mrs. Dawson there was a cold, deadly glint. Quietly Maria resumed her chair.

'This mystery began for me on the day when the supposed Major Hasleigh brought his alleged daughter to this college,' she said. 'I knew he was a fake by his ill-conceived sunburn but let it pass then because I believed he had his own reasons for doing it. The real trouble began when the girl we called Frances Hasleigh was found hanged in Bollin's Wood. From that scratch start I had to determine the why and wherefore. When I examined the clearing I was particularly impressed by the two grooves on the tree branch — the one caused by Frances's weight hanging on the death rope; and the other, of thinner variety, at the extreme end of the branch. It was clear that Frances did not hang herself by perhaps releasing the rope that held the branch down, because by doing that she would have dislocated her neck, and this had not happened. So, what then?

'Whoever had hanged her had not been strong enough to raise her bodily, so had pulled the tree branch *down* instead and then let it rise gradually by paying out at the rope which was holding the branch end. Once it had fully straightened Frances would be about four to six inches from the ground. To this, however, there was a more sinister implication. The groove was a *deep* one, which to me showed that the rope had been embedded in the branch under severe strain for quite some time. Why? Frances had been allowed to rise very gradually, inch by inch perhaps, and that to me meant that she had been tortured to death! With every fraction that the branch straightened out the tighter would become the noose round her neck . . . Yes, she was slowly hanged, and no doubt it was done to try and force a secret out of her. She refused to comply with the wishes of her attacker and so finally died. Since she was gagged and no sounds were heard by the three girls in the lane we can assume that a nod of the head was the signal that could have saved her life.'

'And just what has this got to do with us?' Mrs. Dawson snapped.

'I will make matters a good deal clearer in a moment, Mrs. Dawson. To resume: It was perfectly evident when I went over the clearing that not a single footprint had been caused in the death of Frances. The murderer did not fly or have wings, obviously. There were two girls in the clearing all the time. The stout, unimaginative Beryl Mather I dismissed from my theory, but you, Joan, remained — and for many reasons!'

The girl looked up sharply. 'I? But why?'

'I'll tell you. Like Beryl you were in your stockinged feet and it was therefore unlikely that you would leave any marks in dead leaves and soft ground if you trod lightly. Another thing, when I untied you I found your wrists by no means tightly fastened — just as though you had tied the rope and then slid your wrists into it. You could have wriggled out of them with little effort. And also it seemed odd to me that you had been hit in the jaw and rendered unconscious whereas Beryl had been hit over the head and had a large bruise to show for it. You did not have your jaw examined, I noticed, and while it was possible that no mark had revealed itself, as very often it doesn't, I could not reconcile your story of your being hit in the jaw by somebody coming up from behind you. That would be a physical impossibility, and nobody anxious to stun you would use such a complicated method when the same system that had knocked out Beryl would have done equally well . . . Further, I noticed that although you only took two or three steps in your stockinged feet you lacerated yourself so badly with thorns, as you said, that you limped for several days after-wards — whereas Beryl, who covered the same distance as you, and was far heavier, was hardly hurt at all. It was not luck on Beryl's part that she happened on better ground, but the fact that you had taken *far more than a few strides* in your stockinged feet!'

'I didn't!' Joan declared hoarsely. 'I was lying unconscious, I tell you! I didn't — '

'I'll tell you what I believe you did!' Maria interrupted curtly. 'You wriggled out of your ropes, hit Beryl over the head with the nearest thing handy — a piece of old branch perhaps which you threw away afterwards — and then you reduced

Frances to a brief spell of unconsciousness by pressing on the arteries in the back of her neck with fingers and thumbs, a trick in self-defence you learned in a forestry club before you left it three years ago — oh, yes, my dear, I know all about that,' Maria added, as the girl's eyes widened. 'In fact you no doubt learned how to get out of ropes by the same training . . . You were bent on torture, and I'll tell you just why later.

'Now, you looked about the clearing and saw a figure in a boat on the river. Mr. Lever! How opportune! Back went your mind to the Sixth Form room. You remembered having seen his pen there — and it was probably still there, too. Anyway, worth the risk, and it might pin things on him . . . You had to work fast. Frances was too heavy for you to lift, so you dragged her along the ground to the death tree, maybe covering up the grooves left by her heels, but you forgot her torn stockings would provide the evidence. In doing this you cut your own feet pretty badly, but took little heed of the fact in the urgency of the moment.

'From round your waist, under your frock, you took out a silk rope which you had been keeping there for just such an opportunity as this. You knew what you were about all right. You knew that even if Lever failed to provide a suspect you had three girls who could equally take the blame. You would be the last one to fall under suspicion. Four suspects and you safe! It was just what you had been waiting for. I'll tell you why you had that rope ready so opportunely later on. Let us get back to the moment . . .

'With the rope from your own wrists you pulled down the branch of the death tree and secured it, then when Frances showed signs of returning consciousness you retied her hands securely with triple knots just to be sure, slipped the silk cord about her neck and tied it in triple knots to the centre of the tree branch. In your excitement you used the knot you knew to be the most secure and the most simple — to you. She would not nod her head to the questions you asked, so you let the branch slowly straighten out by paying out the securing rope. Frances finally died by strangulation, and without a sound owing to the gag.'

Maria got to her feet, her face so merciless it might have been carven in ivory. She pointed a steady, accusing finger across the desk at the motionless girl.

'Joan, you murdered that girl, and did not learn a thing! Then you realised that Vera and her friends might be back any moment. You saw that Beryl had not recovered yet. You retied the rope round your wrists after removing it from the tree, made tight loops and wriggled your hands into them, then you lay in apparent unconsciousness until you were rescued. Finally, pale through the emotional strain you had undergone — but which everybody thought was because of your unconsciousness — you were finally 'revived.' You denied everything, then on walking found out how badly your feet hurt. When you got back to the college afterwards you used the first chance to look for that pen of Robert Lever's, and presumably found it. You threw it in the clearing from a distance to avoid any sign of footprints and, when you returned to the school I saw you entering, though it took me some time to decide who it was.'

Herbert Dawson sprang to his feet, his face flaming with rage. His eyes darted to Vaxley as he sat folded in his chair, lost in thought.

'Superintendent Vaxley, why don't you arrest this woman?' he shouted. 'Do you realise the preposterous tissue of lies and insults she is hurling at my daughter? I demand that you stop her!'

'Of course,' Maria said gravely, 'you want proof?'

'You'd better provide it or face a lawsuit for defamation!'

'There is plenty of proof, Mr. Dawson. The silk rope that killed Frances had shreds of varicoloured silk in it, which had come off the frock Joan was wearing that day. Now, electrically, silk attracts silk, but there is a certain scientific angle to that. I suggested that the rope had dragged across her supine body and carried fragments from the surface of her dress with it. Later I realised that would have been impossible. Silk, to become magnetic to other silk, has to be charged. And there is no better medium for the purpose than the human body. That pointed infallibly to the fact that Joan had *worn* the rope close to her. It had no doubt been wrapped round her waist, invisible because of its slenderness, had become so charged that the rubbing of the underside on her dress upon it had drawn off fragments . . . You, Superintendent, can verify that?'

'I can verify the silk shreds,' he nodded, 'but I confess the scientific angle had rather escaped me. I had assumed — as you did at first — that the rope had dragged across the girl. That is a most brilliant deduction, Miss Black.'

She smiled transiently at the compliment, then again became the implacable unraveller of mystery.

'I had two things to go on — Joan had injured feet which three strides could not have caused, and she had worn a silk rope. Now what? Just how long had she had this silk rope? Then I recalled an event mentioned by Vera that might fit it. She said Joan had recently received a parcel of silk stockings from home, but unlike her usual custom, had not displayed her prize to any other girl. *Had it been silk rope and not silk stockings?* I was prepared to believe that this was so — and significant in view of the fact that she got the so-called stockings after the arrival of Frances Hasleigh at this school.'

Joan gave a little start and glanced for a moment at her stepmother's Sphinx-like face. Maria noticed it, but simply went on talking.

'I was faced with a problem. It was hard for me to credit that a mere schoolgirl could have done such a terrible act without a very real and desperate motive . . . Well, as I was trying to sort this out a new angle presented itself in the removal of Frances's corpse. Somebody else was involved in this, clearly. The suggestion of strength about the whole thing ruled out Joan and made me wonder if I was on the wrong track after all . . . You, Super, know of Clive Whittaker's activities in that direction. When the body had gone I reasoned that it could not be Joan who had done it, for several reasons. She had, to my mind, given up all hope of getting anything out of Frances when she died. It was a case of out of sight, out of mind. But, since somebody else had taken the trouble to remove the corpse it was possible that there was something even on the dead body that might be of value. If so, if Joan herself were to find the body, she might discover what the something was and take up her activities again, thereby giving me a chance to go on tracing her actions.

'My reasoning was more or less justified. With Beryl Mather she found the body — and she must have guessed that what she had wanted had been on that forearm. What now? Obviously she must make every effort to find who had moved the body since that person must now have whatever it was she wanted . . . Further, I do not believe that you just found that body, Joan. I believe you saw it being taken to the mausoleum the night before, when you returned from putting that fountain pen in the clearing. You followed Whittaker to the mausoleum, but you had not the courage to go too far. You waited for a while — during which time Whittaker was busy below — and then you decided to risk seeing what he was up to. You made a noise and were afraid. So you ran for it — and it was as you entered the college again that I saw you. I was then on my way to take a look at the corpse in the visitors' wing. Whittaker, too, took fright at the sounds you made and left his job half finished — or at any rate not tidied up.'

Silence. Maria got to her feet and began to pace up and down slowly.

'You knew beyond doubt, Joan, that Whittaker was the body-snatcher and it was about this time that I found the thing you sought was a formula for a high explosive. At that time my job was to find out what Whittaker was doing and his connection with the dead girl, and in the process thereof I found the half of the formula that had been on Frances's forearm. Now I knew why she had been tortured to death. You, Joan, had tried to force from her the whereabouts of the secret, and had failed — unaware that it was invisibly tattooed on the girl's arm . . .

'No doubt you were aware, Joan, that I was looking into the business: you could hardly fail to do so if you were on the watch for Whittaker. Anyway, you saw through the laboratory window one evening that I had the formula — but not complete, as you no doubt thought — in my watch locket. From then on you must have kept an eye on me. From your bed in the dormitory, and in the bright moonlight you could easily see the School House exit, and when that night you saw me going out you resolved to follow and get that formula. Aware that some foodstuffs reposed in the pavilion — from your watching Whittaker's movements in the interval — you made this your excuse to get out and used Frances Hasleigh's shoes, using a bent wire to open her locker. To make yourself further safe — but which really overdid the conviction — you dared the boastful, bullying Vera Randal into saying that she had been out. Most of this story fell to bits in the classroom when you and Vera fought out the issue of my stolen watch. To me it was perfectly clear then that you had known beforehand of the food in the pavilion, which also showed me you knew where Whittaker's rendezvous was. I realised more than ever that you were the one to watch. Possibly fear of me tempted you into inventing such an unconvincing story to explain the return of my watch. You knew I was looking into things and were getting nervous in consequence . . . Yet still at the back of my mind I could not imagine why a schoolgirl was doing all this. There must be something behind it.'

Nobody spoke as Maria reflected for a moment. She noted silently that not a word of denial had so far reached her.

'For the moment, Joan, I will stick to you and fill in the blanks after,' she resumed. 'Next thing, I found you as good as hanged in your own locker — but just prior to this I had heard somebody running from the passage outside my study towards the stairs. This somebody, I realised later, had been listening to my conversation with Mr. Martin, during which I had mentioned that I was going to the dormitory to search the lockers. I believe, Joan, that you raced to your study en route to the stairs, knowing Beryl Mather was busy with a common room meeting, and pulled the rope off her travelling case. You used it to convey the impression you had been hanged. According to your story you had been lifted by somebody you had not been allowed to see. This I regarded as manifestly impossible — and again I recalled that in the clearing somebody had obviously not been strong enough to lift Frances, so there was something wrong somewhere. The three-knot ropes were also suggestive to me and served, if anything, to blacken your own case.

'No, what you really did was to prepare everything to look as if you had been hanged — complete with three-knot ropes round wrists and feet, and one round the neck attached to the top centre hook of the locker. A gag was provided for good measure. But, Joan, you were in the locker until you heard me enter the dormitory, or so I believe, standing on the shoe rack, which would have raised you a good six inches from the floor. You deliberately risked strangulation to make for reality, knowing you'd be immediately rescued. You could not have hanged more than ten seconds before I released you, and you went down with no great jerk. Your shoe marks were all over the ledge, there was a long scratch on the paint where you had let your feet slide; you had knocked one or two pairs of shoes over on to the floor. So, you were so determined to throw me off the scent, you had risked even this . . .

'The next thing I knew you were trying to escape from the school and were overtaken by Whittaker. Since you were trying to escape you must presumably have got all you wanted from Whittaker — and he knew it, too, hence his effort to stop you. So until I knew what the real situation was I locked you in the punishment room, not for safety, but to make sure you could not escape. It also seemed to me that your denial of the fact that it was Whittaker was because you knew that if you accused him it would start an inquiry, which you wanted to avoid at all costs in case you got too involved . . .

'Well, so far, I have outlined what I believe you did, Joan. Perhaps not accurate in every respect, but close enough, I fancy. Now there are other points. From my knowledge of girls I did not judge you as a criminal, murdering type. There still had to be a reason behind all this. I remembered the rope that had possibly been disguised as silk stockings. That had come from home. What was there at home, then, to explain things? I got my first hint when I noticed the colour of your eyes, Mr. and Mrs. Dawson!'

'It can't be any more crazy than what you've said so far,' the woman said briefly. 'Explain yourself!'

'In his theory of the Recessive Unit, Mendel, the famous biologist, has said that it is a physical impossibility for two blue-eyed people to have a brown-eyed child,' Maria stated calmly. 'On this fact I rested a lot of my faith. I had never been told but what Joan was your own daughter. I did not know that you, Mr. Dawson, had married for the second time . . . From then on things began to tie up.

You, Mr. Dawson, only rose to such commercial eminence, I found, after your second marriage, and since her maiden name was Einhart, a distinctly Continental, not to say Germanic patronymic, I began to trace a possible connection. Whittaker had said that he and his sister were on the Continent for many years, and had been in danger many times because of the valuable secret they possessed. When war arrived one particularly determined agent made them leave France in a hurry. The connection between you, Mrs. Dawson, and the Continental agent, seemed too obvious to be missed. There was a link somewhere, but I still did not know what it was. Certainly it did not yet explain the murderous behaviour of Joan. Then I thought of a possible hereditary complex to account for it. I sent my assistant up to London to look into things, and he found that your first wife, Mr. Dawson, died in the Kilbury Hospital for the Criminally Insane five years ago! Am I right?'

Vaxley looked at Maria in wonder, then to Dawson. He nodded, tight-lipped, and there was real grief on his strong face.

'Yes, Miss Black, it's right. That is why I never mention my former marriage.'

'I am going to be very blunt now,' Maria said. 'You, Joan, I had discovered, are a strange girl with a highly developed neurosis. Love of wet days, erratic behaviour, periods of dead calm, sudden fits of so-called nerves, inferiority complex at intervals when all the world is against you — in other words, young woman, the first signs of the terrible mental disease which ruled and at last destroyed your own mother! You knew she was insane, but you were reverent enough to her memory to never mention the fact.'

'Yes,' Joan whispered. 'I knew — But I'm not crazy!' she shouted suddenly. 'I'm as sane as any of you.'

'Keep quiet a moment!' Maria ordered, and the girl sank back into silence again. Then Maria went on, 'It made your action of murder logical at last! But it was still queer for a girl to do such a thing without *direction*. So I came to the real truth . . . You, Mrs. Dawson, were connected with many European endeavours before the war — and no doubt still are if the police interest themselves, as they will. My assistant tells me you still have connections with Germanic Paris even yet . . . I'll tell you what you did. You knew that your stepdaughter had the same inclinations as her mother had had and so you resolved to use her as a pawn for your own purposes. You have an iron hold over her: she told me so herself. You were informed, or otherwise found out through the underground methods you are capable of using, that the bogus Frances Hasleigh, whom you had tried to attack in France along with her brother, was coming to this school. You sent Joan here a little way ahead of time and ordered her — Joan — to inform you the moment a new girl answering to Frances's description appeared. This I believe Joan did.

'You then sent Joan a silk rope, told her to say it was a pair of stockings, and instructed her to learn from Frances where her formula for high explosive was — and to learn, too, the whereabouts of her brother. Joan had got to do it, even to the extent of torture if need be, the silk rope to be used for the purpose. I do not say you prescribed death as the end, but it happened anyway. But no doubt you did tell Joan to watch her chance, wear the rope always about her to keep it out of sight, and to strike as fast as possible. The rope being a product of South France it seemed naturally to point to you. Knowing the girl to be a true replica of her mother you guessed her turbulent mind, given to spells of sadism, would bring you results!'

'In all my life,' Clara Dawson said slowly, 'I never heard such a preposterous story. This is going to cost you very dear, Miss Black! You dare to sit there and accuse me of — '

'It's true!' Joan cried abruptly, leaping to her feet. 'I tell you, it's true! I don't know how Miss Black knows all about it, but I love her, even if she is my Headmistress, even if she has found out all this about me! She's been my one true friend . . . You know it's true, mother — *you know it*!'

'Keep quiet, you excitable little fool!' her stepmother blazed.

'I *won't* keep quiet! I can't hold this back any longer!'

'All right, Joan, speak,' her father said gravely. 'Believe me, Miss Black, I knew nothing of all this. I'm as interested as you to know the facts.'

'You're not going to start talking about me!' Clara Dawson cried: 'What kind of a fool do you think I am?'

'I'd advise you to be quiet, madam,' Vaxley said stonily. 'Go on, Joan.'

'Well, it's more or less as Miss Black has said,' the girl said urgently, her words tumbling over one another. 'I was at school near my home, a day-school, then all of a sudden mother made up her mind to send me here because, so she said, I was not doing well in my studies. She told me that before long a new girl might arrive here — with grey eyes and fair hair, and would probably have a heavy figure for her age. I was to cultivate her all I could and find out all about her, writing the facts back home. So — I did.'

'Why?' Maria asked. 'Didn't you

wonder at such a request?'

'Yes, but I didn't dare do anything to cross mother; so I did as she told me. By return she sent me a length of silk rope and told me to tell anybody who inquired that it was a pair of stockings. I was to wear this round my waist. She then said that if I was a true English girl prepared to help my country I would devise the best way possible to trap this new girl and find out from her the truth about a formula for high explosive that she and her brother had got. The way my mother put it the formula could lose this country the war if I didn't get it somehow. It was in my power to do it. If I didn't do it I'd answer to her!'

'The girl's unhinged!' her stepmother said bitterly. 'It's all damned nonsense!'

'It isn't nonsense!' Joan nearly shrieked. 'I can prove it! I've got your letter — '

Her stepmother started. 'What! Why, you infernal little fool! I told you to destroy it — !'

She stopped abruptly, darted a glance round the merciless eyes fixed on her.

'So you admit you *did* write such a

letter,' Vaxley murmured. 'Thank you very much, Mrs. Dawson. Go on, Joan.'

'I — I didn't really mean to kill Frances!' Joan panted. 'I sort of got one of my attacks of nerves when we were tied up in that clearing. But I realised, too, that I had a chance that might never come again. I got free of my ropes, knocked out Beryl, then used that self-defence trick I'd learned at forestry class to make Frances unconscious while I bound her up. I was planning to frighten her into telling me something, but I hanged her instead! Then I thought I heard Vera and her pals coming back. I lost my head and let the rope go on the end of the branch. Frances swung there, wriggling and choking. It was ghastly! I lost my head, I didn't know whether to release her or what, and by the time I had calmed a bit she had stopped struggling. So I tied myself up again and pretended to be unconscious.

'As I became calmer I realised many things. I'd seen Mr. Lever out on the river and I remembered having seen his pen in the form room. I'd previously killed

Frances and was scared to death. I might save myself by switching the blame, so I put his pen in the clearing later that night. You were right about the thorns, Miss Black. They cut my feet dreadfully.'

'Yet, knowing you had committed murder you stayed on here at the college?' Vaxley asked. 'Was that sheer brazen nerve, or what?'

'No, it wasn't that. I hadn't got what my stepmother had asked for and I had to stay until I had. You remember that when dad and mother came here it was mother who insisted I stay on? I knew that it was Mr. Whittaker who'd taken the dead body of Frances, because I saw him do it when I came back from the clearing — so you guessed right, ma'm. And I knew it was him I wanted — '

'Then?' Maria prompted.

'Well, I didn't know you were up to anything, Miss Black, until you went into the laboratory one evening. I was hidden outside to see if Whittaker came in, because that might give me a chance to get the formula. Instead I saw you take a note out of your locket and then take down several chemical bottles. I realised that I had got to get at the formula somehow. You know how I did that. I saw you leave in the moonlight when actually I was watching for Mr. Whittaker. I used the food pretext and Frances's shoes — '

'And had Vera take the blame?' Maria snapped.

'I dared her into it to safeguard myself. I only returned your watch after attacking you in the mine because I realised things might be much worse for me if I didn't. The trouble was I dare not leave, because I'd only got half the formula even now . . . I watched my chance and tried to find out what you were going to do, Miss Black. I heard you say you were going to examine the dormitory lockers, so I went ahead of you and arranged that little trick. I felt that you did not believe me, though, and it seemed that I had got to act fast. My only way seemed to be to concentrate on Whittaker and get out the moment I could.

'Luck favoured me because later that evening, from my study window — Beryl was out in the common room — I saw

Whittaker go over to the lab. I dashed to his study and found it unlocked, went through the place from top to bottom — and found the formula, or at least a copy of it, behind a picture. I'd just got it when Whittaker came back. I made an excuse about a question, and got out quick. My one aim then was to get the formula to my mother personally as fast as possible. But you know what happened.'

'And where is this copy formula now?' Vaxley asked.

Joan shot a defiant glance at her stepmother's steely eyes.

'In the lining of my travelling case in the punishment room. You can get it any time you want.'

Maria rose, unlocked the door, and left the study. In a few minutes she returned with the case in her hand. Putting it on the desk she let Joan do the rest. Vaxley took the copy formula from her and pocketed it. Then he looked at Mrs. Dawson.

'Well?' he asked curtly.

She remained silent, her thin face sardonic.

Vaxley shrugged. 'With the letter you sent to your daughter and your own admission before witnesses here any confession of yours would be superfluous. We can trace your connections easily enough.'

'If she won't speak, I will!' Herbert Dawson declared. 'I have long had my suspicions that she was somehow involved with certain European factions who would naturally regard the acquisition of a deadly explosive as most desirable, but there was nothing I could prove. Besides, since her influence with certain of these contacts boosted my own business I did not feel justified in questioning anything. I suspected the murder of Frances Hasleigh quite a lot, because I know my wife had many letters with the postmark of this district upon them, presumably from whomever she had tracing the movements of that girl and her brother, by which she knew they were planning to come to Roseway here. Believe me, Miss Black — and you, too, Superintendent — this is a terrible shock to me that my daughter should be used as a pawn for murder.'

He fell silent, obviously too distraught to go any further.

'I shall have to ask all three of you to come down to the station with me,' Vaxley said quietly. 'And before we go I'll come with you and get that letter, Joan. You, Miss Black, we shall need for evidence at the trial.'

She nodded and handed over the dossier.

'For you, Super, with my compliments,' she said gravely.

15

Towards eight o'clock that evening Superintendent Vaxley reappeared at Roseway and was shown straight to Maria's study.

He found her in the armchair, deep in an omnibus volume of *Sherlock Holmes*. She laid the book aside and rose with extended hand.

'Why, Super, this is most pleasurable! Is it purely for the sake of a few words, or is there an epilogue to be written?'

He smiled and seated himself as she nodded to a chair.

'I just wanted to say goodbye, Miss Black. I'm leaving for London in an hour — and I want to congratulate you. You have put up a most extraordinary show in this case.'

'Without my textbooks I'd still be only the Headmistress,' she shrugged.

'Suppose we forget the textbooks and give the credit to your amazing gift of abstract reasoning? I admire you immensely, Miss Black.'

She coughed a little and momentarily wished she were twenty-five years younger. Then she deliberately made conversation as she found his sincere eyes fixed on her.

'Er — tell me, Super. How are things going on now this business has been cleared up?'

'Well, both Mr. and Mrs. Dawson are under arrest, and Whittaker is being detained on various charges but murder is not among them, of course. Lever, I think, will soon be released. Mrs. Dawson finally decided to sign a confession — confronted with such damning evidence, she could do little else. A strange, deadly type of woman, Miss Black, who used a neurotic schoolgirl with a slight mental unbalance as her cat's paw. I think the law will be merciless, particularly as she has connections with the enemy. As to Joan, her age and mental state will probably save her, though she'll be under medical observation for many years . . . And Whittaker? Well, he seems to have had a rough time all round but he'll have to answer for some of his misdemeanours. I imagine he won't get a long sentence and will then enter into negotiations with the Government for his explosive. In any case the matter is finished with. Your own extraordinary analysis of the problem went right to the root. That dossier of yours is a masterpiece.'

'You are full of praises tonight, Super,' Maria beamed.

'By no means unwarranted! If I — '

'Would you like a cup of tea?' Maria interrupted. 'I am afraid it is the strongest stimulant I can provide — or allow.'

'Delighted!' Vaxley said, and sat back in his chair. Then his next words made Maria turn sharply. 'Miss Black you ought to be connected with criminals as a permanent thing instead of being in a college. Why don't you change'

'In what way exactly?'

'I was thinking of a partnership — a private detective agency. I have often thought I'd like to retire from the Yard. To make matters free of embarrassment I — er — I wonder if you would consider marriage?'

Maria got control over herself immediately. She fingered her watch-chain and smiled. It was the first time Vaxley had ever seen her look so womanly.

'You do me a great honour, Super, but — well, I do not think I quite like the idea. Partnership and marriage — we can speak freely at our age, can we not? — are not entirely the correct states for two people with intense individuality and their own way of doing things. I have been a lone wolf all my life, and I have come rather to like it. Nor do I want to leave my school — not for a time anyway. There has been one mystery here, and there may be others. With so many characters at Roseway, anything can happen.'

Vaxley smiled regretfully. 'Well, I've asked you, and, like you, I do not give up easily. If our paths cross again, as assuredly they might, I shall ask again. You won't think it a liberty?'

'No — an honour,' Maria replied quietly; then she seemed grateful that the kettle needed attention. She made the tea, but they had hardly settled to it before there was a knock at the door and Pulp Martin entered in response to Maria's invitation. When he saw Vaxley he hesitated.

'Do come in, Mr. Martin!' Maria exclaimed. 'You know Superintendent Vaxley, I think?'

'Yeah — sure.' Pulp looked uneasy. 'I'm allergic to cops, though. Just thought I'd report, Maria. I've spent the day in London and came up on the evening train. How did things make out?'

'Perfectly, thanks to your excellent work. I'll explain it in full to you at a later time. For the moment, Mr. Martin, your work is over. And here is your money.'

Out came the cashbox and Pulp's eyes gleamed at the notes he received.

'Thanks, Maria — always glad to do me stuff. What's next?'

'Just wander as you will, Mr. Martin, and keep me notified of your various stopping-places. When I need you again — if I do — I'll contact you. Right?'

'Right! And I'll take care I don't get scooped up in no draft that comes my way. I'll be around if you want me.

'Night, Maria — and you, too, flatfoot!'

He went out whistling and Maria gave a faint smile. 'A rough diamond, Super,' she said, stirring her tea.

'I'd sooner give you a real one,' he replied quietly — but she shook her head.

'Not at present, Super. I've two solved mysteries to my credit and I'm thirsting for more. That means more to me at my age than romance.'

Vaxley sighed and raised his teacup. 'To the day when you tire of mysteries, then. When that happens I'll be on your doorstep.'

THE END

CLIMATE INCORPORATED
THE FIVE MATCHBOXES
EXCEPT FOR ONE THING
BLACK MARIA, M.A.
ONE STEP TOO FAR
THE THIRTY-FIRST OF JUNE
THE FROZEN LIMIT
ONE REMAINED SEATED

We do hope that you have enjoyed reading this large print book.

Did you know that all of our titles are available for purchase?

We publish a wide range of high quality large print books including:

**Romances, Mysteries, Classics
General Fiction
Non Fiction and Westerns**

Special interest titles available in large print are:

**The Little Oxford Dictionary
Music Book, Song Book
Hymn Book, Service Book**

Also available from us courtesy of Oxford University Press:

**Young Readers' Dictionary
(large print edition)
Young Readers' Thesaurus
(large print edition)**

For further information or a free brochure, please contact us at:
**Ulverscroft Large Print Books Ltd.,
The Green, Bradgate Road, Anstey,
Leicester, LE7 7FU, England.
Tel:** (00 44) **0116 236 4325
Fax:** (00 44) **0116 234 0205**

Other titles in the
Linford Mystery Library:

THE FROZEN LIMIT

John Russell Fearn

Defying the edict of the Medical Council, Dr. Robert Cranston, helped by Dr. Campbell, carries out an unauthorised medical experiment with a 'deep freeze' system of suspended animation. The volunteer is Claire Baxter, an attractive film stunt-girl. But when Claire undergoes deep freeze unconsciousness, the two doctors discover that they cannot restore the girl. She is barely alive. Despite every endeavour to revive the girl, nothing happens, and Cranston and Campbell find themselves charged with murder . . .